She wanted to be with a man. This man.

Yet fear lingered in her soul. Her self-protective instincts were still strong and ever on the alert. Her body and mind were knotted with conflicting emotions and desires.

Resting her head on Jordan's chest, she heard the wild pounding of his heart; she could feel his muscles tense up as he held her. 'Jordan, I must be driving you crazy.'

She felt a silent laugh rumble deep in his chest. 'You are.'

'If it's any comfort to you, I'm driving myself crazy.'

'Good.' Burying his face in her hair, he whispered, 'I hate being frustrated alone.'

Dear Reader

It's August—the height of summer—and we have some truly sizzling, satisfying reads in the Special Edition™ line-up!

This month, the always-delightful Joan Elliott Pickart brings you our THAT'S MY BABY! title; *Texas Baby* is the final book in her FAMILY MEN series, where the forty-something heroine rediscovers the joy of motherhood when she adopts a precious baby girl. But the dashing man of her dreams has no intention of playing daddy again...

An uncle's will looks set to cause trouble for the McKendrick siblings in Cathy Gillen Thacker's HASTY WEDDINGS. It starts with *The Cowboy's Bride*, when Cody is forced to re-marry the woman who ran out on him just hours after their elopement and *before the wedding night!*

Also this month, fate reunites a family in *A Daddy for Devin* by Jennifer Mikels, and passion flares between a disgruntled cowboy and a tough lady cop in *The Cop and the Cradle* by Suzannah Davis—the second of the SWITCHED AT BIRTH books.

We finish off the month with secret-baby and amnesia stories from Phyllis Halldorson and Judith Yates. Look out for *The Millionaire's Baby* and *Brother of the Groom.*

Happy reading!

The Editors

Brother of the Groom
JUDITH YATES

SILHOUETTE

SPECIAL EDITION®

JUDITH YATES

grew up in a tiny New England town, where she secretly wrote novels after school. After such an early start, she finds it ironic that she didn't get around to 'following her bliss' of writing professionally until after she'd worked for years in Boston and Washington, D.C., married and started a family.

When she's not busy writing and taking care of her two small children, Judith volunteers at local schools and enjoys speaking to young people about writing—especially those who are secretly working on novels after school.

Other novels by Judith Yates

Silhouette Special Edition®

Family Connections
A Will and a Wedding

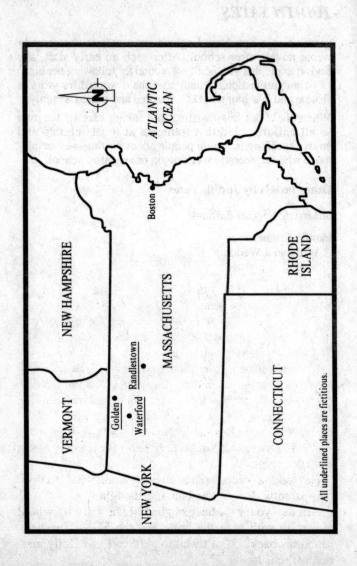

ATLANTIC OCEAN

Boston

NEW HAMPSHIRE

VERMONT

MASSACHUSETTS

RHODE ISLAND

Golden
Waterford
Randlestown

CONNECTICUT

NEW YORK

All underlined places are fictitious.

Prologue

Today was not the day to be late.

Jordan Mason knew he'd never hear the end of it if he muffed up his job as best man for his younger brother. Especially under the circumstances.

Irritated to the hilt by the mess known as Boston traffic, he ran up the steep cathedral steps. Dashing through a side door into the looming arched hallways of the Gothic church, Jordan soon found himself encircled by several excited bridesmaids and the bride's teary mother.

"Whoa there, Jordan. Where's the fire?" one of the women teased.

He took a deep breath, feeling somewhat foolish. "Apparently, I'm not as late as I thought."

All the young ladies laughed. Liza Farrell, who'd grown up with both the bride and the Mason brothers, patted his back. "Can't wait to get Scott and Holly married off, eh, Jordan?"

Jordan held his tongue despite Liza's dig. It was no secret that he had suggested the childhood sweethearts wait a year or two before walking down the aisle. But his advice had been rejected—vehemently. And that, as far as he was concerned, was the end of it. His little brother and Holly were on their own, mistake or not.

He winked at Liza. "I'm counting the minutes."

"Well, your brother ought to be counting the minutes," Holly's mother chided, casting a wary glance at her jeweled watch. "I can't believe he isn't here yet."

"He isn't?" Jordan was surprised. It wasn't like Scott to show up at the last minute. Everyone considered him the Mason brother to rely on.

"That's what they tell me. And Holly's almost finished dressing." Mrs. West pulled a handkerchief from her satin handbag and began dabbing at her eyes. "She looks absolutely lovely in her gown. So elegant...like a real princess."

He fought the urge to roll his eyes. Holly had always been something of a princess in her parents' eyes. From what he'd heard, her bridal regalia would be suitable for an authentic royal wedding. Yet Jordan couldn't picture it. Holly West was T-shirt and jeans and a swingy blond ponytail. To him, she looked more like a carefree teenager than a woman about to be married in a very formal ceremony in front of God, family and half of New England.

As Mrs. West led the bridesmaids away, Jordan checked his watch. He wasn't late, but he wasn't terribly early, either. How in heck had he beaten Scott here?

He meandered back to the main entrance, where six groomsmen had begun ushering the first few guests to their seats. He asked the guys if they'd seen Scott. None of them had. Jordan peered down the aisle, noting the expensive floral displays throughout the sanctuary and on the altar. The ethereal refrains from the cathedral's old pipe organ filled the air.

Turning back to the vestibule, Jordan spotted his father heading toward him. He looked anxious.

"Is it true? Your brother's not here yet?"

"So it seems."

Lawrence grimaced. "He must be stuck in that awful traffic. Can you believe such a mess on a Saturday afternoon?"

"That's what happens when you get married less than a mile from an important Red Sox game," Jordan joked, hoping to ease his father's worry. "He'll be waltzing in any second now."

"I hope so," Lawrence replied, shaking his head. "Your mother, God bless her, would have had him here two hours ago."

Jordan smiled. "She'd have everything under control."

"She loved Holly like a daughter, you know. She'd be thrilled about this marriage."

Jordan nodded, finding it tough to say more about his mother. She'd been on his mind a lot today. In the five years since her death, Lawrence had married a much younger woman and retired from business; Jordan had taken over Mason CompWare, the family's computer software company; and Scott was marrying the girl next door. Their lives were so different now, and certainly not as close.

"Have you talked to Scott today?" Lawrence asked abruptly. "He didn't get carried away at the bachelor party, did he?"

"Spoke with him this morning. He was awake, sober and getting ready."

"You haven't said anything more about postponing the wedding, have you?"

"Give me a break, Dad."

"Sorry. Guess I'm nervous. Never have been father of the groom before." Lawrence shrugged. "It's just unlike him to be late. I'm sure he'll be right along, though. Scott's never given me a day's worry."

Unlike me, Jordan thought dryly. Yet he couldn't help worrying now himself. Where in the world *was* Scott?

Fortunately, a group of New York relatives descended upon them, offering a momentary distraction. When the Reverend Parker—all dressed and ready to perform the ceremony—tapped him on the shoulder, Jordan felt an immediate unease.

The reverend did not look pleased.

"You have an urgent telephone call, Mr. Mason. You may take it in the vestry." He gestured Jordan to follow, adding in a discreet whisper, "I believe it's your brother."

"He hasn't had an accident, has he?" Jordan asked, hurrying down the side hall after the Reverend Parker. He glanced back at his father, grateful Lawrence was too occupied with the relatives to have noticed his departure.

The clergyman shook his head. "It doesn't sound like *that's* his problem."

Jordan winced. Oh, God, please let it be just a matter of a flat tire or good old Boston gridlock. Please.

The Reverend Parker pointed to the telephone on a corner table, closing the vestry door behind him when he left. Swallowing hard, Jordan pushed the blinking button as he lifted the receiver. "Scott, where are you?"

"Home."

"Home? What the hell's going on?" Jordan burst out. Deep down, he already knew.

"I can't do it, man. I can't go through with the wedding."

Forgetting he was in church, Jordan muttered a few choice words.

Scott coughed to clear his voice. "You were right all along. About everything. We're too young...we've just gotten out of college...Holly's the only girlfriend I've ever had. Man, Jordan, I just turned twenty-one."

"Ten minutes before the ceremony is a great time to change your mind. Everybody's here."

"Ever since the rehearsal yesterday, I knew it would be a mistake to go through with it," Scott admitted. "Only, I didn't know how to stop it. I even got all tuxed up, thinking once I got to church I'd be fine. But it's wrong, man. It's all wrong."

Jordan closed his eyes. Suddenly, Scott's heavy drinking at the bachelor party made sense. "Couldn't you have said something last night?"

His brother groaned. "I was scared. And part of me didn't want to admit that, as usual, you were right. But you *are* right. About my not really wanting to help you run the business. About closing off possibilities. About everything."

For the life of him, Jordan wished he hadn't been so right. "What about Holly? Don't you love her?"

"Yes, I love her," snapped Scott. "Except my head is full of questions about *how* I love her. Maybe it's not the marrying kind of love. We're talking the rest of my life here."

"For crying out loud, I suggested you *postpone* the thing, not break it off." Jordan paused, wanting nothing more than to wring his brother's neck. "You're absolutely sure you don't want to go through with this?"

"Absolutely sure."

"Then get yourself over here pronto and tell Holly."

"How can I tell her? I can't face her—and everyone else."

"You owe her an explanation."

"I—I can't go there," Scott sputtered. "I won't."

"So who in the hell do you expect to tell her? Me?"

"Yes."

"Are you crazy? I'm not one of her favorite people these days. She'll think I put you up to this." He shook his head violently, as if his brother could see. "No way."

"Please, Jordan."

"Get over here, you little jerk, or I'll come and drag you by the throat."

"Forget it. You don't have a clue what it's like trying to live up to everyone's expectations. You don't care. Well, I'm tired of being the one who always does the right thing."

"Dammit, Scott."

"I've written Holly a letter explaining everything. I'll talk to her when I get back."

"Back? Back from where?"

"I don't know. I gotta get away from here for a while," Scott said, his voice an emotional whisper. "Just tell her how sorry I am. Really, really sorry."

Stunned, Jordan kept the receiver on his ear several long seconds after Scott had hung up. How in God's name was he going to tell Holly? Where did he even begin?

The dressing room was directly across the corridor from the vestry. He could hear happy, feminine banter through the closed door. Anger kicked back in. Maybe he should tell Holly she was lucky to find out about the miserable little weasel before it was too late. She should be relieved to not be marrying the kind of man who'd leave her standing at the altar.

Despite his anger, however, Jordan had no stomach for the job. As he walked across the hall to knock on the heavy wood door, the last thing he felt like was the best man. He felt like a spoiler.

Liza answered his knock. "Finally," she declared as she swung the door wide open. "Ready to start now?"

He took a tentative step inside. Flanked by her mother and innumerable attendants, the bride stood in the center of the small room, fidgeting with her gown's long white train. A nervous cough erupted in his throat, prompting Holly to turn around.

Jordan stood speechless. It was as if he'd never really seen her before. Was this the skinny pigtailed tomboy who used to follow Scott and him everywhere? The smart-mouthed nuisance he'd known almost all his life? He eyed her from head to toe. This woman with graceful curves swathed in white satin and lace, golden hair swept up beneath yards of veil, her creamy skin glowing as she smiled at him—this lovely, radiant woman was a Holly he could never have even imagined.

At that moment he could have cheerfully murdered his wimp of a brother.

She wrinkled her nose in perplexity—a habit that *was* pure Holly West. Her big brown eyes, suddenly as sassy as ever, glimmered with mirth. "Why are you staring at me like that, you big dope?"

He coughed again as his heart sank. Knowing he was the last person she wanted to hear this from made it that much harder. "Ah, I need to speak to you."

She laughed and reached for the flowing bouquet of flowers in her mother's hands. "It'll have to wait. I'm getting married in exactly one minute."

"Holly, I really have to talk to you—alone."

She searched his gaze for one long, unbearable moment. He could hear his heart pounding in his ear. Then Jordan saw realization flash in her eyes. She knew. The sparkle and spirit that had been the Holly West he'd known forever evaporated before his eyes. She knew.

"Scott's not coming?"

Somehow, the words needed to explain eluded him. His tongue felt like lead. All he could do was shake his head. "I'm sorry, Holly," he whispered. "God, I'm so sorry."

The others in the room were stunned silent.

"How could he? Why?"

The grief in Holly's voice pained him. Jordan reached out, but she shrank back.

"He sent you to tell me?"

In the longest five minutes of his life, he gently revealed what he knew. Holly managed to hold herself together while he explained. But after he left the room, the sound of her weeping seeped through the closed door. As he headed toward the sanctuary to alert the wedding guests, the devastation in Holly's eyes haunted Jordan.

He suspected it always would.

Chapter One

Jordan was lost. And it was no one's fault but his own. After all, he had let himself be snowed by an old man's anxieties.

He shook his head. Jordan Mason never *used* to be a soft touch. And look where succumbing to sentimentality had landed him: driving around in circles in some back-of-beyond town where he didn't want to be, looking for a woman he hadn't seen in five years.

"At this rate it'll take five more years to find her," he muttered, surveying his surroundings one more time.

There were no signs of the landmarks mentioned by the gas station attendant back in town. With a groan of disgust, he pulled a U-turn in the middle of the deserted country road. He was lost, all right. Good and lost.

These days, some might call that par for the course.

Jordan eventually scouted his way back to the center of Golden, Massachusetts. He decided to bypass the service station this time and try his luck at the general store. Maybe he'd get better directions there.

The store's interior, with its sawdust floors, glass cases and merchandise ranging from antacids to zipper pulls, was as quaint as its white clapboard exterior. Too quaint for Jordan's taste. The white-haired gentleman manning the cash register suited the store's Yankee ambience to a tee. Jordan snapped up a six-pack of soda and plunked it down on the checkout counter.

"I need help with directions," he said, pulling out his wallet. "The guy at the gas station got me all turned around."

"That would be Edgar—his mind *is* all turned around." The clerk took Jordan's money. "Where you trying to get to?"

"Old Paget Road. Holly West's place."

"You looking for Holly? Heck of a lot easier to get her at the shop. It's right across the common here."

"I tried. It's closed."

"This early?" Rubbing the back of his neck, the man shrugged.

This nonanswer frustrated Jordan. But he wasn't going to waste more time with more questions. He just wanted to check out Holly's situation as he'd promised and then be on his way. Preferably by dinnertime.

To be on the safe side, Jordan jotted down the clerk's directions. Taking the first right after the Arthur B. Paget Memorial Library, he drove, as directed, over the rickety Golden Creek bridge. Several miles later, he finally reached Old Paget Road. It was winding and narrow. Only the occasional rural mailbox signaled a residence. The homes were hidden by unruly woods full of maples, birches and pines.

Jordan spied the mailbox marked "West" just a few

feet before the isolated road dead-ended at a small pond. He stopped the car for a moment, unable to fathom why Holly had chosen to live in the middle of nowhere. Then again, he didn't know much about Holly anymore. He hadn't seen her since that disastrous day at the church five years ago. He had wondered about her, though.

Because he'd been the messenger bearing the bad news back then, this meeting could prove awkward. Even his stomach was doing a nervous spin as he drove on. Not that Holly's so-called driveway helped any. His car lurched and dipped slowly over the dirt path, while straggly branches from overgrown bushes and trees scraped against it. Jordan clenched his jaw as he steered the car around a blind bend.

"I should've known better," he muttered. "This is the last favor I— What? Damn!"

A blur of pink and white dashed out right in front of him and he slammed the brakes. The car stopped with a screeching jolt. "Oh, God," he gasped, his heart beating double-time.

Frantic, Jordan scrambled out of the car. He thought he'd stopped in time. He didn't think he had hit her. Yet the little girl sat on her bottom at the edge of the driveway, the wheels of her fallen pink tricycle still spinning less than a foot away.

He rushed to the child's side. "Kid, are you okay?"

The girl, more dazed than frightened, looked down at herself and nodded. "I'm okay."

"Are you sure?" His eyes scoured her from head to toe. Besides a couple of raspberries on her knees, she appeared unhurt. Much to his everlasting relief. Jordan felt he could breathe free again.

"Dammit, honey, I almost ran over you."

She stared up at him with a cool eye. "Ooh, you said a bad word." No longer dazed, she got to her feet.

Jordan couldn't help but grin. "Shouldn't somebody be watching you? Where are your parents?"

The girl didn't answer. Instead, she bit her lip and stared at the ground. Fear and guilt spread across her smudged face. She looked as if she'd been caught with a hand in the cookie jar.

Or caught talking with a stranger, Jordan realized as the girl's lip began to tremble. "Look, honey, I know you shouldn't be talking to a stranger, but I'm not try—"

Before he could finish, the child had run away in a swirl of dust. He called after her, but to no avail. Jordan felt bad about scaring her. Still, he was glad the kid had sense enough to fear strangers. Shaking his head, he moved the trike out of the way and returned to his car. This was turning into one hell of an endeavor, just one delay after another. Holly had better live at the end of this seemingly endless driveway. And she had better be home.

As his car snaked along the dirt road, he caught glimpses of a house through the trees. Finally, he reached a clearing of expansive green lawn surrounding what best could be called a large country cottage. He spotted the little girl just a few feet ahead of him. With one frightened glance over her shoulder, she ran furiously—as if the devil himself were after her.

"Wait, kid," he called out his window. "I'm just here to see Holly West."

"Gracie, Gracie," the girl cried, stumbling up the front walkway to the wide-porched cottage.

A white-haired woman barreled out of the front screen door. "What is it, Stephanie? What's happened?" she demanded, appearing as dour as a bulldog and as solidly built.

"That man—that man!"

The woman gazed past the girl and spotted Jordan in his car. Her gaze narrowed.

"Great, this is all I need." Cursing under his breath, he climbed out of the car.

As he approached, the woman took a step back, drawing the girl behind her. "What exactly is going on here?"

"The kid misunderstood. I'm just looking for someone."

She eyed him skeptically. "I'm sure we can't help you."

"Gracie." The child tugged at her apron, but the woman shushed her.

"The guy at the general store gave me these directions," Jordan replied, feeling fairly well fed up with Golden and everyone in it. "And the mailbox—"

"Gracie," the child said again.

The woman paid no attention. "You're the one who's made a mistake," she declared in a no-nonsense, clipped New England tone. "I wasn't told to expect anybody today."

"Gracie!"

The woman gasped in exasperation. "For heaven's sake, what is it?"

"He wants Mommy."

"No, I don't," Jordan snapped, his patience shot. "I don't know her mother. This is all a big misunderstanding."

"Well, then, who are you looking for?" Gracie asked.

"Holly West. I'm an old friend of hers."

The woman's suspicious glare deepened. "If that was true, you'd know Holly West *is* this child's mother."

Suddenly, his mouth was as dry as Holly's dusty driveway. His eyes fell to the little pigtailed blonde clutching the woman's leg. He studied the child from head to toe, the telltale brown-eyed gaze overwhelming him with a dizzying sense of déjà vu.

And, for only the second time in five years, Jordan Mason was stunned speechless.

The golden retriever rubbed happily against Holly's leg as Dr. Gabe Sawyer handed her its leash. "Taffy's shots are all in order for another year. Just make sure you keep up with the heartworm pills," he advised. "Jess gave you a supply, didn't she?"

"She did." Holly smiled at the vet's assistant sitting behind the clinic's reception desk. "And thanks for keeping Taffy while I was at Harvey Kingston's office. Sorry it took longer than expected."

Gabe shot her a hopeful look. "Make any headway with him?"

"My dear landlord is still reluctant to remodel the building, and he absolutely refuses to enlarge the parking lot. Says it'll upset the neighbors."

"He has a point there, Holly."

She couldn't help wincing, although she suspected Gabe was right. As an elected town official, he had a good fix on what would fly with the residents of Golden. Holly sighed. "If I can't expand, it'll be the Randlestown Mall for me."

"You'd really have to relocate the shop?"

"My franchise contract demands I meet all revised standards—including their increased square-footage requirement," she explained as the clinic phone rang behind them. "The nearest available space is at the mall."

Which was twenty miles from Golden and her daughter. She had invested in the franchise so she could live and work in the same community, and be within reach of Stephanie at all times. Her goal had been to make Golden her home in every possible way. With the success of her Bath and Body Essentials Boutique, Holly thought she had achieved it—until now.

"Holly, your baby-sitter's on the line," Jess announced from her desk. "Says it's urgent."

Tossing Gabe a worried glance, Holly took the phone receiver from the receptionist. "Gracie, is Stephanie all right?" she asked at once.

"She is now," the older woman confirmed. "Some man followed her to the house, scared her half to death. I tried to get rid of him, but he claims he's an old family friend from Boston. So I locked him out on the porch until I could call you."

"What's his name?"

"Mason."

Shock clutched her heart. "Are you sure?"

"Yes, Jordan Mason. Tall, dark, kinda good-looking," Gracie said grudgingly. "His clothes look like they cost a pretty penny, too."

It sounded like Jordan, all right. But what was he doing in Golden? "You'd better let him in, Gracie. Give him a cold drink, and I'll be right there."

Holly was flabbergasted by the news. She had had no contact with Jordan after those initial nightmare days following her ill-fated wedding. The rift between the two families had been painful and complete. Not even Scott's death in a motorcycle accident two years later could bridge the wide chasm between the Masons and the Wests.

As Holly drove away from the center of town, apprehension tore at her. Why had Jordan come? Why now?

Within minutes, she pulled up next to the Mercedes parked in her driveway. It had Jordan Mason written all over it. His expensive tastes in cars, clothes, homes had always been testaments to the fantastic success of CompWare, the computer business his father had started more than two decades ago. She smiled. Oh, yes, Jordan had liked being rich. If the accounts she'd been reading in the Boston papers were accurate, he had just become a whole lot richer.

Holly unleashed Taffy, who scampered off into the yard. A fretful Gracie was waiting for her at the front door.

Holly peered into the living room. "Where is he?"

"I put him out in the backyard with a pitcher of lemonade. Then I sent Stephanie up to her room to play. I thought it safer that way."

"Mr. Mason's safe. I've known him all my life."

"Maybe so. But I didn't much care for the way he showed up here, scaring Steph and me like that." Gracie shook her head. "It just wasn't right."

"He could have used better judgment, I agree." Holly patted the older woman's shoulder. "And I'm glad you called me at Dr. Sawyer's."

"If you want me to, I'll stay until he leaves."

"Thanks, but I'll be fine. Besides, you've been here all day."

"I am kind of tired. And I need to feed my cats." Gracie gathered her belongings and donned the wide-brimmed straw hat she wore every May through September. "Oh, I finally got around to making the tuna noodle casserole Steph wanted. All you have to do is heat it up.''

After seeing Gracie off, Holly quickly checked on her daughter upstairs. She just needed to. As was becoming her habit, Stephanie had her nose buried in a picture book as she pretended to ''read'' the story she knew by heart. Then Holly stopped in the kitchen to collect an extra glass before joining Jordan in the backyard.

As she headed outdoors, Holly's nerves began to fray. She felt off keel. Coming face-to-face with Jordan was much trickier than she would have thought. Funny how certain memories could be aroused in an instant, the emotions behind them springing back to life, as vivid as ever. It felt as if she'd been jilted at the altar just yesterday.

Holly spied Jordan sitting in one of the Adirondack chairs, seemingly mesmerized by the distant vista of Summer Pond. Unnoticed, she watched him. As always, his thick dark hair was brushed back and well-groomed. Although casual, his white polo shirt and tan slacks were pressed, crisp and impeccable. His profile was clean, strong, handsome. As always...

Holly had harbored a secret crush on Jordan until she'd turned fifteen. By then, his college sophistication—and the six-year age gap—had become too discouraging. Besides, he'd had a different girlfriend every week and partied all the time. He had never paid any attention to her.

She shook her head. What off-the-wall things to think about at a time like this. With a shrug, Holly took a deep breath and walked over to him. ''Hello, Jordan.''

''Holly...hello,'' he murmured.

He sounded hesitant as he got to his feet. Still, his dark-blue eyes gazed down at her, unwavering, direct.

"It's been a long time."

Finally face-to-face with him after all these years, Holly felt a tad off balance. She stepped back. "You've caused quite a stir here."

"Apparently. Your housekeeper wouldn't let me in the house—even after she called you." A slight smile twitched his lips. "Don't get many visitors, Hol?"

Now it was her turn to smile. "No one like you, Jordan. No one like you at all."

He responded with a laugh that broke through the awkward tension between them. "Sorry about that. Next time I'll call ahead and save us all trouble. This is not an easy town."

"Golden? You can't be serious." Motioning him to sit, Holly pulled another chair up to the wooden table. "You just haven't spent enough time in small towns," she added, refilling his glass with more lemonade.

"Now I know why." He sipped the lemonade, glancing about the yard and nodding back at the house. "I've got to say I'm impressed, Holly—with all this and with what I saw of your shop in town."

"You sound surprised. Didn't think I had it in me to make a life for myself?"

"Not so." He shot her a wry smile. "I always figured you were tougher than anyone gave you credit for."

"Thanks. I could've used that vote of confidence five years ago." As soon as she said it, she bit her lip. *She* hadn't planned on bringing up the subject.

Jordan's expression changed. "I tried to speak with you after that—several times. You would never take my calls."

"I know." Holly stared down at her glass. "Everything was just so hard then. I was in no shape to talk to anyone."

Truth was, Jordan had been the last person with whom she wanted to talk. An oh-so-independent take-charge guy like him—who had always known exactly where he was headed—would have been clueless. He couldn't have understood how lost she felt after his brother had walked out, or how wounded she'd been when Scott had refused her calls months later.

"That was all a long time ago," Jordan offered gently.

Holly gave a nervous laugh. "Doesn't feel that way right now."

When she looked up, she found his gaze on her. She'd never realized how deeply blue Jordan's eyes were. Perhaps the intriguing crinkles and lines of the past years had intensified the color. Perhaps she had simply forgotten. Now, however, their smoky remoteness stirred her in an elusive, undefinable way.

Feeling her skin grow hot, Holly racked her brain for a snappy comment to break the almost intimate silence. But Jordan beat her to it with a wily smile she remembered from long ago. "You've certainly proven you can make it on your own."

"I wasn't aiming to prove anything."

"Really?" His dark brow rose in doubt.

This skepticism was pure Jordan Mason. She remembered that, too. "Jordan, what *are* you doing here? You haven't said."

"I ran into your father last weekend—on a golf course at Hilton Head. Quite by accident. I had no idea he lived there now."

"He retired there after my mother passed away last year."

"So he told me."

Holly eyed Jordan. "What else did he tell you?"

"Not enough, that's for sure." He leaned back into the wooden chair. "But he kept after me until I finally agreed to come out here and see how you're doing."

"You mean check up on me?"

"Ted's very worried about you. And, frankly, I was surprised to hear he's barely seen you since your mother died."

"That's his choice," Holly said, trying not to sound defensive. "I've left the door open. He can come anytime."

"But you don't go see him?"

She stiffened. After all this time, what was her father playing at by sending Jordan Mason around?

"Did he happen to mention why I don't visit?"

"Your father didn't mention a lot of things." His voice rose. "Like the tiny fact that you have a five-year-old child."

"Stephanie is only *four*."

Again, skepticism glinted in his eyes. "He didn't bother to let me know that you've been married, either."

"Because I haven't been." She looked away.

"Then tell me, Holly, why would Ted beg me to come see you, yet not say a word about your daughter?"

"He must have his reasons." Holly plunked her glass down and started out of the chair. "You'll have to ask him."

"No, Holly. Now that I've come this far, I'll ask you." Jordan clamped his hand over her arm, his vivid blue eyes pinning her back down. "Is it my brother? Is Scott Stephanie's father?"

She stared back at Jordan, each breath barely escaping her tight throat.

"Well?"

Holly heard the back screen door slam. Yanking her

arm from Jordan's grasp, she turned toward the house. *Oh, Steph, not now.*

Yet, as she watched her daughter skip across the lawn, the most tender of loves welled up in her heart—as it always did. Since before Stephanie's birth, this love, with its inherent fears and protectiveness, had influenced every choice Holly made. As Steph drew closer, small and sweet and laughing, Holly realized more was at stake than a secret. Right or wrong, this love overrode everything—even honesty.

''Mommy!'' her gleeful daughter called, mere steps away from leaping onto her lap.

Quickly, Holly looked at Jordan. ''Don't fool yourself,'' she said in an urgent whisper. ''Scott's not her father.''

Chapter Two

Jordan glared at Holly as the kid pounced on her lap. *Fool himself?* It was not something he tended to do. In this case, he flat-out didn't believe her, and only the little girl's presence kept him from saying so.

Cuddling her, Holly nuzzled the giggling child's neck. Jordan concentrated on Stephanie. Blond, brown-eyed and honey-skinned, she appeared to be an exact miniature of her mother. Yet, as she wiggled in Holly's arms, he continued to study her expressions, her voice, her laugh, her movements. Try as he might, Jordan failed to detect the slightest hint of his brother in the child.

Still, he wasn't convinced.

Mother and daughter discussed tuna casseroles and the dog named Taffy, among other things. Jordan felt as if they'd forgotten he was there, which did not sit well. He wanted answers. With impatience getting the better of him, he leaned over to whisper in Holly's ear. "Why should I believe you?"

She looked up at him, her nose scrunched in perplexity. This familiar gesture brought back the Holly West of the past, a Holly so different from the independent single mother he'd found here in Golden. Jordan found an odd comfort in the reminder.

Holly slid the child off her lap. "Honey, see Taffy sitting by the back door? She looks so glum. You know, she's been cooped up at Dr. Gabe's clinic all afternoon."

Stephanie set her big brown eyes on the golden retriever. "Poor Taffy."

"I bet she could use a good run around the house."

The kid bobbed with excitement. "I'll do it, Mommy. I'll take her for a run."

"Go for it." Holly waved her off.

"Taffy! Come on, Taffy, come on!"

The dog came to life as Stephanie ran toward her, and yipped playfully when the child started circling the house. Holly chuckled. "That's one of her favorite things to do. She loves leading Taffy around."

Which was all very nice, but it couldn't have interested Jordan less. "I'm waiting for an answer."

"You haven't changed. You still can't take anything at face value, can you?"

"Not this, Holly." He shook his head. "Not this."

Yet the challenge on her face made him wonder. Could there be more at play here than the obvious? After all, the very notion that Scott and Holly had a child together without anyone in his family knowing *was* a stretch. In those days, the circle the Masons and the Wests had moved in was small—too small to hide such a momentous event.

Holly sighed. "This isn't easy to talk about, Jordan.

You can't imagine how worthless I felt when Scott walked out on the wedding.''

Actually, he could well imagine it. He had never forgotten the moment when her glowing bride's smile had crumbled into disbelief and pain. He had never forgiven his brother for hurting and humiliating Holly so.

"Because I was absolutely miserable, my parents sent me off on a cross-country trip with my cousin," Holly continued. "Remember?"

"Yes. The last time I tried to call you, your mother told me you would be gone for the summer. But by summer's end, your parents had sold the house and moved to Connecticut. It was pretty sudden."

"They moved because I was pregnant." She looked down at her hands.

"Holly?"

"Not by Scott."

"Then *who* for Pete's sake?"

A flash of embarrassment colored her face. "A student I met while my cousin and I were traveling. Someone who paid a lot of attention to me at a time when my self-esteem was about zilch. Guess you could call it a rebound affair."

"I see."

"Do you?" Holly asked, fidgeting in her chair. But before Jordan could even think of how to answer, she continued, "By the time I discovered I was pregnant, he was long gone."

Jordan was stunned. This was beyond anything he had imagined about Holly. Could it be true?

"So you, ah, decided to—to—"

"Keep the baby?" she said, finishing for him. "Of course. There was never any question. I wanted her more than anything."

"I don't know what to say. No one knew..."

She nodded. "That's what my parents wanted—they had a tough time with the...situation. And after everything that had happened with Scott and the wedding, who could blame them? We all thought a fresh start was best."

Jordan studied Holly's face. Her explanation seemed plausible. Any woman left at the altar the way she had been would be vulnerable to another man's attention. Yes, it could have happened as she said...except for one thing that didn't connect. "Then why did your father want me to come find you?"

"Ah, my father." Holly closed her eyes for a moment. "My father has a hard time believing that I've built a good life for myself, even after all these years. He's always been uncomfortable with my being an *unwed* mother. Maybe that's why he didn't say anything to you about Stephanie."

"Ted did seem to be holding something back."

"Poor Dad. In the past, my mother did the worrying for him. But now that she's gone..."

"He's worrying again?"

"Because he can't or won't accept that I'm doing fine on my own," she said with a shake of her head.

"But he was so anxious about you."

"It's difficult to take Steph to see him. He moved into a very small condo in an adults only development down in Hilton Head," she explained. "And he won't come here to see us out of sheer stubbornness. But I keep hoping he'll give in. Then he'd see for himself how well we're doing."

Jordan was blown away by it all.

Minutes ago, he would have bet his life Scott was Stephanie's father. But now Holly's explanation made more sense than the harsh notion that she'd keep a baby secret from Scott or his family. Despite the bitterness created by his brother's actions, the two families had been too close for something like that.

"The father never knew?"

"Oh, Jordan, I tried. It was just impossible to get through to him. It wouldn't have mattered anyway, but I did try—I—" Her voice broke, and she quickly bit down on her quivering lip.

"It's okay, Hol." Jordan reached across the table for her hand. After hearing the sadness in her voice, feeling the tremble of her hand, any doubts he had all but vanished. He couldn't help but believe her.

Holly watched him, her brown eyes pensive. A gentle afternoon breeze wafted through her fine golden hair. Jordan recalled the last time she had looked at him like that, dressed in her frothy wedding gown, standing in a room of shocked silence. He blinked away the memory to focus on the woman here with him now.

"Do I look sadder but wiser to you, Jordan?" Holly asked, slipping her hand out of his.

Jordan shook his head. "You look wonderful. Very much your own woman."

A smile lit her face. "Thank you for that."

He meant it. Time had refined her face's youthful roundness with delicate angles; experience had graced her coffee-colored gaze with an intriguing expression. Leaning back in his chair, he took in the lithe line of her body. It was hard to miss how motherhood had softened her girlish shape with supple curves. The spoiled, bothersome kid from next door was history now, as was the weeping abandoned bride. Holly had transformed herself into a self-sufficient woman.

And more power to her, Jordan thought, even if she had chosen to bury herself away in this speck of a town.

"Look, when I get back to Boston tonight, I'll call Ted and tell him all is well."

Her eyes widened. "Don't do that!"

"But Holly, I should—"

"He won't listen to you. Let me handle it."

Suddenly, the panting dog ran up to Jordan, rubbing enthusiastically against his leg.

"Taffy!" Holly issued another sharp reprimand and the retriever slunk away. "We're trying to teach her not to do that."

"No harm done." Jordan brushed a patch of reddish brown dog hair from his slacks.

"Now, where's Stephanie?" she wondered aloud as she got to her feet. She began calling her daughter.

Finally, Stephanie's small voice came floating across the yard. "I'm in my house, Mommy."

Jordan turned to Holly. "Her house?"

"Tree house." She grinned. "Come see. This is something you'll appreciate."

He followed Holly to the other side of her house and to a big old oak with low, wide-spreading limbs. He scarcely believed what he saw. On the thickest, lowest branches was a tiny playhouse built on a sturdy platform. The pitched roof was actually shingled, the exterior was whitewashed and the door and window shutters were painted Dutch blue. Five steps built on low risers made it an easy climb for pint-size legs.

Holly glanced up at him. "Look familiar?"

"Sure does," Jordan admitted, as a tree house from the past came to mind. "Looks like a duplicate."

"Well, it comes as close as memory allowed. Of

course, since you're the one who designed the original, you'd know best.''

"That was a million years ago, Holly.''

He'd been eleven, maybe twelve, when the carpentry bug had bitten him big time. Tired of building bird feeders and step stools, he had set his sights on the big chestnut tree in the Wests' backyard. He had designed a plan, thrilled the six-year-old Holly with his drawings and then persuaded Ted West to let him build it.

But his vision had proven greater than his rudimentary carpentry skills. After Jordan struggled for weeks to erect the tree house, his father and Ted West had taken over and finished the job. That had pretty much ended his participation. Although he helped with the final painting, his enthusiasm for the project had faded. Now Jordan remembered how childish and incompetent he had felt.

"I loved that tree house so much,'' Holly continued, "that I wanted Steph to have one just like it.''

"Hi, Mommy.'' Little Stephanie popped her head out the front window. "Are you coming in?''

Holly looked to Jordan. "Would you like to see inside? We can all fit in if we scrunch down low. It's been done.''

"Yeah, when Dr. Gabe came to our tea party,'' Stephanie announced.

"Dr. Gabe?'' This was the second time Jordan had heard the name mentioned.

"The friend who helped me build this.''

The little girl giggled. "Mommy, you helped *him*.''

Holly laughed, too. "Okay, okay. But I was the one with the idea.''

Jordan had forgotten the chimelike quality Holly's laugh possessed. The easiness of it brought back the carefree exuberance of their childhoods. The sweetness of it filled him with regret for happier days when his brother had been alive and his father healthy.

"Jordan?" Holly touched his shoulder. "Do you want to go in?"

Jordan glanced from mother to daughter and back. That Holly had re-created this special memory was all very touching. But it wasn't for him. "I think I'll take a pass, Hol."

"Sure, Jordan," Holly answered right away. "It's pretty grimy up there anyway, and you're not dressed for it." With a glance down at her long, gauzy print skirt, she added, "Neither am I."

Holly's quick response failed to cover her daughter's audible sigh of disappointment. Jordan felt a stab of guilt—which he resented. He wasn't used to being around kids. Maybe he *had* been insensitive about Stephanie's invitation. Still, why would the kid care if he came inside or not?

Jordan looked up at the little girl, trying to think of an excuse to appease her. But Stephanie stared right past him. "I'm hungry, Mommy."

Holly checked her watch. "Oh, gosh, it's almost six-thirty! You must be starving, honey. Good thing Gracie made dinner for us tonight."

"Yeah, Gracie's tuna noodle casserole. Ya-aa-ay!" Stephanie cheered, jumping excitedly inside her little house, making the tree branches bounce.

"Take it easy, Steph," Holly warned as she turned to Jordan. "It's her favorite. She's been after Gracie to make it for weeks."

"With that kind of enthusiasm, it must be quite the dish."

"I don't know about that," she replied with a shrug. "But if you'd like to, ah, stay…"

Stephanie picked up on this immediately. "Gracie bought ice cream for dessert," she said, meeting Jordan's gaze this time. "Peanut butter ripple—from the dairy farm."

Tuna noodle casserole and peanut butter ripple ice cream? It wasn't exactly cuisine he had a taste for, and he had planned to be on the road by now. The drive back to Boston was long and tedious. Yet the kid was staring at him with expectant eyes from her perch at the tree house window. For some unfathomable reason, she wanted him to stay.

"It would be good to have a meal before I hit the road," he said, recognizing a second chance when he saw one. Jordan didn't want to remain in this little girl's doghouse, although he wasn't sure why he felt it mattered. Somehow, it did.

"Then you'll be staying?" Holly sounded surprised.

"If it isn't too much trouble."

"It's no trouble at all. But if you have someone waiting for you…"

"Not tonight."

Stephanie let out a whoop of delight. "Mommy! Can we use the pretty dishes? And candles, too?"

Chuckling, Holly nodded. "My daughter loves having company for dinner," she said to Jordan. "It can get awfully quiet around here sometimes."

So that's why the kid wanted him to stay, Jordan mused silently as he followed Holly into the cottage. Well, the two of them did live a somewhat isolated existence way out here in the boonies. Their home was a good five miles from the center of town, with no neighbors within earshot. Stephanie, too young to go to school, stayed home all day with a senior citizen baby-sitter. No wonder she was hungry for company. And what about Holly? Despite her obvious pride in her rein-vented life, was she lonely, too?

"Hey, this peanut butter ripple stuff isn't bad," Jordan announced after his first taste of Stephanie's favorite ice cream.

Holly almost laughed at the amazed look on his face. Of course Jordan would be surprised that a superb ice cream could be produced by the local dairy farm. "Actually, Houghton Farms ice cream is considered just about the best in this part of the state," she said, feeling compelled to tell him. "People come from all over to buy it."

"But it's 'spensive," Stephanie offered, causing dribbles of melted ice cream to ooze down her chin.

"Not with your mouth full, young lady," Holly admonished, reaching to wipe her daughter's face with a napkin.

She noticed Jordan had averted his gaze and was now staring down at his ice cream dish. Well, four-year-olds were often messy when they ate, she thought. But Jordan wouldn't know that. He was the epitome of the businessman bachelor—urbane, fastidious and clueless.

On second thought, Holly realized she wasn't being fair. All through dinner, Jordan had been in fine humor. For a man of sophisticated tastes, tuna noodle casserole had to be something of an indignity. But he had eaten his entire serving without complaint, and his refusal of seconds was so gracious it even made Stephanie smile.

That was another thing. Her daughter tended to be reserved around adult males. Except for Gabe Sawyer, so few were present in her day-to-day life. But Stephanie was taking quite a shine to Jordan, despite their earlier dustup. And, surprisingly, Jordan seemed to grow more at ease with Steph as the meal progressed.

This observation pricked at Holly's conscience. The relief she'd felt when Jordan accepted her story about Stephanie's conception felt shallow now. Doubt gnawed at her. Good Lord, she'd done what was best for her daughter, hadn't she?

A single sharp knock at the front screen door gave Holly a start.

"Holly, may I come in?" a familiar male voice called.

"It's Dr. Gabe!" Stephanie announced brightly.

Jordan looked across the table at Holly. "The famous Dr. Gabe?"

Unsure what he meant by that, she turned away and beckoned Gabe to come inside. "This is a surprise," she greeted as her friend joined them in the dining room.

Gabe took a long look at the candlelit dinner table before his gaze rested on Jordan. "Seems I've come at a bad time."

Holly assured him he had not. "This is Jordan Mason, an old family friend. We grew up together," she explained. "Jordan, this is Gabriel Sawyer, our good friend."

"And Taffy's doctor," chimed in Stephanie.

"And tree house builder extraordinaire." Jordan stood up to shake Gabe's hand.

Catching the edge in Jordan's voice, Holly frowned.

"Jordan was the neighborhood boy I told you about," she reminded Gabe. "The one who designed the first tree house."

Gabe nodded as Stephanie tugged on his elbow. "Why didn't you bring Jenny?" she asked.

"Her mom actually made it home for supper tonight,

so Jenny and Matt wanted to stay with her. Sorry, honey.''

''Jenny and Matt are your children?'' Jordan asked Gabe.

''No, they're my sister's. The three of them live with me.''

''Ah, I see.''

See *what?* Holly wondered, puzzled by the expression on Jordan's face.

Stephanie sighed, shaking her head. ''Too bad. Jenny really likes peanut butter ripple.''

''So does Dr. Gabe, as I recall,'' Holly added, motioning him to sit down.

Jordan watched the easy familiarity between Holly and *Dr. Gabe.* And little Stephanie also appeared to be quite comfortable with him.

''So, Gabe, what brings you here tonight?'' Holly inquired as she fetched another crystal dish from the china cabinet.

''I may have some good news for you about the old apple packing plant. There's a chance it could be rezoned for commercial retail.''

''A chance?'' Holly echoed as she scooped out more ice cream. She had considered the small, rather dilapidated old packing plant as a possible site for her shop. But its neglected condition and the zoning issue proved daunting. That was months ago, however, and now she was getting desperate. ''What happened?''

''After we spoke this afternoon, I discussed your location problem with the other selectmen. The packing plant came up, and George Woodbury mentioned he's been getting a lot of complaints about it,'' Gabe said as Holly handed him the dish of ice cream. ''People say it's an eyesore and possibly a safety hazard. Some want it torn down.''

"But some people don't," Holly countered, recalling the tidbits she'd heard around Golden. "They're afraid someone will put up a bunch of ticky-tacky houses on that land."

"Exactly. That's why a rehab of the building might be a good compromise. As long as the plans meet a town meeting approval, that is."

"You think that's possible, Gabe? This town doesn't take change well."

"People might be persuaded if a developer comes up with good plans. And the board of selectmen is willing to propose it to the town," Gabe advised. "We've already agreed on it—unofficially, you understand."

This was the best news she had heard in weeks. It gave her hope. Maybe, just maybe, she could keep her business in Golden and be near Stephanie throughout the day. That was what she wanted more than anything. While Jordan asked Gabe about the packing plant, Holly found herself daydreaming about how she'd design the new shop, where she would place her products and how she would display them. She could hear the two men talking, but she was too caught up in her imaginings to listen.

"Holly. Holly."

A tap on her arm jolted to attention. "I'm sorry," she gasped, looking from one man to the other. She felt her skin grow warm with embarrassment. "Doing a little dreaming, are we?" teased Gabe.

"Sort of. What did I miss?"

"Gabe suggested a walk down to Summer Pond," Jordan explained. "I know I'd like to stretch my legs before driving back to Boston."

"Ooh, can I go? Can I, Mommy?" Stephanie peered up at Holly with beseeching eyes.

"I thought we could all go," Gabe added.

Holly quickly realized that this was her chance. She was determined to reach her father before Jordan got back to him, and she needed to be alone when she made the call.

"Look, why don't the three of you go ahead while I clean up here?" she suggested.

After some back and forth, she had overcome their objections to leaving her behind. She waved them out the back door, smiling at the sight of her tiny blond daughter sauntering along between the two tall, dark-haired men.

As soon as they had disappeared from view, Holly reached for the kitchen telephone. Her father answered on the first ring. "How could you send Jordan Mason here?" she demanded, letting loose the resentment she'd kept pent up all afternoon. "Why did you do it?"

"He did come to see you?" Ted inquired with a whisper of disbelief. "I wasn't sure he'd actually follow through."

"Oh, Jordan followed through, all right. He's still here, in fact," she revealed. "He showed up at my house unannounced, he saw Stephanie—"

"Did you tell him?"

"No!"

"No? But, honey, the Masons have to be told."

"Why?" Holly asked. "We settled this matter years ago. You promised Mom."

"Against my better judgment. And, under the circumstances, I'm regretting it now more than ever."

"I don't understand what you mean."

"Didn't Jordan tell you about his father?"

"No. He hasn't said a word about Lawrence." Her head had begun to ache, and she didn't like the alarm in her father's voice. "What's wrong?"

"Apparently, Lawrence had a severe heart attack and had to undergo emergency bypass surgery," Ted explained. "He's been very ill. Jordan was on his way back from visiting him in Florida when I ran into him at Hilton Head."

"He's going to recover, isn't he?" Holly felt sick at heart. She had held a special affection for Lawrence Mason. He'd been like a second father to her.

"He's home now, recuperating, and Jordan said the doctors are optimistic."

"Thank goodness."

"Holly, the man almost died—without knowing that his dead son had fathered a child, without knowing he has a granddaughter. I can't live with that anymore," Ted insisted. "Lawrence Mason was once my closest friend."

"Oh, Dad." Unable to continue, Holly swallowed hard.

"You know I never liked keeping Stephanie a secret from the Masons. Especially after Scott was killed. But you were so upset, and your mother was so adamant..."

She took a deep breath in an attempt to steady her voice. "That's why you sent Jordan here?"

"Yes. Because as much as I wanted to tell him, it's not my place. You and your mother made that clear long ago," he said with unmasked bitterness. "But you have to. You have to tell Jordan so that he can break the news to his father. Please, Holly, before it's too late."

Holly's hand trembled as she hung up the phone. The ache in her head was now a full-blown throb. How naive she'd been to think she could keep Scott's child a secret from the Masons forever. And she'd been wrong to try—terribly, terribly wrong.

She sat on a kitchen stool and stared out the window. Lawrence Mason's illness weighed on her heart. Why hadn't Jordan told her? If only he had said something...she grimaced at the thought of the elaborate lie she had told him just a few hours ago.

Noticing the sky was darkening, she realized a spring thunderstorm was headed their way. The walk to Summer Pond would be cut short, and the threesome would be returning any minute. Holly knew she had to have a serious talk with Jordan before he left. Finally, after five long years, the time had come to speak the truth—as painful and as difficult as that might be.

Despite the rumblings of fast-moving thunder, Holly heard voices approaching. Then the back screen door slammed and Stephanie ran into the kitchen.

"Mommy, Mommy," she called in a panic, "the angels are bowling again! And they're so noisy!"

Holding her daughter close, Holly tried to soothe her anxiety. "Maybe they've got a big tournament tonight, so they're playing extra hard."

Stephanie answered by burying her face in Holly's shoulder.

Gabe and Jordan made it inside seconds before the rain began to pour. "This was unexpected," Gabe said, peering out the window. "Looks like it's going to be a big one."

A crack of thunder resonated through the room. Stephanie hugged Holly tight. "I don't like bowling."

Gabe gave Stephanie a comforting pat on the back. "I'd better get home. My gang's not fond of thunderstorms, either."

"I should be going, too, Holly," Jordan added. "I'll follow Gabe out to keep from getting lost this time."

"You can't leave yet, Jordan," she blurted out.

"I can't?" He appeared startled. "I've got a long drive ahead of me, and this rain isn't going to help any."

"Then wouldn't it make sense to wait out the storm? It'll pass over."

"I've already stayed longer than I'd planned."

"Please, I really need to talk to you."

He shrugged in resignation. "All right, I'll stay—but just for a while."

After saying goodbye to Gabe at the door, she and Jordan watched him run through the rain to his truck. By then, Stephanie was half asleep in Holly's arms.

As soon as Gabe pulled out of the driveway, Jordan turned to her. "Okay, what is it you want to talk about?"

She glanced down at the golden head resting on her shoulder. "I've got to put her to bed," she whispered. "It shouldn't take long. She's so tired the thunder isn't even bothering her anymore."

With a restless sigh, he leaned against the doorjamb and promised to wait.

Upstairs in her bedroom, Stephanie rallied a bit when Holly started undressing her. "Have the angels stopped yet, Mommy?"

Her daughter's sweet, drowsy voice filled Holly with tenderness. Earlier today, she had wanted to protect Stephanie above all else. She *needed* to protect her. But from what? A loving grandfather? Because now that she had finally allowed herself to consider him, Holly knew that's exactly what Lawrence Mason would be.

And Jordan? Although he'd made the effort to get along with Stephanie at dinner, Holly sensed he had no real affinity for children. They played no part in his world. So what did she have to fear from him? As an uncle, his interest would be minimal at best.

After tucking Stephanie in bed, Holly sat holding her hand in the dark. The thunder was now nothing more than a distant echo, and soon her little girl drifted off to sleep. Holly kissed her baby-soft cheek.

Then, mustering up every last scrap of her courage, Holly went downstairs to face Jordan.

Chapter Three

She found him standing at a living-room window, gazing out at the bleak night. Jordan turned when her footsteps sounded on the wood floor. "The wind is gusting up again. I think we're in for another round."

Now that they were alone, Holly's courage lagged.

"Let me get a pot of coffee brewing before we sit down." She hoped a few extra minutes would calm this attack of second thoughts.

"Holly." Jordan put up his hand to stop her. "I'd like to get out of here tonight. Another storm is heading in."

The rising wind could be heard now, whipping through the trees and rattling the outside window shutters. Jordan's point taken, Holly gestured to the living-room sofa. "I called my father while you were out with Stephanie and Gabe," she began as they sat together on the camelback sofa, "and he told me about Lawrence. You should've said something."

"God, Holly, I meant to. But when I got here and learned about Stephanie, it threw me. And then seeing you again…"

As he reached for her hand, their eyes met. "I got sidetracked, I guess. I'm sorry."

Her pulse sprinting into double time, Holly felt caught by the clear deep blue of his eyes. She did believe him, yet the warmth of his hand on her skin blurred the direct connect between thought and speech.

"Holly? You know I wouldn't keep that from you," Jordan added when she was slow to respond.

The concern in his voice cleared her head. "I know that. I was stunned when my father told me, though. It was so unexpected."

With a low sigh, Jordan leaned back into the sofa. "This day has been full of the unexpected."

As swift as the flash of a camera, a stroke of lightning brightened the room. Then a long, lumbering roar of thunder rumbled overhead.

Holly gasped, rising from the sofa. "That's close. I've got to check on Stephanie."

The electric lights flickered for a second before everything went dark.

Jordan muttered a curse. Then he came to her side, brushing against her in the dark. "I hope you have a flashlight or two around here."

"In the kitchen. I can find it."

She felt her way through the darkened rooms, side-stepping chairs and tables, skirting corners. Just as she reached the kitchen, a small flare of light glowed from the adjoining dining room.

"Here we go," Jordan said, carrying in the stubby candle left from their candlelight dinner. "Luckily, you left the book of matches on the table."

He directed this sole source of light over her shoulders as Holly groped through an upper cabinet. When she located the heavy-duty flashlight, she was relieved to find the batteries weren't dead. Next, she pulled out a box of emergency candles. "These should fit in those candlesticks." She handed the box to Jordan. "I'm going upstairs."

With the flashlight illuminating her way, Holly hurried up to her daughter. She found Stephanie curled up in a deep sleep, apparently undisturbed by that first crash of thunder and oblivious to the current, more muted rumbles. Her breathing was gentle and even. Holly envied her child's peace. And she worried about it, as well. Stephanie's secure little world was bound to change once Jordan and Lawrence knew about her. But how much, and in what ways?

Her resolve wavering, Holly pushed the thought out of her mind. She *would* tell Jordan the truth, and then she'd hope and pray all would come out right in the end.

"She's okay?" Jordan asked when she returned to the kitchen.

"Sound asleep. She didn't hear a thing."

"That's some kid you've got there," he said with a shake of his head.

The wry inflection in his voice made her wonder if he meant that as a compliment. It had always been like that with Jordan. Holly remembered the many times she'd been unsure of what he had meant. She wondered if Jordan did it on purpose—to keep people off balance and at arm's length.

A muffled ringing echoed from another room, breaking into her thoughts. Jordan gave her a puzzled look. "Is that your telephone?"

"I think it's my cellular phone," she said, somewhat puzzled herself. "It's in my handbag."

Holly aimed the flashlight toward the front hall, where she had left the bag. Jordan followed her with one of the sturdy white candles in hand.

She was surprised to hear Gabe's voice on the other end of the static-filled line. Since the connection was poor, he quickly delivered news for Holly to pass on to Jordan. Switching the phone off, she turned to Jordan with a small amount of dread. He was not going to like this.

"That was Gabe. The phone lines are down, too."

"He used your cellular number to check on you?"

"Not really," she replied, baffled again by his tone. "He wanted to know if you were still here."

"Why should it matter to him?"

"*Because,*" Holly continued, bracing herself against his inevitable displeasure, "lightning struck a couple of old pines by the creek bridge—the one you crossed on the way here. They've fallen right across the road, blocking the bridge."

"Don't tell me," he said, his expression cool. "That's the only way out of here, right?"

"'Fraid so. Gabe says the road crew won't be able to clear the way until morning."

Jordan groaned and leaned against the front door. "An apt ending for this day, wouldn't you say?"

Expecting biting irritation, Holly found his resignation made her feel worse. "I'm sorry, Jordan. If I hadn't asked you to stay..."

"Forget it, Holly. Even *I'm* not going to hold you responsible for acts of nature." The slightest of smiles crossed his lips. "Guess you'll be putting me up tonight."

"Guess so. There's a sofa bed in the den. I hope you won't mind it too much."

"I've never slept on one."

"Oh, you're in for a treat," she said diplomatically, brushing aside the temptation to tease him. "I'll go make the bed up."

"Holly." Jordan caught her by the wrist. "It's not even nine o'clock yet. I don't know about you, but it's way too early for me to turn in."

She looked back at him with disbelief and then shined the flashlight on his wristwatch to check.

Jordan chuckled. "I know how you feel. This day never seems to end."

Holly had to laugh. "All right. I won't make you go to bed yet. But since it's my fault you're stuck here, I'll lend you my cellular phone for as many calls as you need to make. You probably want to notify your office of your whereabouts."

"I don't have an office anymore."

"You? Oh. That's right," she sputtered, "you sold CompWare."

Jordan didn't say a word.

An uncomfortable silence hung between them as Holly mentally kicked herself for her gaffe.

"Well, why don't I open a bottle of wine and then we can sit back and relax," she finally said, pointing the flashlight toward the kitchen. "Besides, you still have to tell me about your father."

And she still had to tell him about Stephanie.

The candles at each end of the coffee table flickered and danced in the dark as she and Jordan drank red wine. The thunder and lightning had passed, but the rain rapped a steady rhythm on the windows. As they sat on the sofa, stocking feet resting on the low table, Jordan explained about his father's heart attack and surgery.

"I'm glad to hear Lawrence is getting better. Although it sounds like it was touch-and-go for a while."

"Yeah, we almost lost him." Jordan's thumb traced the rim of his wineglass. "He still has a long recovery ahead, and he has to be very careful. But Rachel is taking great care of him."

Holly remembered Lawrence's young second wife fondly. "He's lucky to have her."

"Thank God he has her, especially after losing Scott and all."

The slight catch in his voice both moved and troubled her. "He has you, too, Jordan."

"I'm not much of a comfort to him, Holly. You of all people should know that."

Indeed, Holly knew quite a bit about the stormy years between Jordan and his father. Jordan had been just about the wildest teenager their staid neighborhood had ever known. Lawrence always seemed to be bailing him out of one kind of trouble or another. And the loss of Jordan's mother had created even more strain between them. Yet after Jordan had joined Mason CompWare, their relationship mellowed. Or so Holly had thought.

"Scott's death should have drawn you two closer."

"It had to, didn't it? After all, we're the only two left."

"Jordan." Holly reached for his hand. Regret for the family she had once felt part of, and her own painful memories of Scott, filled her with sorrow.

Jordan's hand slid from hers as he moved off the sofa. "Don't make it out to be worse than it is, Holly. Okay?"

"Sorry. I didn't mean to."

After a moment, he turned back to her. "I didn't mean

to jump down your throat. Talking about almost losing Dad is hard—especially after what happened with CompWare. He wasn't exactly one hundred percent behind the sale.''

''Actually, I was surprised that *you* would part with the company,'' she revealed. ''When your father retired, you took over without a hitch. Scott joked that it was as smooth as a royal succession to the throne.''

''Did he?'' Jordan said, his smile wistful. Then he shrugged. ''The business world moves with amazing speed these days, Holly. One has to be able to move with it.''

''Still, selling out couldn't have been an easy choice.'' Unless the money was too tempting to resist, she considered ruefully.

''Selling out never is,'' he replied, his voice dry and direct as he sat down beside her again. ''Look, Dad and I went back and forth about this sale. He wanted to hold on to the company. But, in the end the decision was mine to make. And I made it. End of story.''

The shadow of regret in his eyes hinted that there *was* more to the story. Holly was surprised. Regret was an emotion she would not have associated with Jordan Mason. Guilt was another. She sensed he was feeling that, too—particularly in regard to his father. For the first time, Holly realized there might be one or two chinks of vulnerability in that well-fortified persona of his.

''Well, Jordan, what are your plans?'' she asked, changing the subject. ''Perhaps some travel now that you're a free man, so to speak?''

''I considered it. But I don't want to stray too far until Dad's condition has been stable for a while. The next few weeks of recovery are crucial,'' he explained. ''And to be honest, endless months of travel doesn't hold that much appeal. I need—I *want* to get back to work, Holly.''

She should have known he'd be itching to get back in the saddle. Aimlessness was not in Jordan's nature. "What do you propose to do?"

He tossed back his head and laughed. "That is the million-dollar question, isn't it? Suddenly, I have all the free time in the world, and more money than I know what to do with."

A cutting irony laced his words, and Holly couldn't understand why. Most men would give anything to be in his position.

"You must have some ideas," she offered gently.

"A few. And I've received plenty of suggestions from an eager army of potential partners." He reached for the wine bottle. "More for you?"

Shaking her head, she watched Jordan refill his glass.

"I've looked into a few of the more interesting prospects, but nothing's grabbed me yet. Maybe CompWare is just too hard an act to follow."

She studied his profile out of the corner of her eye. The clean angle of his jaw, the firm set of his chin, exuded a strength that belied the possibility that Jordan was at loose ends. He was even more attractive than she'd remembered. The callow good looks of his youth had deepened into something infinitely more appealing. He was confident, yet approachable. At ease with himself and sexy. Jordan still had it all—and then some. Tall, dark, handsome—and rich—the kind of man women flocked to. They certainly used to! Holly recalled wryly.

As she focused on his dark-blue gaze, however, Holly sensed a certain despair—a despair she was sure Jordan kept buried inside. He was not the kind of man to wear his heart on his sleeve. But this day had been much too full of surprises and too ripe with evocative memories to leave either of them untouched. It was natural for all kinds of emotions to rise to the surface. Holly felt as if she'd been through the wringer herself.

But what now?

Jordan's uncharacteristic moodiness, combined with his concern for Lawrence's recovery, made Holly wary. Perhaps this wasn't the best time to blurt out the truth about Stephanie. They were both on edge. And she'd wager he was as exhausted as she was. No, she decided, neither one of them was in shape tonight to deal with the aftershocks of this particular announcement.

Holly felt no relief at postponing the truth. The fact that Scott was Stephanie's father had to come out. It was time. Still, it seemed more prudent to wait until they both had a chance to rest from this roller coaster of a day. But in the morning she would, at last, tell Jordan everything.

Jordan cursed as he contorted his body in yet another attempt to find a comfortable position on the thin mattress. Sofa beds had to be the most wretched contraptions to befall a good night's sleep. Or any sleep at all. For most of the night he'd been staring into the dark, mulling over yesterday's turn of events and the changes in Holly. Talk about unexpected…

Jordan had had his fill of tossing and turning. He climbed out of the low foldout bed and lifted the blinds to look outside. The sun was rising in the gray sky. Restless to get out of the small, closed den, Jordan decided to take a walk. After showering quickly, he brushed his teeth in front of the bathroom mirror with the extra toothbrush Holly had given him. The sight of his shadowy morning beard reminded him of the spare shave kit stashed in the trunk of his car.

The house was still as he passed through on his way out to his car. Outside, the beginning of a knockout spring day enveloped him in its early warmth. Jordan leaned against the Mercedes, gazing at the flowers and the grass and the trees, all fresh and glistening after last night's rain. Yet he couldn't imagine waking up to this *every* morning—his glassed-in high-rise view of busy Boston Harbor suited him just fine.

Giving in to impulse, Jordan got into the car, rolled down the windows and slid open the moon roof. Driving was a passion of his. And this unusual morning was calling him to take to the country roads. He figured he'd drive to the closed-off bridge at Golden Creek to check out the extent of the damage. He'd be back before Holly even noticed he was gone.

By the time Jordan reached the bridge, the fallen trees had already been removed and the road was clear. A solitary worker was tossing debris into the back of a town pickup truck. Jordan drove up to him and expressed surprise that the bridge had already been cleared.

''We get to work real early around here,'' the man said, his gaze roaming over Jordan's car. ''Trees hit the road, not the bridge. Didn't take us long to move 'em out. I'm just cleaning up a bit. Rest of the crew's headed for the lake. Supposed to be a mess over there.''

''So the bridge is safe?''

''Sure. Go right on ahead.''

Jordan checked his watch. ''Is there any place I can get coffee?'' He wanted a cup badly.

''General store opens at seven. Always got a pot brewing there,'' the worker said, waving Jordan on.

At the store, Jordan located the self-serve coffee set

up and poured himself a large cup. As he stirred in a packet of sugar, the discussion among the four old men hanging out at the front counter became louder. The mention of Gabe Sawyer caught his attention. After listening for a moment, Jordan realized they were talking about Holly's apple packing plant.

"It's falling apart. They should tear the durn thing down."

"That's good, valuable land it's built on. What do ya think will happen to it?"

"Ah, people from the city are always looking to move out here. Somebody will build a big house on the property just so they can say they live in the *country*."

"Don't be a fool. Someone will come along and build a whole slew of houses on that land. Mark my words."

The old men continued arguing, ignoring Jordan as he passed between them to pay at the counter. He was amazed to hear them debating the details Gabe Sawyer had mentioned last night at Holly's. News sure traveled like wildfire around this town.

Jordan realized this building seemed to inspire a lot of excitement and interest, not only in the men at the store, but in Holly, too. She'd been practically starry-eyed when Sawyer talked about it at the dinner table last night. As he drove up the hill to the gas station, Jordan decided he wanted to see the building. He asked for directions after filling up his tank. Fortunately, Edgar, the befuddled attendant from yesterday, wasn't on duty. Today's directions were as clear as a bell.

The apple packing plant was less than half a mile from the center of town. The flat-roofed, one-story building looked as if it had been abandoned years ago. It stood alone and desolate, half-hidden by overgrown bushes and thigh-high grass. Jordan got out of his car and took a walk around. The cement block building had been neglected too long. Its condition was dismal. The site had only two things going for it as far as he was concerned—its proximity to the town center and a sizable parking lot. He shook his head when he thought of Holly's hopes for the place.

When Jordan got back into his car, the time glowing on the dashboard clock came as a jolt. Holly was probably wondering what had happened to him. He automatically reached for his cellular phone. Only he didn't know Holly's phone number.

Jordan sped back to the house. When he arrived, he saw that Holly's compact car had been replaced in the driveway by Gracie's big old sedan. "Great," he muttered, grabbing the shave kit that had lured him out to the car in the first place.

"Well, there you are," Gracie growled when she opened the front door. "We thought you had left."

"Mommy was mad," Stephanie chimed in as she ran up behind Gracie.

"I went for a drive and lost track of the time," he said, trying to explain to the two dour faces. "Holly's left already?"

"She opens the shop early on Saturdays," Gracie announced. "It's her busiest day."

"Cuz people get paid on Friday," Stephanie added with an air of authority.

"I'll go see her as soon as I shave. Maybe I should call her first—to tell her what happened."

Gracie frowned. "I'll call her. You go shave." Then she stalked off.

Jordan headed for the downstairs bathroom, feeling the sooner he got out of there the better. He could just imagine the spin Gracie would put on his explanation.

He lathered up quickly and began shaving with the sharp disposable razor.

"Doesn't that hurt?"

Jordan flinched. Instantly, he felt a sting on his chin. "Damn!"

"You said a bad word again!"

He snapped off a sheet of toilet paper to press against the bloody knick. "Kid, never sneak up on a man with a razor in his hand," he grumbled.

"I didn't sneak in. The door was open," she replied, indignant. "What's a razor?"

Giving his small wound one last dab, Jordan sighed, realizing he had left the door open. He held out the black plastic razor for her to see.

"My mom has one of those for her legs. 'Cept it's pink." Without missing a beat, Stephanie lowered the toilet seat cover and plunked herself down. "That's because she's a girl, huh?"

"That's usually the reason." Resigned to the half-pint's presence, Jordan leaned over the sink and resumed his shave.

"What's that on your face?"

"Shaving cream. It's kind of a foamy soap."

"My mom has lots of foamy stuff at the store. And it smells better than that stuff."

"Uh-huh," he murmured as he stroked the razor along his jaw.

"Mommy calls it moose. But that's crazy," Stephanie said with a slip of a giggle. "Mooses can't use it."

Jordan shot her a glance and grinned in spite of himself. "You've got a point there, kid. A real good point."

After he finished shaving, Stephanie stayed right on his heels as he went looking for Gracie. She was in the kitchen, flipping pancakes on a hot griddle.

"I'll be on my way now," he told her. "Thanks for, ah, everything."

"Hold on there, Mr. Mason. Who's gonna eat these?" She jabbed the plastic spatula at the cooking hotcakes.

"Those are for me?"

"Who else?" she barked. "Holly insisted you get a decent breakfast before you left this house."

Jordan knew he was already on the housekeeper's bad side after yesterday's misunderstanding. Although he'd probably never see her again after today, he figured it was best to appease her. Besides, the doughy aroma wafting in the air taunted his empty stomach. He sat down at the kitchen table as ordered.

While Gracie served him a plateload of buttermilk pancakes, Stephanie dragged her plastic booster seat from the dining room and plopped it on the empty chair next to him.

"You've already had breakfast, dear," Gracie reminded her before announcing she was off to put the den back in order.

The kid climbed up onto the booster seat. "I'm just gonna watch, Gracie."

And watch she did. Jordan had never known what it felt like to be on display—until now. Her big brown eyes followed his every move as he patted butter on each pancake, then doused them with maple syrup. But when she fixed her gaze on his mouth as he was about to take the first bite, Jordan put his fork down.

"Would you like some?"

Stephanie's eyes widened, and she cast a furtive glance over her shoulder.

"Don't worry about Gracie. It'll take her a while to pick up in the den," he said in a low, conspiring voice. "How about it? Want some?"

"Yeah," she whispered, her pale-blond pigtails bouncing with her excited nod.

Jordan grabbed a clean plate from the sink drainer and quickly scooped out a small portion from his own dish. While they ate in companionable silence, he was struck anew by how much Stephanie physically resembled Holly. Watching her eat with gung-ho enthusiasm, Jordan was glad there wasn't any little girl prissiness in this kid. Yeah, he thought with a smile, Stephanie was a tomboyish squirt, all right—just as her mother used to be.

As soon as they finished eating, Jordan told Stephanie he had to be going.

"When will you come back?"

"When?"

The utter earnestness on her face threw him. He wasn't planning to ever come back, yet he couldn't bring himself to tell *her* that.

"Maybe tomorrow?" she asked. "Mommy will be home all day."

Jordan's mind went blank. For whatever reason, the kid had taken a liking to him, and he wasn't sure what to do. Her watchful gaze, however, demanded a reply. "You see, Stephanie, I live way over on the other side of the state. It's too far for me to just turn around and come back tomorrow."

"Oh." Stephanie stared down at the table until, suddenly, her face brightened. She looked up at Jordan with a big smile. "Can you come the day *after* tomorrow?"

His heart sank. "I don't think so."

"Then when?"

As her smile faded, Jordan didn't know what to say. He didn't want to lie to the kid. But delivering the news straight to that hopeful little face was too much—even for him. He gave her shoulder a gentle squeeze. "I don't know, honey."

Stephanie nodded, her disappointment clear. Jordan half expected her to start crying.

He felt like such a heel. Still, what else could he have said or done? Geesh. How had he ended up in this position anyway? This brief visit to Golden—his favor for an old family friend—had gotten out of hand. Without a doubt, it was time for him to leave.

Stephanie still followed him as he collected his belongings and said goodbye to Gracie. The kid didn't say much, though, not even when Jordan said goodbye on the front porch. When he started up his car, she was still there, sitting on the top step, watching.

She looked so small and lonely. He felt bad about leaving her. But that was crazy—he barely knew the kid. Before driving away, he rolled down the window and waved. To his surprise, Stephanie's face lit up once more and she waved back with both hands flapping buoyantly.

But damn, *that* made him feel worse.

"This is ridiculous," Jordan muttered, stealing a last look at Stephanie from the rearview mirror. Lack of sleep was doing this to him, he concluded. A decent night's rest would restore his perspective.

So would getting the hell out of this town.

Holly spotted Jordan parking in front of the shop, while she was showing a new line of vegetable shampoos and conditioners to the Sanderson twins. The girls were two of her best customers. Being the most sought-after teenaged baby-sitters in town, they never failed to show up at the shop on Saturday mornings, flush with their Friday-night earnings. Today, it seemed they were sampling and sniffing every product in the store. But now that Jordan was here, Holly wished the twins would hurry up and make up their minds. Unfortunately, her Saturday sales assistant had called in sick, leaving Holly to manage the shop alone.

She would need a private moment to tell Jordan about Scott's being Stephanie's father. Guilt had kept her awake most of the night. But his disappearance this morning had dashed her chance to talk to him at home. Now—somehow—she had to tell him here in the store. And she had to do it before the retirement home van arrived with its Saturday-morning shopping group.

The wind chimes above the entrance announced Jordan's arrival. Turning away from the girls, Holly met his gaze right away. The intense blue of his eyes made her pulse thrum with disconcerting unevenness. She chalked it up to nerves.

"Hi," Jordan said, his voice sounding a shade raspy. He looked tired, too.

"I'll be right with you," she promised.

His slightly rumpled clothes and tousled dark hair didn't escape her notice. She found the effect appealing. Certainly, this unintentional disarray seemed more approachable than his usual groomed crispness.

Holly returned her attention to the twins. "So, ladies, have you decided what you want?"

The girls didn't answer. Apparently, they found Jordan infinitely more interesting than vegetable shampoo. Anxious about the time, Holly distracted them with an offer of free samples. The twins were thrilled with all the freebies, which eased her guilt about pushing them out the door.

"You'll never stay in the black if you give stuff away like that," Jordan observed with a sly wink.

Holly chuckled. "Those two *keep* me in the black."

Jordan took a long look around the room. "You've got a great setup here, Holly. You wouldn't expect to find a store like this in—"

"In the middle of nowhere?" she asked, teasing him a little.

His lips curved into a knowing smile, and Holly felt her pulse taking off again. She didn't think it was from nervousness this time. What it *was* from, she refused to consider. Too many memories and a five-year secret stood between her and Jordan. And once she revealed the truth, their lives would be turned upside down.

"Jordan, I really wanted to talk to you at the house this morning."

His smile faded. "I apologize for disappearing on you like that. I was just driving around and—"

The trill of the door chime cut him off, as Annette from the bakery across the street poked her head in. "Holly, did you get more peppermint foot powder yet?"

"The foot powder? Oh, yes. The shipment came yesterday morning. Hold on a second."

Holly hurried into the crowded stockroom to fetch the product. The retirement home group would be descending upon the shop soon, and she had to talk to Jordan before it did. Quickly ringing up the sale, she sent Annette on her way.

"Sorry about that, Jordan," she said, joining him over by the display of natural bristle brushes. "Now, about this morning," she began slowly, in an attempt to control the anxious tremble in her voice.

"Please, let me explain," Jordan insisted before she could continue. "I had every intention of getting back to your place before you left for work. But I stopped at the apple packing plant and lost track of the time."

Holly was astonished. "You went over there? Why?"

"To get a look at it, of course," he replied. "You sounded serious about the place last night. And after what I heard at the general store, I decided to check it out for you."

"For me? I never asked you to do that."

"I took it upon myself, I know. But you'll be glad I did, Holly. Because you're in for a big disappointment if you pin your hopes on that building. It's in terrible condition."

Holly stiffened. "I'm well aware of its condition."

"Are you?" he asked with his typical skepticism. "Then you're also aware of the kind of money you're talking about—not only to reconfigure the building for retail use, but for all the repairs, as well?"

"Oh, please." She glared at him, annoyed. "I've been considering every possibility, every angle, for months. Give me a little credit, will you?"

"I'm just trying to help." Jordan began pacing in front of the brush racks. "You seem so intent on moving your business to that dilapidated old building, I can't help wondering—what *are* you thinking?"

"I'm thinking I want to keep my business here in Golden because I want to have as much time with my daughter as possible. I'm *thinking* the apple plant is my last best hope for that." Exasperated, Holly started re-arranging the hairbrushes on the display.

"I'm glad to hear that, Holly." Jordan stopped pacing and his tone was calm. "Because it's clear to me your little girl is hungry for attention."

Holly stepped back, stunned. "She has all my attention, Jordan. How dare you question that?"

"I'm not. I think you're a great mother. All I know is that your kid followed me around like a shadow this morning. To me, that says she's lonely."

"Oh, she's just curious about you, Jordan. Someone like you doesn't show up at our door every day, you know."

Jordan shook his head. "It was more than that. You didn't see her face as I was driving away."

His concern bewildered Holly. He hadn't seemed all that interested in Stephanie last night. Indifferent was more like it. "Stephanie has several little friends. And she has a wonderful baby-sitter. Gracie just dotes on her."

"I don't doubt it. But seems to me that your daughter spends an awful lot of time on her own, with just an old woman for company. That's hardly a perfect situation," Jordan proclaimed. "Don't forget, I almost hit the kid with my car yesterday when she wandered too far from the house. And what if something happens to Gracie while the two of them are alone? Don't you worry about that?"

Of course she worried about that, and a zillion other things, as well. She was a single working mother, doing her best to give her child a secure, balanced life. Holly could barely contain her resentment. Perfect situations were few and far between. Besides, she'd stopped believing in *perfect* the day Scott had abandoned her at the altar.

The memory of Jordan's part in that dark act of her life fueled Holly's resentment. She marched back to the front counter, trying to compose herself. It didn't help.

"It's one thing to criticize my business decisions, Jordan. But questioning how I raise my daughter is off-limits. Because, believe it or not, this is something you know nothing about."

He followed her across the room. "Holly, I was just trying to point out my concern—"

"No, Jordan! You're telling me I'm making mistakes and what I should do to fix them—just as you did when you told Scott we were too young to get married and that he should postpone the wedding."

She expected more protest. But none came. Only when she looked directly at Jordan did Holly realize the blow her words had dealt. His face was ashen, his gaze stricken with an anguish that surpassed remorse.

Holly gasped. "I'm sorry."

"Why? That's how you feel."

"I shouldn't have said it."

"You have every right to say it, Holly," he replied, his voice low. "Besides, it doesn't come as shocking news. I've always known you blamed me for what happened."

Chapter Four

"You weren't the one who walked out on me, Jordan."

Jordan's eyes narrowed with skepticism as Holly struggled to keep memories of that long-ago anguish at bay. Those memories represented the folly of a vulnerability she vowed never to experience again.

"I did resent the way you interfered before the wedding," she admitted. "I resented it for a long time. But blame you? Why? You were right."

"I wish I hadn't been so goddamned right. Then maybe Scott would be alive and you two would be married and have a fam—"

"Jordan, please don't." Talk like that would make it harder to tell him about Stephanie. "There's something we have to discuss before you leave."

But the doorbell chimed again, this time announcing the arrival of the retirement home van. A dozen or more senior citizens streamed in, chatting happily and full of questions that needed her immediate attention. Holly's heart sank. How could she tell Jordan, now that her shop was bustling with activity?

As she attended to her customers, Holly caught a glimpse of Jordan leaning against the front counter. He appeared to be fascinated by the small group of women avidly comparing notes on the various skin moisturizers on the shelves.

"I've never seen anything like this," he said when Holly snatched a spare moment. "You've got yourself a nice business here, Holly. I hope the apple packing plant works out—if that's what you really want."

"I think it can be a winner."

"Then more power to you." He curved an arm around her shoulders, his blue eyes glinting with sincerity.

Holly was sure this was nothing more than a brotherly gesture on his part. For several intense moments, however, it didn't feel that way. Jordan's eyes drew her in and warmed her with an errant cloak of intimacy. She was aware of little else except the heat of his body when he brushed against her and the weight of his muscular arm on her shoulder. The buzz of a dozen shoppers in her little store had faded. Holly heard only the low, steady cadence of Jordan's breathing and the insistent beat of her heart.

"I have to leave soon, Holly," Jordan murmured, pulling her back to reality. His arm slipped from her shoulder. "What was it you wanted to discuss?"

The shop had come alive again. Sadie Campbell and Phyllis Peters stood less than a foot from Holly, arguing over who was entitled to the last bar of strawberry soap. And Frank Elliot, with two expensive shaving brushes in hand, seemed to be heading straight for her. Holly realized it was too late. The time to tell Jordan the most intimate secret of her life had come and gone.

Except Jordan was waiting to hear what she had to say.

Holly improvised quickly. "It's about your father. How long will it be before he's fully recovered?"

"Another month or two—if he follows doctor's orders and avoids any real stress. Why?"

"I'd like to give him a call when he's back on his feet. It's been so long."

"He'd like that a lot, Holly. You were very special to him."

Holly winced. Lawrence had always called her the daughter he never had. But what would he call her once he learned the truth? Would he ever forgive her for keeping his granddaughter from him?

With Scott's death, Lawrence had been the one most wronged by her sin of omission. Holly realized *she* had to be the one to tell Lawrence about Stephanie, not Jordan. As soon as Lawrence was deemed well enough to hear it, that's exactly what she would do. Although she felt horrible about it, this missed opportunity with Jordan was—probably—for the best.

"Will you jot down your dad's address and phone number for me?" she asked as Frank Elliot approached her.

After Holly explained the difference between two shaving brushes to the older man, Jordan handed her a white business card. "Dad's address is on the back."

Holly glanced at the address. Turning the card over, she noticed Jordan had scratched out the office telephone number printed beneath the old Mason CompWare logo and had written in a different one.

''That's my home number,'' he said. ''If you ever need anything, call me.''

He really meant it. Holly could tell. And it made her feel worse. Guilt roiled inside her. Would *Jordan* forgive her once he learned the truth about Stephanie? Would he understand why she had deliberately lied to him yesterday?

''Since you spoke to Ted last night, I gather there's no need for me to call him,'' he continued.

Her throat felt tight. Not trusting her voice, she simply shook her head.

''Holly, I'm ready to check out,'' Sadie Campbell called from the front of the shop.

''I better go.'' Jordan lowered his lips to her cheek.

It was the briefest of kisses, yet it made her skin tingle. As he turned for the door, he murmured something about being in touch.

Holly sensed that was just a way to say goodbye. Jordan had no reason to get in touch with her—at least not until after she made Stephanie's existence known to his father. What would happen then? she wondered.

Cupping her hand to her cheek, she could still feel the warmth of his kiss. A flicker of regret taunted her. As she watched Jordan wend his way past her customers, Holly felt a bewildering stab of loneliness. She found herself wishing things could be different between them.

But that could never happen. Her terrible lie and the cold truth about the past five years made such a wish impossible.

Holly shook her head as she studied the latest spreadsheet. Her idea to pool resources with two other business owners to purchase the apple packing plant had held such promise. Both Susan Leary, owner of the cramped fabric store next to Holly's shop, and Nancy Barron, who'd been searching for space to open a new-and-used bookstore, had jumped at the chance. But now, with the final figures in front of her, Holly felt her hopes sinking fast.

"It doesn't look good, Susan." Holly slid the spreadsheet across her kitchen table. "See for yourself."

Her friend skimmed the numbers and groaned. "It's worse than I thought. Wait until Nancy sees this."

Holly glanced at the clock on the stove. "She should be bringing the kids back from the library any minute now. Do you want to break the news to her?"

"Are you kidding? I'd rather not even be here when she finds out. You know how excited she is about the bookstore," Susan said, reaching for her glass of iced tea. "Besides, you're much better at things like that than I am."

"Gee, thanks a lot." But Holly figured it was her responsibility anyway. She was the one who had thought up the idea in the first place.

Susan peered down at the spreadsheet again. "The rehab costs are killing us."

"I know. They're exorbitant." Just as Jordan had warned five weeks ago.

Holly pressed her own icy glass of tea against her forehead. The afternoon had turned surprisingly hot, and hours of combing over the discouraging numbers had made her head ache. Thinking of Jordan didn't help. His appearance in Golden had stirred up her past and put one big question mark on her daughter's future. Thinking of Jordan reminded Holly that so much in her life was up in the air.

Yet she thought about him every day. And she thought about his father, too.

She had decided to call Lawrence Mason around the middle of July. Then, if his health permitted, she would fly down to Florida with Stephanie and tell him everything. Her projected scenario for this trip was as detailed as her business plan for the shop's new location. She prayed that the trip would meet with more success than her wilting project.

The jangle of children's voices roused Holly from her thoughts. She heard the squeak as the front screen door opened and five rambunctious preschoolers rushed into her kitchen. A weary and crumpled Nancy Barron dragged in after them.

"They were all perfect angels during story hour," she said as she plopped herself down at the table. "But all hell broke loose as soon as they got in the car. My two are in time-out as soon as we get home."

"Mommy, I'm thirsty. Can we have pink lemonade?" Stephanie crooned. The other kids echoed the request.

Susan poured Nancy a tall glass of iced tea as Holly got the lemonade out of the fridge. Leaning back lazily, Nancy used her hand to fan her face. "Whose turn is it to have the kids next?"

"Mine, I think," Holly volunteered, mentally reviewing their play-exchange schedule. "This Friday afternoon, right?"

Nancy smiled. "Perfect. I'm going to make an appointment at the mall for a facial and a manicure. Then I'll get one of the Sanderson girls to baby-sit and make my husband take me to Green Hill Inn for an expensive dinner."

"You're in the mood to pamper yourself, eh, Nance?" Susan commented as Holly gave each child a lidded cup of lemonade and sent the group out to the enclosed side porch to play.

"After a day like today, I need it." Nancy sat up straight, looking from one friend to the other. "You know what? We should all go to the Green Hill on Friday to kick off Memorial Day weekend. Phil and me, you and Jamie, and Holly, you could ask Gabe."

Susan immediately voiced her enthusiasm for the suggestion, but Holly held back. Although Gabe had become a close friend, she disliked the idea of calling him whenever she needed a male escort.

Nancy turned to her. "Holly?"

"I'll take a pass on that one."

"But why?" Susan asked. "Because you and Gabe quit dating ages ago?"

Holly nodded. "He's not an escort service, you know. Besides, he does so many things for me. I don't want to bother him with something like this."

"Will you listen to yourself, girl?" Nancy chuckled, pulling Holly down to sit in the chair next to her. "You make it sound like it would be a hardship for him or something. And you forget—Gabe's our friend, too. I bet he'd enjoy a night out with us."

"*I'll* invite him if you want," Susan offered.

"Or maybe Phil and I can fix you up with the new associate at his firm," Nancy added.

Holly laughed. "You guys are relentless. You know that?"

Her two friends exchanged glances. Nancy leaned closer to Holly and patted her hand "We just want you to get out and have some fun. Between running the boutique and taking care of Stephanie, you have so little time for yourself."

"So humor us and come out and play," Susan said with a wink.

"Okay, okay. You win," Holly declared, raising her

hands in resignation. "But there'll be no fixing me up with Jamie's associate. And I'll call Gabe myself."

Nancy and Susan agreed.

Listening to them chat about dinner reservations and baby-sitters, Holly felt lucky to have these two women for friends. They had welcomed her when she had first moved here—no questions asked. They, along with Gabe Sawyer, had helped her ride out that first rough year in Golden.

The rest of the town hadn't been as accepting. Part of this reception, Holly later learned, had to do with the oldtimers' innate Yankee wariness of strangers. She had no family or connections to Golden. Who was she to come into *their* town and start up a business selling bubble bath and body creams of all things? The fact that she was six months pregnant—with no father in sight—aroused curiosity, as well. Small, conservative Golden was leery of such matters.

Despite the initial coolness, Holly never regretted moving here. The townspeople might have been wary of her, but they were never unkind. They might have kept their distance at first, but they also allowed her the chance to prove herself as a businesswoman and a citizen. In time, the town accepted her as one of its own. With that acceptance, Holly won what she'd been after all along—a secure, supportive community for her child, a place where Stephanie would never feel alone, a place they could both call home.

A high-pitched wail pierced the kitchen table conversation. Then another child's voice began hollering from the porch.

Susan grimaced. "Good Lord, that sounds like mine."

"I should've known this peace was too good to last," Nancy said as Susan scurried out to save the children from each other. She glanced at the spreadsheets on the table. "Maybe you should tell me what you and Susan found out from these before *all* the kids fall apart."

With the sound of Susan's scolding reaching them from the porch, Holly pulled her chair closer to the table. "You're not going to like this," she warned before delivering the disappointing news.

She had almost finished explaining the figures to Nancy, when Gracie arrived at the front door, carrying a watermelon and an insulated bag of ice cream in her arms. "I brought some treats for Stephanie."

Holly went to the door and took the heavy watermelon from Gracie. "But this is your afternoon off. Why aren't you out doing something fun?"

"I *was*—with Sadie and Phyllis. While we were out driving, we stopped at Houghton Farms for a dish of ice cream. And I couldn't leave there without picking up some peanut butter ripple for my little girl."

Holly smiled. "You really do spoil her."

"I know, I know," Gracie said as she followed Holly into the kitchen. "But since I have no kids or grandkids of my own and she has no grandma, we both get something out of it."

Her innocent remark made Holly flinch. Outside of Holly, Gracie was the closest thing to family Stephanie had here in Golden. Gracie adored Stephanie, and Holly was grateful for that. But her child's lack of real family ties had been troubling Holly more each year. Jordan's surprise appearance only shoved this concern to the forefront of her mind.

"Hey, what's with the watermelon?" Nancy asked when Holly and Gracie came into the room. Susan was back at the table and all seemed quiet out on the porch.

Gracie pulled up a chair. "They just got some beautiful ones in at the general store. I couldn't pass it up."

"Watermelon is one of Steph's favorites," Holly informed her friends as she put the ice cream and the melon away.

"Anything for Steph, eh?" Susan tossed Gracie a playful wink.

"Never mind that. You should be glad I stopped by the store today, ladies," Gracie admonished. "Wait until you hear what they're all talking about there."

"Are those old coots grinding out another rumor?" Nancy asked with wry grin. "Wasn't the last one about the new librarian and the stash of X-rated videos she supposedly keeps locked up in the library safe?"

Holly couldn't take Gracie's remark so lightly. She knew her housekeeper didn't have much use for town gossip. Holly had a sinking feeling that something was wrong. "What did you hear, Gracie?"

"Somebody has bought the apple packing plant."

Nancy and Susan gasped. Holly blinked in astonishment. "Who?"

Gracie shrugged. "Some out-of-towner. That's all anybody seems to know. But if you heard the fellows down at the store jawing about it, you'd think the devil himself was coming to Golden."

"I wonder what the buyer plans to do with it," Susan said.

"What does it matter?" Nancy slumped low in her chair. "Holly's figures already prove we're doomed. This just seals the coffin."

Her friends' distress upset Holly more than her own disappointment. Sure, the numbers were discouraging, but there remained a few more avenues to explore. She hadn't been prepared to give up earlier and she wasn't going to now. At least, not until she had some answers.

"This situation may not be as hopeless as it seems," she declared with as much conviction as she could muster. "Who knows? The guys at the store may have gotten the story all wrong."

During the next few days, Holly tried to find out everything she could about the sale of the apple packing plant. In the end, however, she found out absolutely nothing. Not even Gabe Sawyer could help. The entire board of selectmen was clueless about the identity of the seller. They knew a commercial agent from Boston had brokered the deal, but that was all. Although Gabe promised to try to find out more before the dinner at the Green Hill Inn, he didn't sound optimistic.

On Friday afternoon, Holly closed up shop an hour early. She wanted the extra time for a relaxing bath before gussying herself up for her rare night out. Holly stopped at the general store for panty hose and snapped up a pair of extra sheer. On her way to pay at the front counter, she noticed the four older men gathered around the coffee machine—the General Store Four, as they were affectionately known around town. Eager to get home, Holly smiled and waved, but kept walking.

"Hello, Miss Holly," silver-haired Clyde Barker called out. "How's business?"

"Just fine, Clyde. Thanks."

Percy Daws, leaning on his cane, motioned her to come over. "Give us old fools a moment, will you, Holly?"

With a silent sigh, Holly gave up her place in the checkout line. "What can I do for you, gentlemen?"

"You know the old apple plant's been sold, don't

you?'' Earle Stacy asked, his voice deep and dry, his New England accent thicker than anyone else's in town.

Howie McGovern shook his gleaming bald head and muttered at his friend. "Of course she knows. She wanted to buy it herself. Remember?"

"Yeah, yeah. It was just a way to get the conversation going," Earle barked.

Percy shot a disparaging look at his cohorts. "Have you any idea who bought it, Holly?"

"I'm afraid I don't. It's quite the mystery."

Emitting a pronounced harrumph, Clyde rubbed his grizzled chin. "All this secrecy. I don't like it."

"It spells trouble, believe you me," Earle said.

"I hear they're gonna tear down the building and put up a shopping center or maybe even a mall," Howie advised, his tone sharp with resentment.

Percy grunted in disgust. "We don't need any shopping mall in this town. Could you imagine the traffic? The noise?"

"This whole thing gets me steamed," Earle groused.

"Outsiders just can't waltz in and force things down our throats," declared Percy, tapping his cane on the floor for emphasis. "We'll put a stop to that malarky, at the town meeting."

As the old men griped among themselves, Holly slipped away to pay for the panty hose.

The General Store Four were still going at it when she left the store. It wouldn't be long before the rest of the town joined their chorus of resentment. Holly felt kind of sorry for the purchaser of the packing plant. Whoever it was probably hadn't bargained on anything like the good people of Golden, Massachusetts.

Jordan pulled into Holly's driveway and parked behind her car. Although an amazing number of stars glittered in the night sky, it was very dark out. He sat in his car, staring at the small house, wondering how Holly would react when she found him at her door.

Damn! Jordan gripped the locked steering wheel. He didn't know why he was even concerned about it. It was just *Holly,* after all. But reminding himself hadn't slowed his quickening excitement when he had crossed the Golden town line. Nor was it doing a heck of a lot to ease the tightness in his chest.

"Oh, what the hell." Jordan climbed out of the car.

The single porch light illuminated his way to the house, while a clamoring chorus of crickets drowned out the sound of his boot heels on the front steps. He rang the doorbell and within seconds he heard Holly unlatching the locks.

"Hi, Hol—" The name died on his lips when Gracie's white hair poked out from behind the door.

"You're back?" With a wary sigh, the housekeeper unhooked the chain lock and opened the door wider. She made no move to open the screen door.

Somehow her less than cordial greeting didn't surprise him. "Hello, Gracie," he greeted from his side of the screen. "I didn't see your car in the driveway."

"It's in the shop."

"I'm sorry to hear that." She just stood there peering at him through the screen. "Ah, could you tell Holly I'm here to see her."

"Don't you know how to use a phone?"

Jordan couldn't suppress a chuckle. He hadn't planned to pop over tonight. He'd thought he would call Holly in the morning. Yet when he had reached Golden after the long drive from Boston, he felt like a kid about to burst from excitement. All of a sudden his news couldn't wait. He had headed straight for this house.

"You've got a point, Gracie. I should've learned my lesson after the last time, but—"

"Holly's not here this time, either. She went out to some fancy do with Dr. Gabe."

"Oh." Thrown off by the hard thud of his heart, Jordan looked away from the woman. "She'll be late, then."

"I expect so."

"And Stephanie?" he asked impulsively, facing Gracie again. "Has she gone to bed yet?"

"Goodness, yes. It *is* after nine o'clock," she replied with an indignant roll of her eyes. "Do you want me to tell Holly you dropped by?"

Keeping a rein on his disappointment, Jordan shook his head. "No point in bothering her about it tonight. I'll call in the morning."

He could feel Gracie's eyes on his back as he returned to his car. The woman had no use for him that much was clear. But her unsurprising iciness didn't explain the deadweight of dejection lingering in his gut.

An unshakable image of Holly and Stephanie all alone in their isolated cottage in this nothing little town had propelled him into action. That Holly might actually possess a social life didn't mesh with the picture fixed in his mind. And in the rush to get his brainstorm off the ground, he'd forgotten about Dr. Gabe.

As he headed for the motel he'd spotted out on Route 16, Jordan reminded himself that Holly's personal life had no bearing on what he'd come back to Golden to do. His time here was limited. He needed to get on with the rest of his life—as his father had pointed out after CompWare was signed, sealed and delivered to its new owners. Jordan regarded this upcoming project as the first step toward moving on. It would help Holly, and it would help him.

After he'd spent a restless night in a thin-walled room, the rumbling of heavy trucks on the nearby state highway woke Jordan unmercifully early. He drank two cups of coffee at the motel café, but had no stomach for their big, greasy-spoon breakfast. He'd pick up something at the bakery on the common or at the general store. By then it would be late enough to telephone Holly.

Jordan was surprised by the temporary No Parking signs posted around the town center. Last night, he hadn't noticed these signs as he cruised through in the dark, nor had he seen the red, white and blue buntings draped across every storefront on the common. While he parked behind the white steepled church located at the foot of the expansive green, the lights in Holly's shop caught his eye. Could she really be out and about already? Especially after her big night with Dr. Gabe?

The lights drew him across the common like a magnet. A flash of excitement pumped in his veins as he neared the door and peered inside the window. Holly stood at the front counter, busy tying colorful fat bows on a row of big wicker baskets. She didn't notice him until the wind chimes trilled as he opened the door. Her eyes widened with surprise.

He smiled. "I know Saturday's your busiest day. But isn't seven-thirty a bit too early even for you?"

"Jordan—what on earth?"

Her genuine astonishment proved Gracie had taken him at his word, Jordan thought dryly. She hadn't told Holly about his visit to the house last night. But something felt off here. Holly's surprise seemed more apprehensive than amazed.

"You don't look so happy to see me, Holly." He closed the door behind him. The inside of the shop smelled fresh and sweet, like the rows of blossoming apple trees that lined the road into town.

"No. It's not—it's just—it's just so—*unexpected,*" she stammered. "Why are you here?"

"To see you, of course." This wasn't the reception he'd anticipated. Glancing at what she'd been working on, he realized the problem could be his timing. "I've interrupted you."

She looked down at the baskets. "I'm donating these to the preschool's silent auction at the chicken barbecue. I need to get them done before the parade this morning."

"Ah, that explains the buntings and the No Parking signs. I'd forgotten Monday was the holiday."

"Golden always holds the parade on Saturdays. Then the local Rotary Club sponsors a barbecue out at the high school." Moving from behind the counter, Holly stooped down for a box marked "Kiwi Shampoo."

"Here, let me take that." Jordan strode across the room and lifted the box from her arms.

Closer to her now, Jordan was struck by how much Holly resembled this late-spring morning. Her hair was twisted back into a thick golden braid that grazed the back of her slender neck. The pale-green dress she wore, light and graceful, flowed almost down to her ankles. Beneath its short sleeves, her arms were gently muscled, yet delicate. Her skin was taut and looked as smooth as creamy fresh honey. Imagining just how soft she would be to touch, he felt a stirring ache low in his body.

Swallowing a quick, sharp breath, Jordan pulled back. He put the box on the table behind the counter as Holly directed. "I can help you with the baskets," he suggested, despite the sudden rawness in his throat.

Holly took him up on the offer. "Place one of every product in each basket," she instructed, pointing to the array of colorful tubes and jars on the counter. "And try to make the basket look nice."

Even with Holly's guidance, it took him a while to get the hang of her artful arrangement. As they progressed through the baskets, she described the purpose for each lotion, powder and gel. Being a straightforward bar-soap kind of guy, he found the variety of bath products mind-boggling.

"So Jordan, *why* did you come back?" Holly asked as she checked each basket, tactfully tidying up his handiwork without comment.

The slight tremble in her voice was perplexing. If he made her that nervous, he'd like to know why. But Jordan suspected it had to do with Scott, and that irked him. He resented the idea of forever being linked in her eyes and in her mind with the man who had left her devastated. No way was he going to bring up the subject of his brother. Not now.

Besides, his news was too good to spoil with talk of the past. Holly was going to be thrilled. Jordan reached inside his sport coat pocket for the folded wad of documents. "This is why I came."

She took the papers and skimmed them. "This is a sales contract for the apple plant," she said, bewildered.

"I know. I bought it."

"You! You're the one?"

"Yes. I'm going to remake it into a first class facility."

She stared at him in disbelief. He looked back at her, completely baffled. She sank back against the counter with a sigh.

"Holly, what's wrong?"

"Oh, Jordan," she groaned, shaking her head. "You don't know what you've done."

Chapter Five

Jordan was floored by Holly's reaction.

"What's the problem? The building was up for grabs, so I bought it."

"But why?"

"I thought about it a lot after I left here, and I realized you were right. The building has great potential as a small retail center," he explained. "And I have the money to make that happen."

Holly's eyes darkened with disapproval.

"Waltzing into town and throwing your money around smacks of arrogance." She tossed the sales contract at him. "Do you have any idea of the uproar you've created around here?"

"Uproar? What kind of uproar?" Jordan couldn't believe it. "All I did was buy the building so you could relocate your shop."

Her eyes widened with shock. "You bought it for me?"

He nodded. "You made it clear the building was your best hope. But I knew you'd never be able to afford it on your own—not with all the renovations it needs."

"You should've consulted with me before deciding that."

"Maybe I should have. Except I didn't think it would be an issue. You wanted the building and I had the money to invest. It was the answer to the problem."

Holly's nostrils flared with indignation as she moved back behind the counter. "That was *your* answer, Jordan. But the problem was *mine*." She began fussing with the bows on the baskets. "Hard as it may be for you to believe, I've been managing on my own just fine. I don't need anyone—especially you—buying my way out of problems."

He knew she took great pride in her independence. Yet he had to wonder if something else was behind her strong reaction. As he gazed at her from across the counter, his eyes were drawn to the wispy blond tendrils caressing her flushed cheeks. Her delicate beauty undermined Holly's claims of strength, and it tripped the switch on a protectiveness he'd rarely felt.

Jordan leaned in closer and apologized. "I can see I presumed too much. It never occurred to me that you'd feel this way."

She met his eyes, and slowly, the tension eased from her face. "Oh, Jordan," she said with a sigh. "What am I going to do with you?"

A dozen tantalizing things suddenly sprang to mind, catching him off guard. He'd never thought of Holly in that way before. It would take some getting used to.

Aware that she was watching him, Jordan brushed

these surprising and lustful notions aside. They had nothing to do with why he'd come back to Golden. Clearing the tightness in his throat with a cough, Jordan wished he could clear the confusion in his head as easily.

"We should sit down and talk about it."

Holly nodded. "But when? There's so much going on today with the parade and the barbecue. I don't see how we're going to find time."

"It can wait until tomorrow."

"You'll still be here?"

He couldn't help laughing. "Since I'm now the proud owner of the building in question, I thought I'd stick around—for a little while anyway," he said. "Why don't we meet at the building tomorrow? Say about ten o'clock?"

"Eleven would be better. We have church tomorrow."

"Oh. Sure," he replied, feeling embarrassed. He had forgotten tomorrow was Sunday, and that for a lot of people, the day meant more than sleeping in or reading the funny papers over leisurely cups of coffee.

At that moment, a frazzled woman with long, salt-and-pepper hair bustled into the shop. "I'm running late as usual. Are the baskets ready?"

Before Holly could answer, the woman looked at Jordan. "Who are you?" She eyed him from head to toe.

Holly jumped in, introducing him to Karin, the preschool director. "Jordan's a childhood friend," she took pains to add.

The characterization made Jordan wince.

Karin glanced around the shop. "Where's my little pumpkin, Stephanie?"

"Over at Gracie's apartment, playing with the cats.

She and Gracie should be popping over here any minute.''

"Tell your daughter that the face-painting lady will be at our booth at the barbecue after all. Steph must have asked me about it fifty times this week." Karin looked Jordan's way again. "Hey, big fella, can you help Miss Karin carry these baskets to her car?"

Wondering if "Miss Karin" talked to all adults as if they were preschoolers, Jordan caught Holly's eye. She confirmed his suspicion with a wink and a smile. The preschool director continued chattering as he loaded the baskets into her big station wagon. After she drove off, Jordan heard a high-pitched squeal of delight coming from across the road. He turned to find Stephanie running toward him.

"Jordan!"

Her giggles filled the air as she darted away from Gracie. Clutching a floppy stuffed rabbit in her arms, she rushed up to him, oblivious to her baby-sitter's warnings to look both ways.

"Whoa there." Jordan caught her by the shoulders before she ran right into him. Gazing into her dancing brown eyes, he was struck again by how much she looked like Holly.

"You came back!" Her voice was full of glee. "The parade's today."

Fast on the kid's heels, Gracie snapped out her name.

"Uh-oh," Stephanie exclaimed, her eyes wide.

"Uh-oh is right, kid," he replied as the grim-faced baby-sitter approached. "Looks like you've gotten us both in trouble."

Ignoring Jordan, the woman scolded Stephanie for running out into the road. The child stared down at her rubber-toed sneakers until Gracie finished reprimanding her. Then she lifted her bright face. "Look, Gracie. Jordan's here."

"Hi, Gracie," he said, offering her a smile.

She acknowledged him with a cool nod.

"Now, child, where's your mother?" she continued as if he weren't there. "We've got to find a good spot for watching the parade."

Holly emerged from the shop, carrying a folding chair in one hand. "Are you coming to the parade with us, Jordan?"

Stephanie grabbed his hand before he had a chance to answer. "You hafta come, Jordan."

She tugged his arm until he fell in step behind Holly and Gracie as they headed toward the town common. The kid's pudgy palm was so soft and her stubby fingers felt so small in his hand. Jordan was sure he'd never felt anything like it.

Still, he hadn't a clue why the kid had latched onto him like a long-lost buddy. Maybe it *was* because she lacked a male presence in her life—other than Dr. Gabe, of course. And if Gabe Sawyer did show up now, who was to say Stephanie wouldn't dash off to him?

Jordan caught himself. Why was he even worrying about it?

The number of people drifting onto the common from all directions surprised him. Crowds in Golden was an oxymoron in his mind. This Memorial Day festivity was probably one of the town's social highlights of the year—one of the few things to actually do here. No wonder people were pouring out from the woods. Young parents pushed strollers and chased after runaway toddlers. Long-haired teenaged girls hung together, watching shaggy-headed teenaged boys lounging on the hoods of their cars, watching them. The more senior residents relaxed on folding lawn chairs, chatting among themselves. Jordan even recognized the old guys from his stop at the general store the last time he'd been in town.

"This looks like a good spot," Holly announced when they reached a clear area directly across from the Congregational Church. She positioned the folding chair for Gracie and then sat on the curb, her knees curled up beneath her billowy skirt. Stephanie plopped down next to her mother as Holly gestured to the curb. "Have a seat, Jordan."

No sooner had he lowered himself onto the curb than the steady beat of a marching drum echoed from afar.

Stephanie hopped to her feet in excitement. "I hear it, Mommy! I hear it!"

The kid remained standing, nestled between him and Holly, her thin little arms curved around both their shoulders. "I see them now," she chanted. "See the flags! Here they come."

Jordan peered down the main road. A color guard of four aging veterans in snug-fitting, faded military uniforms led the way. Next followed what had to be the high-school band, playing a reedy-sounding "Stars and Stripes Forever." On the heels of the band came more service veterans, some in uniform, some not.

"Mommy, look!" Stephanie tugged on Holly's arm and pointed to the classic red convertible trailing behind the marching veterans. "Look! Dr. Gabe."

Jordan glanced over his right shoulder. Dark-haired Gabe Sawyer sat at the wheel of the gleaming old car. Two men rode with him, and all three waved to the crowd as they passed by. Plastered across the front hood of the car was a banner identifying the three men as the board of selectmen. As if anyone in this town didn't already know, Jordan thought dryly.

"Hey, Gabe!" Holly called out, waving and laughing. Stephanie and Gracie joined the chorus until Dr. Gabe located them in the crowd. Jordan couldn't miss the broad smile Gabe aimed at Holly before waving back to Stephanie.

"Here you go, Steph!" With a toss of Gabe's arm, a half dozen or more pieces of brightly wrapped candies flew across the road, landing right at Stephanie's feet.

In the blink of an eye, the kid scooped up the candy in her hands. "Mommy, Dr. Gabe threw me candy! Gracie, look at all the candy Dr. Gabe threw at me!"

As the two women oohed and aahed with the thrilled child, Jordan felt an inexplicable irritation jabbing his chest. It was such a small thing—why was the kid so excited about a few morsels of candy? He watched the three females with their heads bowed together as Stephanie very slowly counted out each piece.

Yet if it really *was* such a small thing, why was he sitting there feeling like the proverbial fifth wheel?

The three shiny fire engines following behind the selectmen's car made Stephanie forget all about the candy. Members of the Golden Volunteer Fire Department walked beside the trucks, handing out kid-sized fireman hats to every child along the parade route.

Stephanie pulled the red plastic cap down over her silvery bangs. "Look at me, Jordan. I'm a firegirl!"

But when the passing trucks revved up their sirens, her eyes were stricken with panic. "Mommy, make them stop," she wailed, hiding her face in Holly's lap.

"They'll be gone soon, honey," Holly soothed, patting Steph's thin little back.

Jordan looked away. The sight of Holly mothering her child still seemed strange. He told himself to get over it.

The sirens faded as rows of Girl and Boy Scouts,

dressed in uniforms of browns, greens and blues, began marching by. Stephanie, dry-eyed and none the worse for the experience, perked up immediately. Holly got to her feet and Gracie began folding up the lawn chair. Surprised, Jordan turned to Holly.

"The parade's over," she stated.

"Already?"

"That's what's nice about small-town parades. They're short but sweet."

The people around them were falling into line behind the scouts. "Where's everybody going?"

"To the War Memorial and the cemetery for wreath layings and then on to the barbecue." She led them onto the street to follow the crowd.

People seemed to be moving along in a respectful silence. Shotgun blanks echoed loudly at the War Memorial, and at the cemetery the bugle song "Taps" wove a plaintive duet with the steady, low whistle of the morning breeze. The stillness and the solemnity moved Jordan. The townspeople seemed to be taking very much to heart the honoring of lives lost. Even restless children and blasé teenagers stood straight and quiet during the ceremonies.

Afterward, the crowds drifted farther along the road, until the smoky aroma of broiling chicken filled the air. Jordan's stomach growled, reminding him he hadn't eaten that morning.

Although Holly kept urging her to keep up, Stephanie dragged several feet behind them. "I'm tired, Mommy. I can't walk anymore."

Holly held out her hand to her. "Come on, honey. It's not much farther now."

Bypassing Holly, Stephanie walked up to Jordan. "Will you carry me? Please?"

He stared down at her corn-colored head. "If that's what you want," he said, reaching out to gather her up in his arms.

But Stephanie pulled away. "Not the way moms do it."

"What?"

"Carry me the way daddies do. Please?" she quickly added.

The way daddies carried kids? Jordan looked to Holly for help.

"She means on your shoulders," Holly explained, sounding as wary as she looked.

"Yeah! On shoulders. Like that. And that." Stephanie pointed at every man she saw carrying a kid on his shoulders.

Suddenly fathers toting children on high seemed to be everywhere. From what he could see, two-parent families predominated around here. He wondered if four-year-olds were aware of things like that. Jordan kind of felt for the kid. No way was he going to disappoint her this time.

"Okay, sweetheart, a ride on the shoulders it is."

This was a first for him. Unsure of exactly what to do, he awkwardly crouched so Stephanie could climb up on his back.

"Good Lord, I can't watch this," Gracie muttered. "I'll see you at the barbecue."

"Bye, Gracie," Stephanie crooned as she scooted onto his shoulders.

"You don't have to do this, Jordan." Holly hovered close by as he slowly stood.

As he circled Stephanie's legs to his chest, his first few steps were on the wobbly side. Afraid that he'd drop her, Jordan held on to the kid for dear life. But Steph was so light. Within minutes, he got the shoulder ride down pat.

Eventually, Holly relaxed, too. She walked alongside them without her arms half-raised, ready to catch Steph *just in case.* "Jordan Mason, I wouldn't have believed this if I hadn't seen it with my own eyes," she declared. "You are just chock-full of surprises today. You know that?"

Between Stephanie's bubbling giggles and Holly's intrigued glances, Jordan felt lighthearted. He liked the notion of being full of surprises. Up until a few months ago, his life had been too damn predictable.

Holly held her daughter at bay for as long as possible. But as soon as Jordan had finished eating his chicken dinner, Stephanie grabbed his hand and led him away to the pony rides. Jordan didn't balk. In fact, he seemed more than happy to go off with her. Holly's heart was in her throat as she watched them stroll across the playing field. The increasing affinity between Stephanie and Jordan was startling, to say the least. And worrisome.

"So your friend came back," Gracie commented from her lawn chair, which she had set up next to the picnic table. "Kind of a surprise, isn't it?"

Holly nodded, her gaze fixed on man and child as they drifted farther into the crowd. Jordan had returned because of the apple packing plant—or so he said. But was there more to it than that? Had he, somehow, found out about Stephanie? Was he waiting for just the right moment to confront her with the truth? That's what she had feared when he appeared in the shop this morning.

"Is he going to be sticking around long?" Gracie asked.

Before Holly could answer, however, Nancy and Susan descended upon her. "You've been holding out on us, girl," Susan accused. "Who is this tall, dark and handsome guy everyone's talking about?"

"And where is he?" Nancy added.

Gracie uttered a scornful harrumph and turned her attention to acquaintances at the next picnic table.

Holly explained to Susan and Nancy that Jordan was an old family friend. She said nothing about his purchasing the apple packing plant. It was too sore a subject in Golden these days. Unfortunately, this omission left her the target of their conjecture, which was highly romantic. Her two friends didn't let up on the questions until their husbands showed up and dragged them away.

Their notion that Jordan was her secret lover astounded Holly. She was grateful he hadn't been around to hear that. Heaven knows what he would have said.

Holly offered to get Gracie a cup of coffee. While waiting in line at the beverage table, she spotted her daughter having her face painted at the preschool booth. Jordan stood nearby, observing the process with great amusement. Holly found herself watching him. He looked different today in worn jeans and navy polo shirt. His bare arms were tanned and long and muscular— much more muscular than she would have thought. Stephanie pointed to him, laughing. In response, he cracked a smile so warm it took Holly's breath away. Her pulse quickened as he shifted his weight from one long, lean leg to the other.

Jordan was a handsome man. She'd always known that. Yet *feeling* it was altogether different. Her heart beat faster, her skin felt warmer and her head was swirling with heightened awareness. No, she had never, ever looked at Jordan in quite this way. But now, exhilarated by the moment, Holly could not look away.

Gradually, she realized Jordan was having a similar effect on the ladies hovering around the preschool booth. These women—mothers all—appeared to be basking in the warmth of that smile of his. Apparently, they were as susceptible as she was to Jordan's charms. Holly found no comfort in the realization. Those ladies should know better. And so should she!

Still, Holly wished they would stop ogling the poor man.

"Holly, there you are!"

Gabe's voice gave her a jolt. Catching her breath, she mustered a weak smile. "Gracie and I wanted coffee to top off our dinner. But this line is so slow—it's taking forever."

"At least you've eaten already," he said, showing her the meal tickets in his hand. "Jenny demanded a pony ride right away, and my sister gave in to her. Janet's been working a lot of extra hours lately."

"Ah, yes, guilt. It's a mother's curse, you know," Holly said, feeling nothing but empathy with Janet Sawyer.

"We saw Stephanie riding the little palomino. I noticed your friend Jordan was with her."

"Yes, he sort of popped in this morning."

"Surprised you, did he?"

Holly chuckled in spite of herself. Gabe didn't know the half of it. She was tempted to tell him the mystery buyer of the apple plant had finally revealed himself. Yet an odd sense of loyalty to Jordan held her back. Gabe, and everyone else in town, would know soon enough.

When Gabe moved on to the food line, Holly stole another look at the preschool booth. The face painter appeared to be putting the finishing touches on Stephanie's butterfly face, and Jordan was still the center of attention with the preschool moms. She shook her head. Jordan didn't have a clue about what he was in for once the news broke.

Holly realized she had to warn him before it did.

The Sawyer kids invited Stephanie over to play after church, allowing Holly to get to the old apple building early. Jordan had already arrived. She found him inside, a heavy-duty tape measure hooked onto his belt and a worn old set of building plans tucked under his arm. He was jotting furiously into a small spiral-bound notebook, unaware of her presence.

"Been here all morning, Jordan?"

He glanced up from the notebook. A startled look melted into an expression so welcoming it made her heart skip. She could almost feel the heat from his gaze as it traveled down the length of her body and back.

"You look very nice," he murmured finally.

"I came straight from church," she said, smoothing the hem of her pale-gold suit jacket with her hand. Right away, she realized it was an inane response to a pointed compliment. But the butterfly dance swirling low in her stomach was too distracting to allow for clever replies.

Jordan shut the notebook and reached for her hand. "Come on. I want to walk you through some of my ideas."

He led her through the empty building, detailing proposed renovations, suggesting layouts. He was full of purpose and excitement as he outlined the possibilities. Despite her reservations about his buying the building, Holly liked many of Jordan's ideas, and his enthusiasm relit the fire beneath her fading hopes. Still, she couldn't help wondering why he was so enthusiastic. Surely for him a project like this was small potatoes.

Then she remembered. Jordan was no longer part of Mason CompWare and it was no longer part of him. "You really are at loose ends these days, aren't you?" she remarked, not unkindly.

Jordan looked away. "Maybe I have been somewhat adrift—what with selling the company and then Dad's heart attack. Guess I was thrown off my game."

"Perhaps what you really need is a good long vacation. Time to relax and regroup."

"Relax and regroup?" He turned to her, shaking his head. "Trust me, Holly. I need this project a hell of a lot more than I need a summer in the Hamptons."

Holly could see the sense in that. Jordan loved to work. After he'd found his niche at CompWare, his youthful wild shenanigans stopped. She remembered how his transformation into a hardworking businessman had stunned everyone.

"But why *this* building?" she asked.

"Does it really matter?" he replied, seeking her gaze.

"It does to me." Although she couldn't say why. Was it because of her concern for Stephanie? Was it because of what might happen with the town? Or because of the way he was looking at her right now?

"I couldn't get it out of my mind. Or your hopes for it," he said, his eyes still locked on hers. "Or maybe even you."

Holly felt her cheeks burning. She was unsure of what he meant.

"Maybe I just really wanted to help out an old, old friend," Jordan concluded.

His comment confused her even more. As a deep breath of relief rushed through her lungs, a silent sigh of disappointment singed her throat. Holly tore away from his gaze. She couldn't imagine what was the matter with her this morning. Her feelings were never this muddled.

"Holly? Is there something wrong with that?"

Pushing away her confusion, she turned around to face him. On this subject she intended to make herself clear. "It's wrong if it's done out of a misplaced sense of guilt, or out of pity. I won't have you feeling sorry for me, Jordan."

"I don't. Honest," he claimed with much forthrightness. Still, a slip of a smile teased his lips. "Well, except for the fact that you're stuck in this hole-in-the-wall town. I do feel badly for you about that."

Jordan's smile felt like a soothing balm on the tension cracking inside her. It put her back on an even keel. And it reminded Holly that she had come to warn him.

"Maybe I should be feeling sorry for *you*," she said gently. "People around here are wary of three things— rich people who throw their money around, change and newcomers."

"I'm not throwing money around."

"It's a matter of perception."

"Warped perception, if you ask me."

"In any case, Jordan, I'm afraid you're in for a tough rezoning fight with this place."

"Even if it's all for you?"

"To a lot of people, I'm still a newcomer," Holly revealed. "As a matter of fact, the real old-timers may even consider us partners in crime in this project."

Disbelief glinted in his eyes. "But you've been in Golden five years. You own a business here."

She knew Jordan wouldn't understand. "It's a small-town quirk—if you haven't lived here all your life, you're a newcomer."

"Then Stephanie is considered a newcomer, too?"

"No. Being born here means she's accepted, one of

the fold." Actually, Golden valued all its children, which was the thing she loved best about the town. If something should happen to her, Holly knew the community would rally around Steph. As a single mother with no family nearby, this knowledge gave her great peace of mind.

Jordan Mason, however, was an altogether different matter as far as Golden was concerned. Holly told him more about the rumors flying around and the resentment many townspeople already felt toward the nameless buyer.

"After you apply for a zoning change for this property, a vote will be taken at the town meeting," she advised. "Be ready for a lot of resistance."

"Ah, small towns—how I love them." Jordan dropped his notebook and the building plans on an empty steel shelf in what used to be the plant's office.

"Sorry to put a damper on your enthusiasm. But I thought you should know."

"Hey, I'm glad you told me. And don't worry," he added with a wave of his hand. "After the way you reacted when I broke the news, I gathered something like this was going on."

"Did you?" She thought he was being rather blasé about the whole thing.

Nodding, he pulled a slightly crumpled snapshot from the back pocket of his jeans. "That's why I signed a contract to buy a house to live in until the project's completed."

"You bought a house here in Golden? When did you do that?"

"Yesterday, after the barbecue." He handed her the photograph. "I figured owning a home here will show that I have a personal interest in the town. So, I called the guy who owns Golden Real Estate and he offered to help me right away. This is the first house he showed me."

Holly took one look at the picture and shook her head. "You bought the old Paget house."

"Yeah." He came up beside her. "You know the place?"

"Oh, yes, I know it," she said, wanting to give Jordan a good hard shake. "Everyone knows the Paget place. And *everyone* knows it's the most expensive lakefront property in Golden."

"Well, it comes fully furnished and I can move in by the middle of the week. That's all I needed to know." He stuffed the snapshot back into his pocket. "If I stay in that motel out on Route 16 much longer, I'll turn into a zombie."

The absurdity of the entire situation finally struck Holly. Jordan had purchased the apple packing plant to help her. He chose the Paget house because he wanted a good night's sleep. Yet who in town would believe his motives were as simple as that? It was actually kind of funny. She couldn't help but laugh. As the newest resident of Golden, Jordan was in for one interesting adventure. But then again, so was Golden.

Jordan looked at her as if she were crazy. "Why are you laughing?"

"Because," she began, breathless from trying to *not* laugh anymore. "Because—you're impossible."

"I've been told that before, Hol," he remarked with that dry tinge of irony she remembered well. "But this is the first time anyone's said it doubled over with laughter."

She tried hard to temper her smile. "I'm sorry."

"Don't be. You have a great laugh."

Before Holly realized what was happening, he had curved his arm around her shoulders.

"I haven't heard it for a long time."

Jordan was smiling as he drew her to his side. As she peered into his ink-blue eyes, her own mirth melted. She couldn't think of what had been so funny. In fact, she couldn't think of anything but the distinct masculine smell of his skin, and the reassuring weight of his arm on her shoulders.

"You're not thrilled I bought this building, I know that."

He stood so close she could feel his breath on her forehead as he spoke. "I'm not thrilled that you bought it for me," she corrected, hoping to God she sounded more coherent than she felt.

"*You're* the one with the dream, Holly. But I can help make it happen. Besides, what good is having money if I can't use it to help a friend?"

How could she respond to such a remark? Who was she to doubt his sentiment, no matter how much it differed from the materialistic bent of the Jordan she used to know?

"We'd make a good team on this project, Holly. And don't worry about what people in town think. You and I will make them come around." He squeezed her shoulder gently. "Come on, Holly, be my partner in crime."

She smiled in spite of herself. The man was persuasive; she'd give him that.

Jordan's face brightened. "Does that smile mean you're in with me?"

Holly found it difficult to remember the drawbacks when he was all around her like this. "You are so impossible," she repeated out of a halfhearted frustration.

"C'mon, Holly, yes or no?"

Yes or no? She wished it were that simple. The situation with the town would be dicey enough, but Holly wondered what might happen with Jordan living in

Golden and working with her. It could be a disaster. She bit her lip and gazed into his eyes. Only then did she realize the choice was clear. The gift and its bearer were too irresistible to turn down.

"All right, Jordan. You can count me in."

With a whoop of delight, Jordan swooped her up in an exuberant hug. "You won't be sorry, Holly."

She laughed. His excitement was contagious. "I know I won't!"

His arms tightened around her when he smiled into her eyes. "We'll turn this mess into a showplace," he proclaimed before planting an enthusiastic kiss on her mouth.

Holly stared at him, wide-eyed, as his lips brushed hers. Their gazes caught. Jordan's eyes widened, and instead of pulling back, he pressed closer. The first kiss flowed seamlessly into a second, deeper, kiss, and Holly, closing her eyes, flowed right along with it. His smooth, strong mouth fanned a stirring warmth low in her body, making her limbs feel weak. Yet she stayed with Jordan's kiss, mindless of anything but the sizzling probing of his tongue and the aching pressure of his hard body.

It had been so long since she'd been held like this, and so long since she had kissed... Her skin grew hot as her need intensified, and a soft moan hummed from deep in her throat. Jordan groaned in reply, clutching her even more tightly.

His groan reverberated off the cement walls of the empty old office, and the echo shook her back to her senses. Her eyes flew open. She lifted her hands to Jordan's cheeks and pushed his mouth away with trembling fingers.

"Jordan, we can't," Holly gasped, pulling herself out of his arms.

Breathing fast and hard, she stepped back. She was

stunned, horrified and embarrassed, too. She couldn't believe she had kissed Jordan like that. Of all people.

Battling awkwardness, Holly made herself look at him. Although wisps of dark-brown hair fell over his eyes, she saw a startled confusion that mirrored her own.

"I'm sorry, Holly," Jordan whispered, still a little breathless himself.

Sorry? So was she—especially for responding like a love-starved idiot. "We both got caught up in the excitement of the moment. That's all it was."

Jordan nodded, his fingers combing the hair back from his eyes. "It never should've happened."

"You're right. Business partners shouldn't get carried away. Not even partners in crime," she added lightly, hoping to ease the tension between them.

He smiled. "Certainly not with each other."

As she drove home, Holly knew the impact of Jordan's kiss was not her only problem. There was the matter of Stephanie. Jordan's return to Golden had forced her to reconsider her plans for informing Lawrence Mason about Scott's child. She had stayed awake all last night thinking about it. How could she continue keeping Stephanie's paternity secret now that Jordan had practically planted himself on her doorstep? It wouldn't be right. She would have to tell him soon.

But a new dimension had been thrust into the situation. It complicated *everything*. Telling Jordan the truth now would not be as straightforward as it had seemed several weeks ago. Not after what had happened back in the building. And certainly not after the way his kiss had made her feel.

Chapter Six

On Wednesday, Jordan went about his business with single-minded determination. There would be no more ruminating over what had happened between him and Holly. He'd done enough of that during his last restless nights at the motel.

Besides, this was moving day. When the cleaning crew van pulled away from his new home, Jordan settled in with two suitcases of clothes and a bag of groceries from the general store. He devoted the afternoon to business-related calls, using his cellular phone until a technician arrived to hook up several new lines in the house.

As he microwaved his dinner, Jordan poured a beer and congratulated himself on how much he had accomplished. He had succeeded in putting Holly and that indescribable kiss out of his mind. He was doing fine.

But on his way into town for a 7 p.m. meeting with Gabe Sawyer, Jordan drove past the apple packing plant.

That was all it took. The memory of those few hot moments in that cold, empty building flooded his thoughts with a vengeance. Everything came back to him—how good it had felt to hold Holly's soft, scented body; how sweet her lips tasted and how inviting they'd been. The suddenness of the kiss, how the heat in it had sent his pulse soaring.

And he couldn't forget Holly's uninhibited reaction...the way she had opened up to him....

Yesterday, the sheer shock of her eager response had excited him tremendously. Tonight, the mere memory of it was driving him to distraction. A meeting with Dr. Sawyer was the last thing he wanted to sit through now.

Gabe was waiting for him in the selectmen's office at the Golden Town Hall. "I usually have people just come over to the house to talk," Gabe said after offering Jordan a seat at the small round conference table. "But my nephew's Scout meeting is at our place. A dozen eight-year-old boys aren't conducive to discussing zoning changes."

Jordan couldn't believe a town official was apologizing for meeting in his office. He figured it was another of those small-town quirks Holly kept mentioning. "I take it you know I bought the apple packing plant," he said, selecting a seat across the table from Gabe.

"Holly told me this morning, and I have to admit I was surprised. I was under the impression you didn't care much for Golden."

"She told you why I'm doing this, didn't she?"

"To help her out," Gabe confirmed. "Which makes complete sense. Believe me, I understand."

I just bet you do, Dr. Gabe, Jordan thought with a twinge of resentment. Yet he knew he must keep Holly's relationship with Gabe—whatever it was—separate from the matter at hand.

Once he did, the meeting proceeded better than he'd expected.

Gabe believed they could get the zoning approved at the upcoming town meeting. "I'm not saying it won't be close," he warned. "And you'll hear a lot of belly-aching in the next few weeks. But people will come around eventually—as long as you don't try to shove anything down their throats."

In spite of himself, Jordan liked the man. Sawyer was a straight-shooter, and it was obvious he thought a great deal of Holly. Quite obvious. Yet what about what had happened three days ago? How did that kiss he and Holly had shared fit into the picture?

"You and Holly seem to be, ah, close," Jordan ventured, attempting to get a fix on the situation.

Gabe hesitated. "You could say that, I guess."

"Well, I'm not aiming to horn in on you and Holly. I want you to know that."

"That's decent of you, Jordan. But there's nothing to horn in on."

"There isn't?" He felt an absurd flicker of relief.

"Holly and I went out for a while when she first came to Golden. But we didn't really *click,* if you know what I mean." Gabe leaned back, clasping his hands behind his head. "She was still hung up on some guy at that point."

"Stephanie's father?" Jordan asked, although he didn't know why. Holly had made the nature of that relationship painfully clear.

"No. She said it was someone else. Someone she was supposed to marry. Holly didn't say much more than that.'' Gabe shrugged. ''Besides, you probably know what happened back then better than I.''

''Yeah, I do,'' he mumbled.

Gabe gave him a strange look. ''You didn't come back just to help Holly out financially.''

''The hell I didn't.''

''You've got a thing for her. Don't you?''

''You don't know what you're talking about.'' Jordan moved restlessly in the uncomfortable chair. He was tired of sitting and the air in the office felt stuffy.

''That's it,'' Gabe noted with a smile that was all too wry for Jordan's taste. ''*She's* the real reason you've come to Golden.''

''Holly and I go too far back,'' Jordan said, waving the notion off.

''I'll tell you what I think.'' Leaning forward, Gabe peered at him from across the table. ''If Holly ever looked at me the way she was looking at you at the barbecue, this conversation would be moot. She and I would have definitely clicked.''

''What are you talking about?''

''When you were at the preschool booth with Stephanie—I could barely get Holly's attention. She couldn't take her eyes off you.''

Jordan got to his feet. ''Her eyes were on Stephanie. She idolizes that kid.''

''Too bad I'm not a betting man,'' Gabe said with a laugh. ''I'd make a killing off you.''

Jordan refused to argue.

Apparently, Gabe didn't know Holly as well as he had first thought. Nor did Gabe know him. True, helping Holly wasn't his only reason for buying and rehabbing the apple packing plant. After the past few wasted months, he needed to find something productive to do. After losing CompWare, he needed a reason to be.

None of this was Sawyer's business, and Jordan offered no further explanation. Although the meeting ended with a friendly handshake, Jordan was none too pleased with the grin on Gabe's face.

Still, Jordan found it tough to put everything Sawyer had said out of his mind. Especially after the way Holly had kissed him. Could Gabe have been right about how she had looked at him at the chicken barbecue?

As he walked out to his car, Jordan glanced toward Holly's shop. A few lights shined through the front window. Since everything else along the common was closed up tight, he grew concerned. With the glow from the three-quarters moon to guide him in the dark, he crossed the sloping green in no time. He peered inside the shop window, and his apprehensions vanished. Holly was busily unpacking boxes. She appeared to be alone, but safe.

Jordan watched her move about as she took the colorful bottles and jars and stocked the shelves. She wore a simple white T-shirt tucked into blue jeans; her pale hair was swept back in a loose ponytail. He could almost feel his heart smile. That was the Holly West he'd known all those years ago.

Well, it was and it wasn't. The luscious figure bending and lifting now bore little resemblance to the gangly, flat-chested teen he remembered. Hell, nothing resembled what used to be, least of all his feelings toward Holly. Even as she wore her "uniform" of old, he found it impossible to think of her as the girl whom he'd grown up with, the girl who had almost married his brother.

And the memory of that damn kiss didn't help.

Jordan tapped his knuckles on the window. Holly

turned, her brows lifting in surprise. He couldn't tell if she was glad to see him or not.

"What are you doing here?" she asked after unlocking the front door.

He told her about his meeting with Gabe Sawyer. "When I saw the shop lights on, I thought I'd better check. You're here pretty late, aren't you?"

"I spent the morning on a field trip to the library and post office with Steph's preschool class," she explained, returning to her boxes and inventory list. "I'm trying to catch up with this latest shipment."

"Can I give you a hand?"

Holly looked at the many unopened cartons stacked behind the counter. "I hope you meant that, Jordan. 'Cause I'm taking you up on it."

"At your service, ma'am," he replied, glad to help and happy she hadn't sent him on his way.

He didn't want to go back to an empty house right now. Although he couldn't think why. After all, he'd been returning to empty hotel rooms, apartments and houses most of his adult life. Only occasionally had someone been waiting for him.

Holly pointed to the boxes marked "Summer Sunflower Gold," directing him to cart them over to the front shelves. "Then you can pull whatever's left of the spring strawberry line and shelve the new summer line."

Jordan got to it, and before long the two of them were working in companionable silence. He couldn't help stealing a look at Holly every so often. When he wasn't preoccupied with her soft curves and fluid moves, Jordan observed how hard she worked. Diligence like that he understood. Diligence had been his hallmark at Mason CompWare, and perhaps his downfall, too.

With only half a shelf left to fill, Jordan ripped open

the last sunflower line box. Lifting a slim gold-colored canister of hairstyling mousse from the box, he was reminded of Stephanie's "moose" for mooses. He chuckled.

Holly came over. "Something's funny?"

"Not really. It's just that mousse is an odd thing to call this stuff. Don't you think so?"

Bemused, Holly wrinkled her nose and shrugged. But even after she had returned to her paperwork, Jordan felt her eyes on him.

"I've been thinking about you today," she finally said, gazing at him from the counter, chin in hands.

"Hmm. Good or bad?" He gathered up the empty boxes. If she only knew how he'd been thinking of her!

"I was wondering what you've been up to these past few years. I mean, we've certainly talked about my life at length," Holly added, slyly. "But you haven't said much about yourself."

"There's not a helluva lot to say." He tossed the cartons into the back room with the trash. "I had my hands full running CompWare."

"Oh, Jordan," she declared with impatience. "A person would think you were married to that business."

"Interesting you should say that. My former fiancée used to call CompWare my mistress."

"You were engaged?"

"For about a year." Drawn by the rich velvet of Holly's eyes, he leaned against the counter and let his gaze drift in their brown softness.

"What happened?"

"All hell broke loose with CompWare, and that sort of exposed the chinks in the relationship. The *many* chinks."

Holly wrinkled her nose. "If your fiancée resented CompWare, wouldn't she be happy about the sale?"

"Very happy. Allison wanted me to take the money and run. Instead, I held off—I wasn't sure selling CompWare was what I wanted. That was the last straw for her. She walked out."

"But I don't understand. You did sell the company."

"Too late as far as Allison was concerned."

"Didn't you go to her after the sale, Jordan? Didn't you try to get her back?"

Jordan stiffened. He could see how much the point mattered to Holly. Perhaps she still believed every woman had to be as madly in love with her fiancé as she'd been with Scott. "Look, Holly, Allison wanted things that I just couldn't give—like my undivided attention. And I wasn't about to retire and go on permanent vacation, no matter how much money I made off the sale."

Holly said nothing, but her distress compelled him to keep explaining. "Allison isn't totally to blame. In the first place, my reasons for asking her to marry me weren't the best. Unfortunately, I figured that out a little late. I'd already asked and she'd said yes."

"What kind of reasons?"

Holly's gaze was so intense, so expectant, Jordan couldn't brush her off with his usual cynical retort. She wasn't the kind of woman to whom you did something like that.

"Mainly, I just thought it was time to settle down. I had no life outside of CompWare. My father and his wife had moved to Florida, most of my friends had families of their own, and there I was—alone."

"And lonely?"

"I didn't think so. Not at the time." Jordan shifted

his position until he was no longer directly facing Holly. "Allison and I had been dating off and on for about a year. She was beautiful, willing and there. On the surface, getting engaged seemed so right. Our families thought it was great." He shook his head. "It was hard for everyone to accept how wrong it turned out to be. Even Dad didn't understand."

Holly put her hand on his shoulder. "I understand."

Moved by the gentleness in her voice, Jordan met her gaze. "I believe you do," he murmured, sliding his hand over hers.

He held her soft slender fingers against his chest, wishing he had told her more. He wanted Holly to know how he had longed for someone to share the everyday highs and lows; for someone whom he could cherish the way his father did Rachel; for someone who would love him the way she had loved Scott.

But he felt something powerful as he gazed into the tender depths of her eyes. It was that link, that connection he'd been searching for with Allison—and perhaps with every woman he'd met. Now Jordan felt it and recognized what it was and what it meant.

Holly West?

He was too overwhelmed to dwell on the irony of it all. Yet her warmth filled him with a sense of both belonging and acceptance. And there were other feelings, too—like desire, freshly sparked and spreading through his loins like wildfire.

Holly?

Jordan stepped back. The strength of the emotions coiling around his heart shook him badly. He placed her hand back on the counter, relieved that the smooth marble top stood wedged between their bodies.

"I didn't mean to go on like that," he said, stuffing

his hands in his jeans pockets so he wouldn't be tempted to touch her again. "Bet you're sorry you asked."

"I'm not."

Those big browns of hers kicked his heart into overdrive. He could practically feel his blood racing through his veins. Did Holly have any idea what she was doing to him? If he told her, she'd be astonished. To her, he was and always would be Scott's big brother.

Holly finally broke the prolonged silence between them. "It's getting late. I can finish the rest of this in the morning."

After helping her close up shop, Jordan walked Holly to her car. Now that it was time to say good-night, however, he was loath to let her go. "I talked to several contractors today and picked up some good figures," he informed her, hoping to buy more time. "The notes are in my car. Why don't we go someplace and have a look at them—somewhere we can get a cup of coffee or even a drink."

"Nothing's open at this hour on a weeknight, Jordan."

"Of course. I should've known," he said dryly.

"Besides, I have to get home to relieve Gracie." She unlocked her car door. "But I do want to see the notes. You can drop them by anytime."

Jordan stood on the curb, watching until the taillights of her car were out of sight. He took a deep breath and the cool evening air filled his lungs. As he walked back to his car, a slight breeze rustled the leafy branches of the large old oaks and maples scattered across the common. The noise drew his attention to the night sky, sapphire blue and sprinkled with stars. Everything seemed sharper to him now: the crispness of the air, the sound of the wind in the trees, the cloudless view of the late-spring moon. Even the fresh warm scent of Holly stayed with him, making him feel more alive than he had for a long, long time.

With all that had gone down in his life these past few years—Scott's death, his own broken engagement and the tough, year-long fight for Mason CompWare—he'd been too busy to feel its emptiness. Tonight, everything appeared in sharp relief—not just his surroundings, but the desires of his heart, as well.

Jordan conceded that Gabe Sawyer might have been right. Perhaps he had come to Golden because of Holly, not for her. Yet what about Holly? Could she put away the past and look at him with different eyes? Could she accept him as a man who wanted her?

He took one more deep breath of the cool night air before climbing into his car. "Oh, hell," he muttered, slamming the door and gunning the engine. "I've got to find out."

Holly stuffed several file folders' worth of work into an oversized tote bag and headed home for lunch. The shop was closed on Thursday afternoons and she had decided to use the time to catch up on the paperwork accompanying the new shipment. It was such a beautiful day, too. She could see herself sitting in the backyard beneath the warm sun, going over her papers while Stephanie played alongside her.

But the cars she found in her driveway weren't part of her idyllic plans. Nancy Barron's station wagon was parked rather haphazardly—as was her habit—behind Gracie's old sedan. Then there was the late-model Mercedes. The sight of it made Holly's stomach flutter. After last night, she didn't expect to see Jordan this soon. After the emotional level set by their conversation, she wasn't sure she was ready.

Entering the house, Holly felt as if she were crashing a party. Stephanie and Nancy's two boys were galli-vanting from room to room, eating huge chocolate chip cookies. Nancy and Jordan sat at the dining-room table, drinking iced tea, talking and laughing. The sight of them together like that peeved Holly, which she knew was crazy. Nancy was her very married best friend and Jordan was...what was Jordan?

Nancy spotted her first. "Hey, Holly, you've finally made it. We were wondering what was keeping you."

It was too noisy to explain about her last dawdling customer. "What's going on?" She tried to make herself heard above the din of overexcited children. "And why are the kids eating cookies now? It's lunchtime."

"It's my fault, Holly," Jordan volunteered. "I brought a dozen over for Stephanie. But the kids spotted the bakery bag—"

Gracie's gruff voice boomed from the kitchen. "I told 'em it was too early for treats. Stephanie hasn't had her lunch yet, and now all three of them are flying from the sugar."

"Don't blame Jordan," Nancy piped in. "I said it was okay. Stephanie was so tickled that Jordan brought her a surprise—you should've seen her face. I didn't think you'd mind this one time."

Holly let her friend off the hook. "Okay, but why don't we send the kids outside to run around the house a few times? That should wear them out."

"You're right. I probably should have sent them out before this," Nancy said, getting up from the table. "But once we started talking about the apple plant, I lost track.

And besides, you didn't tell me this wonderful man was going to make my bookstore happen."

Holly shot a wary look at Jordan. He spread his arms out in a sheepish shrug.

Letting Nancy shoo the kids outdoors, Holly sat next to Jordan. "So, you're the man who's going to make Nancy's bookstore happen, eh?"

"Her words, not mine. I just told her why I dropped by," he explained, oozing innocence. "Frankly, I was surprised you hadn't told her about the plant."

"I figured she'd find out soon enough."

The truth was she didn't want her friends misconstruing Jordan's motives, or her own for that matter. Gabe Sawyer was the only one she trusted not to jump to wrong conclusions. Nancy and Susan were wonderful women, but they were also incurable romantics. Besides, Holly was their one single woman friend—the only one for whom they could play matchmaker.

"By the way, why did you drop by?"

"The notes I mentioned to you last night." Jordan patted the worn spiral-bound notebook on the table. "I said I'd get them to you. Remember?"

Barely. Probably because that conversation was overshadowed by what she did remember. Like how her heart had begun to pound when she saw him rapping on her window. Like how she had enjoyed working with him in the shop. Like how surprised she'd been to learn about his ex-fiancée. And how she had almost melted on the spot when he held her hand against his chest.

"I'll look them over tonight," she said, bristling at the way last night's memories made her feel.

"I thought we could review them together. Over lunch."

"Peanut-butter-and-jelly sandwiches are all we have on the menu today. I couldn't subject you to that."

"Holly, I'm asking you out for lunch. Someplace nice, quiet."

"I can't go out to lunch today."

Suddenly, Nancy reappeared at the table. "Of course you can, Holly. The shop is closed. It's your afternoon off."

"I still have work to do." Holly glared at her friend. "And Stephanie to take care of. Gracie's washing all the floors this afternoon and I said I'd keep Steph out of her way."

"We could take Stephanie with us," Jordan offered, but with a noticeable lack of enthusiasm.

"No, no. That's ridiculous," Nancy insisted, shaking her head vehemently. "I'll take Stephanie this afternoon."

"I wouldn't dream of intruding upon you like that, Nancy."

"Well, you're not intruding, Holly. The reason the boys and I came over was to invite Stephanie home for lunch and—and—to play under the lawn sprinkler."

If Nancy was making this up as she went, the lawn sprinkler idea was inspired. The afternoon promised to get hotter, and running under the garden hose was one of Stephanie's favorite things to do—which Nancy knew.

"All right," Holly said, relenting. "If that's what you intended all along, Stephanie can go with you."

"Does that mean you'll go to lunch with *me?*" Jordan asked with a smile.

"She'd better." Nancy cast a warning glance her way before turning to Jordan. "And take her to the River

House Tea Room over in Waterford. It's small and intimate but has tons of atmosphere.''

"He said quiet, not intimate," Holly muttered.

Nancy ignored her. "The food isn't half bad, either—if you like small portions.''

Jordan looked to Holly. "It sounds fine to me. Would you like to go?''

At least he asked. Which was more than she could say for her pushy pal. "Of course I'd like to go. The River House Tea Room is very nice—if that's what you had in mind.''

"It's exactly what I had in mind.''

The intriguing twinkle in his eyes made her pulse thrum madly.

Apparently, Nancy saw the look in his deep blues, too.

"Okay, we're out of here," she announced, jumping up from her chair. She called the kids through the screen door.

Packing Steph's bathing suit and an extra set of clothes, Holly arranged to pick her up later in the afternoon. Stephanie was so excited to be going to Nancy's she gave her mother a peck on the cheek and dashed off to join the Barron boys in the car.

"Don't rush back," Nancy said as Holly walked her out to the front porch. "I can keep Stephanie for dinner, too.''

"We're only having lunch, Nance.''

"Well, take your time and enjoy it. You deserve some fun.''

"We'll be discussing business," Holly reminded her. "But thanks for having Steph over.''

Nancy put up her hand. "It's just a happy coincidence." She started down the steps but stopped midway and began digging through her purse. "Oh, Holly, I almost forgot the earrings I borrowed. I've been meaning to bring them back for days.''

Nancy dropped the small jeweler's box into Holly's hands and rushed off. Nancy had been promising to return the gold earrings since their big night out at the inn last week. In fact, Holly now suspected bringing back the earrings had been the real reason her friend had stopped by. Inviting Stephanie over had had nothing to do with it.

Holly had to laugh. The only ''happy coincidence'' going on around here was that Nancy had finally gotten an honest-to-goodness shot at playing matchmaker.

Chapter Seven

After getting them the best table the River House Tea Room had to offer, Jordan went through his building notes so fast it made Holly's head spin. With their business concluded well before the entrées had arrived, Holly realized now was the time to inform Jordan that Stephanie was his niece.

She had wanted to tell him before this. But since his return to Golden, they'd been alone only twice. And each of those times something had held her back—like the kiss at the apple packing plant, or Jordan's tale of his broken engagement.

"Tell me about this place," Jordan asked, pulling back Holly's attention. "It had to be somebody's mansion in its former life."

"It was the summer home of Elizabeth C. Paget, a railroad and shipping heiress from Boston. She built it in the 1890s."

"Paget? Any connection to my new house?"

"She had it built for a distant cousin shortly before she died. But they tell me the cousin never lived in it."

"And it's the same Paget of Paget Library and Paget Road in Golden?"

Holly nodded. "She gave lots of money to the surrounding towns. When she died, she willed this mansion to the town of Waterford, along with a trust to maintain it," she explained. "They turned the summer ballroom into this restaurant, and the rest of the mansion is rented out for weddings, corporate meetings, even proms."

"It's a magnificent place, even if it is off the beaten track," Jordan noted. "And this view overlooking the river is amazing."

Holly followed his gaze to the gorgeous panorama outside the huge bay window by their table. The lush green bluffs, the clear, narrow river below and the perfect blue sky overhead were typical of the area in spring and summer. It was almost like a bit of heaven.

"I can understand why old Elizabeth C. kept coming back," she mused, losing herself in the hushed peace of the countryside.

"You really love it around here, don't you?"

She met Jordan's eyes, finding them as blue as the sky she'd been admiring moments before. "I do," she admitted. "It's home to me now."

"Why?" he asked, his voice intent as he leaned toward her. "What is it about here—about Golden—that makes you feel that way?"

Holly didn't have to think twice. She'd known why since the first time she walked along the common with her baby in the stroller. "Because here my slate was clean. It didn't matter what I used to be or who my parents were. It was irrelevant that my fiancé left me standing at the altar on my wedding day or that my baby's father didn't know she existed. Without all that baggage, I could raise my daughter and run my business on my own terms."

Jordan seemed to understand. "Here you can just be who you are. The past doesn't get in the way."

She nodded, adding gently, "At least it didn't until you showed up."

The slightest of smiles twitched his lips. "Are you sorry I did?"

"I was at first, but now that you're here..." she replied with a teasing shrug.

Holly figured this was a good opening for telling him about Scott and Stephanie. Before she could even think of how to begin, however, the hostess seated a party of four at the next table—too close for comfort when it came to revealing a painful secret. Then the waitress brought their food, discouraging Holly for the time being.

While they ate, Jordan asked about the people he'd met in town so far. Yet he didn't talk about them in connection with the building or the town meeting vote. It was as if he'd decided to avoid discussing business in any way, shape or form now that his notes were out of the way. Holly didn't mind. She'd rather talk about her good friends and wonderful neighbors than about how to win votes on the zoning change.

After indulging themselves with strawberry shortcake for dessert, Holly suggested a walk around the grounds. "There's a lovely little landscaped park down by the river. Very shady, very cool. And walking back up the hill to the car will burn up the gazillion calories in that rich whipped cream."

The walk would also give her another chance to tell Jordan that Scott was Stephanie's father.

The path down the side of the bluff was steep and rocky. As it narrowed, Jordan stepped ahead, taking her by the hand to guide her over the bumps and dips along the rugged route. His solicitous gesture—although unnecessary—delighted Holly. It was nice to know that, in this instance at least, someone was there to catch her if she stumbled.

But would Jordan be there for her when he learned how she had lied to him?

"This was definitely worth the hike," Jordan declared when they reached the small park. Ignoring the rough-hewn log benches, he plopped down on the grassy riverbank. "You were right, it feels ten degrees cooler down here."

Holly was glad to see they had the park to themselves. No distractions. And Jordan seemed very relaxed. Leaning back on his elbows, his long legs stretched out on the grass, he gazed at the slow-moving water. Holly felt a reassuring calm. She could do it now. No excuses.

The lazy smile Jordan gave her when she sat beside him snagged Holly's heart. She prayed it wouldn't be the last smile. "I'm glad we have this chance to talk, Jordan."

He turned to face her, resting his cheek in his hand. "Me, too. I thought you would want to rush right home after we ate." Plucking a bright buttercup out of the grass, he held it under her chin. "Remember these?"

The playfulness of his voice made her wince as the soft flower tickled her skin. "Aha!" he cried. "Even after all these years, you still like butter, Holly."

"Who eats butter anymore?" she asked blithely, trying not to laugh.

Holly liked this lighthearted mood of his. Still, she couldn't allow it to distract her. "You and I haven't talked about Scott yet."

Jordan flicked the wilting buttercup to the ground. "No, we haven't."

"It's time we did."

"No."

Holly was taken aback. "No?"

"Not now, anyway."

"We need to."

"We probably do. But not today." He looked at her, the expression in his deep-blue eyes appealing to her to reconsider. "It's a beautiful day—we're having a good time together. Why spoil it?"

Her heart sank. "That wasn't my intention."

She must have sounded dejected, because Jordan frowned. "Let me explain," he said, pushing himself up to a seated position. "I've been thinking about what you said—about clean slates and being accepted for who you are now, not who you used to be. That's how it should be for us today."

"Is that possible, Jordan? I mean, we've known each other forever."

"Holly, I feel as though I've just met you. Everything you say and do is new to me. Everything you are now is—is—" Raising his eyes to the sky, he appeared to be searching for just the right words.

"So un-Hollylike?"

He chuckled and reached for her hand. "I like the Holly you are now. I've enjoyed being with her today."

Her pulse tripped as his long fingers curled around her hand. Before now, she hadn't realized he'd looked upon her as anything other than his brother's old girlfriend or the kid who used to live next door. Yes, there had been the kiss on Sunday morning. But Holly had written that off as a fluke reaction to an emotionally exciting moment.

True, her attitude toward Jordan had gradually altered over the past few days. But sentiments about the Jordan she used to know always seemed to muddy the picture. Perhaps it was time for her to change the lens. If Jordan was able to regard her in a new light, Holly felt she should return the favor. After all, no longer was he the high-powered owner of CompWare, Inc. For all intents and purposes, he was Jordan Mason, independent contractor and the newest resident of Golden, Massachusetts.

"So, it's a clean slate you're after, is it?"

"With all my heart," he bantered back, the slant of his slight smile sexy enough to take her breath away.

"Then it's the new Holly and Jordan for the rest of the day," Holly agreed, reluctantly tucking away her secret one more time.

He squeezed her hand. "Thanks."

His touch warmed her skin, causing Holly to wonder just how much change Jordan had in mind. As tempting as it seemed, she wasn't ready to spend the afternoon gazing into his eyes. Slipping her hand from his, Holly hugged her legs to her chest. She watched the river, rolling languidly but crystal clear and looking cool. Suddenly a wicked impulse seized her. What came to mind was certainly un-Jordanlike. *Un-old-Jordanlike.*

"The water looks too good to pass up," Holly declared, sliding her canvas flats off her feet. "Let's go wading."

Jordan's eyes narrowed. "You're joking."

"It'll be fun."

"I haven't done anything like that since I was a kid."

"Just what I thought," she said, getting to her feet. "Time to start on that clean slate of yours, Jordan."

"I see. This is some kind of challenge, eh?"

Holly nodded. "Put your money where your mouth is, Mason."

"Easy for you to say—you're wearing a dress," he grumbled. But he yanked off his expensive leather shoes and rolled the legs of his tan slacks up to his knees. Then he stood up and held out his hand. "Shall we?"

She led him down the sloping bank to the graveled shoreline. Stepping into the sun-warmed water first, Holly felt the refreshing rush of the river's flow against her ankles. She looked back at Jordan. "Ready?"

"Yeah, I'm ready. I just hope I don't look as ridiculous as I feel."

"You? Look ridiculous? Not with great legs like that," she shot back with a wink. "Besides, this feels so good you'll forget all your cares."

As he followed her into the water, Jordan's mouth broke into a broad grin. "Very nice."

They waded in farther, stepping carefully over and around slippery rocks. Holly felt like a kid, kicking her feet through the water and teasing Jordan to keep up with her. What would Stephanie think of her mom now? she wondered with a laugh.

"What's so funny?" Jordan asked.

As she told him, she noticed how his dark hair had fallen over his eyes, his shirttail spilled partway out of his waistband and the thick, rolled-up cuffs of his pants were getting wet. This was a new Jordan, to say the least. Still, as disheveled as he was, Holly found him more handsome than ever.

"The kid would probably hop right in with us," he

said, oblivious to her admiring gaze. "Now, Gracie, on the other hand, would tell us we're out of our minds."

She heard the edge in Jordan's voice. "Gracie means well. She's just on the cautious side."

"Protective, too," he added, brushing the hair from his eyes. "I don't think she has much use for me."

"She's leery by nature—it's the old Yankee in her." Lifting her skirt up her thigh as the water grew deeper, Holly took a step back. "Give her some ti—oh!"

Her heel hit against one of slimy rocks beneath the water and she slid off balance.

"Whoa there," cried Jordan, clutching her waist from behind as her body pitched forward. It was too late. Sheer momentum plunged her into the river and it pulled Jordan in with her.

Pushing her head up above the surface, Holly coughed away the water she had swallowed. Jordan emerged a split second later, his arm still around her.

"Are you all right, Holly?"

"Yes," she gasped, each breath too short and quick. Her soaking-wet hair was plastered against her cheeks. "I tripped on a rock. Can you believe it?"

Jordan sat back, drawing her to his side. The shallow water just covered their shoulders. "I was afraid something like this would happen," he said with a shake of his head. "Just look at us."

Holly pushed her hair off her face. "We're a mess, all right. But you've got to admit it feels great to cool off." She waved her arm to and fro beneath the water.

"Better than running under the sprinkler."

"That's the spirit, Jordan." She patted him on his wet-shirted back. Then she felt a chuckle vibrate through his upper body, and it made her feel like chuckling, too. "Okay, why are *you* laughing?"

"I was thinking about Gracie again. What would she say about this?"

Holly didn't think her housekeeper would consider this funny. She envisioned Gracie standing on the bank, her arms crossed and her eyes glowering with disapproval. Or was she the one who actually disapproved? A "mommy" should know better than to frolic in the water with a man who makes her take leave of her senses. But Holly had been watching her every step for five long years. She had worked so hard to build a secure, respectable life for her daughter, and there were times she felt very weary, indeed. Caught up in the day-to-day grind, she would often forget she was only twenty-six.

"Gracie would probably give us a good scolding," Holly answered, curving her arm around his back. "But I don't care. I'm having fun."

"I suspect that's a very *un-Holly*like thing to say," Jordan murmured, his chin nuzzling her neck.

A delicious weakness penetrated her slick, wet skin, awakening every nerve ending in her body. Holly sank against him. Beneath the water, Jordan tightened his hold on her waist. He pressed his lips against her neck, sending a shiver rippling down her spine.

"Cold?" he murmured, his breath warm on her skin. He kissed her shoulder.

"No." She leaned into this kiss, feeling all breathless and steamy. As his mouth brushed a slow trail of caresses along the curve of her neck, Holly felt a pulsing heat deep inside her. Despite the languorous beat of her heart, her body was coming alive.

Jordan kissed her jaw, then her cheek. His right hand slithered through the water to her breast, molding his palm to her round softness while his thumb circled the

NO RISK, NO OBLIGATION TO BUY...NOW OR EVER!

CASINO JUBILEE

"Scratch 'n' Match" Game
Here's how to play:

1. Peel off label from front cover. Place it in the space provided opposite. With a coin carefully scratch away the silver box. This makes you eligible to receive three or more free books, and possibly another gift, depending upon what is revealed beneath the scratch-off area.

2. Send back this card and you'll receive specially selected Silhouette® novels from the Special Edition™ series. These books are yours to keep absolutely FREE.

3. There's no catch. You're under no obligation to buy anything. We charge nothing for your first shipment. And you don't have to make any minimum number of purchases – not even one!

4. The fact is thousands of readers enjoy receiving books by mail from the Reader Service™, at least a month before they're available in the shops. They like the convenience of home delivery, and of course postage and packing is completely FREE!

5. We hope that after receiving your free books you'll want to remain a subscriber. But the choice is yours – to continue or cancel, any time at all! So why not take up our invitation, with no risk of any kind. You'll be glad you did!

YOURS FREE!

You'll look a million dollars when you wear this lovely necklace! Its cobra-link chain is a generous 18" long, and the lustrous simulated pearl completes this attractive gift.

ENLARGED TO SHOW DETAIL

CASINO JUBILEE
"Scratch 'n' Match" Game

SCRATCH HERE ?

PLACE LABEL HERE

CHECK CLAIM CHART BELOW FOR YOUR FREE GIFTS!

E8HI

YES! I have placed my label from the front cover in the space provided above and scratched away the silver box. Please send me all the gifts for which I qualify. I understand that I am under no obligation to purchase any books, as explained on the back and on the opposite page. I am over 18 years of age.

MS/MRS/MISS/MR _____ INITIALS _____

BLOCK CAPITALS PLEASE

SURNAME _____

ADDRESS _____

_____

POSTCODE _____

CASINO JUBILEE CLAIM CHART

🍒	🍒	🍒	WORTH 4 FREE BOOKS AND A FREE NECKLACE
🍒	🔔	🍒	WORTH 4 FREE BOOKS
🍒	-BAR-	🍒	WORTH 3 FREE BOOKS · CLAIM Nº 1,528

Offer valid in UK only and not available to current Reader Service subscribers to the Special Edition series. Overseas and Eire please write for details. We reserve the right to refuse an application and applicant must be aged 18 years or over. Only one application per household. Offer expires 28th February 1999. Terms and prices subject to change without notice.

You may be mailed with offers from other reputable companies as a result of this application.
If you would prefer not to receive such offers, please tick box. ☐

MAILING PREFERENCE SERVICE

Silhouette is a registered trademark, used under license.

THE READER SERVICE : HERE'S HOW IT WORKS

Accepting the free books and gift places you under no obligation to buy anything. You may keep the books and gift and return the despatch note marked "cancel". If we don't hear from you, about a month later we will send you 6 brand new books and invoice you just £2.50* each. That's the complete price - there is no extra charge for postage and packing. You may cancel at any time, otherwise every month we'll send you 6 more books, which you may either purchase or return - the choice is yours.

*Prices subject to change without notice.

THE READER SERVICE™
FREEPOST SEA3794
CROYDON
Surrey
CR9 3AQ

sensitive tip. She closed her eyes, riding with the sensation, until her body began to tremble.

"Oh, Holly."

His throaty whisper stirred long-forgotten yearnings. A hunger, unfamiliar, yet insistent, rumbled in her chest and pounded in her ears. Wanting nothing more than to fold her body into his, Holly swung around to get closer. Her violent turn made the water slap against their bodies. But before the sound registered in her consciousness, Jordan had captured her mouth in a breath-robbing kiss.

With a moan, she opened her lips to his tongue. Her limbs turned to liquid as his embrace grew stronger, tighter. Driven by this newfound hunger, she drank deeply of his kiss. They knelt thigh to thigh in the riverbed sand, water up to their waists. Holly felt the Jordan's cold wet shirt through the thin cotton of her sundress bodice, and her breasts tingled.

As if he sensed her spiraling excitement, Jordan slid his hands beneath the water to her bottom. A groan vibrated in his throat and his hips moved hard against hers, his desire evident. The water flowing around them couldn't douse the burning heat spreading through her like wildfire. Her body had never responded like this before. The sensations had never been so intense. Holly knew she had to get herself under control. She just wasn't sure she could.

And that scared the hell out of her.

Pressing her hands flat against his chest, she tried to push herself away. Jordan held fast to her waist. "Please, don't," she moaned after dragging her mouth from his.

"This is crazy, Jordan." She stumbled to her feet and he rose with her.

"Crazy or not, it's happening." His voice was raspy, his breathing labored. Jordan pulled her to him, piercing her with the glint of desire in his eyes. "I want it to happen. I think you do, too."

Want it to happen? She had heard that before. The passion and heat and desire in her soul cracked into brittle pieces. "No, I don't."

Holly freed herself with a strong, angry shove. Staggering to shore, she tugged at her dripping-wet dress.

"Holly, wait."

Jordan splashed through the water behind her, but she ignored his calls. Her eyes smarted—from tears or dripping water she didn't know. And she didn't know what disturbed her more—Jordan's aggressive advance or her uninhibited response; Jordan's remark or her guilty secret. Holly yanked on her canvas slip-on shoes with an anger that added to her confusion.

Jordan emerged from the river, water streaming all over his body as he rushed over to her. "Holly, please. You have to talk to me."

Did she ever! Except now, she was far too upset to tell him about Scott and Stephanie. Or anything else, for that matter. "How can I when we're both sopping wet like this? I'm going back to the car."

Jordan caught her arm. "I'm sorry for getting carried away out there. I'm sorry if I scared you."

Holly made the mistake of looking into his eyes. The desire that had shimmered in them moments before had deepened into an emotion she couldn't quite decipher.

She sighed, unable to walk away. "You didn't scare me, Jordan."

"Then what is it?"

"This whole thing between us—it is *crazy*. I don't want to get carried away by it. I can't." She slid her arm from his grasp. "Just because I've been that route before doesn't mean I'll make the same mistake twice."

"Are you saying I think you're easy?" Disbelief flashed across his face. "Now, *that's* crazy."

"It isn't to me." She felt her face redden with resentment. "And I'm not about to stick around here like a drenched idiot and explain it to you."

Holly bolted back up the steep hill to the mansion. She needed to put space between them, even if only for a few minutes. It was impossible to think straight when her gaze was drawn to the soaked knit shirt clinging to his taut, chiseled shoulders, or when she wanted to curl her fingers though his thick wet hair.

As Holly waited by Jordan's locked car, a late-afternoon breeze kicked up. It felt like a blast of iced air on her bare arms and damp dress, and she couldn't stop shivering. Not even when Jordan caught up with her in the parking lot.

Digging the keys out his pocket, Jordan scarcely looked at her as he walked to the rear of the car. He pulled a blanket from the trunk. "Here," he said, unfolding the blue-and-green wool. "Put this on before you freeze to death."

No words were exchanged as she wrapped the blanket around her trembling body and Jordan unlocked the passenger door. They drove back to Golden in complete silence, the tension between them buzzing like electrified wire.

Holly managed to stop shivering by the time they pulled into her driveway. Shifting the car into Park, Jordan waited for her to get out. But Holly couldn't leave him like this, not with what was left unsaid. Finally, when she made no move for the door, Jordan cut the engine.

"I think you're a wonderful woman, Holly. I admire what you've done more than I can say." Jordan's was voice solemn and low as he stared over the steering wheel. "I also have other feelings for you, which are no secret after this afternoon. I won't apologize for those."

Holly stared down at her hands. "I'm not asking you to."

"You've got to believe that what happened with you and Stephanie's father never entered my mind. That has nothing to do with how you make me feel."

"I know."

"But you were angry."

"Mostly at myself." She looked up to find him watching her. "Pretending the past doesn't exist is okay—up to a point. Yet there are some things I can't afford to forget."

"I should have realized that." He reached out to brush a stray lock of hair from her cheek. "I was only thinking about what I wanted. That's not fair to you."

Fair? He was concerned about being fair, when she had out-and-out lied to him about Stephanie? Good God, she had to tell him.

"Jordan, I'm sorry, but I haven't been—"

"You have nothing to be sorry about." He pressed a finger to her lips to quiet her. "I set up this whole outing because I couldn't get you out of my mind. Since Sunday, all I could think about was kissing you again. I just wanted to be with you. But I got greedy and pushed for more."

"I wasn't exactly an unwilling participant." Moved by his confession, she had to say it. She was being dishonest enough as it was.

A ray of hope flickered in his eyes. "I still want to be with you, Holly. Anytime, any way you say."

"Oh, Jordan," she whispered, her mind reeling with conflicting emotions. "You don't make things easy."

Capturing her gaze with the full force of his midnight-blue gaze, Jordan cupped her cheek in his hand. ''Easy is never worthwhile.''

Holly searched his face, wanting to find some sliver of insincerity that might save her, knowing she'd be devastated if she did. But the earnest set of his jaw was real; the hope gleaming in his eyes was true.

''All right,'' she breathed in uneasy surrender. ''But please, let's slow it down a notch or two.''

They agreed to see each other the following evening. As Holly watched Jordan drive away, however, regret overshadowed the pleasure of anticipation. Another chance to tell him the truth about Stephanie had slipped through her fingers, and she felt terrible.

Jordan's tender admissions had touched her deeply. He had drawn her back to him with all the right words. But now that he was gone, guilt distorted everything. Now, all those warm, precious words were like needles piercing her heart.

Chapter Eight

"Stephanie, please stop crying. These things happen."

Holly dialed yet another number, mentally crossing her fingers. Jordan would be arriving any minute to take her out to dinner and a movie. Unfortunately, replacement baby-sitters were hard to come by at six o'clock on a Friday night.

"I want Kelly to come," Steph sniffled as she crawled onto the sofa. "She was gonna play hairdresser with me."

"She got sick, honey. I told you that." Holly grimaced when she reached another answering machine.

"Can't Kristen stay with me, then?"

"She's sitting for someone else tonight."

After Gracie, the Sanderson twins were her daughter's favorite baby-sitters. She always had a ball when one or the other took care of her.

Holly glanced at the last name on her list. "I'll try Roger Franklin. You liked him. Remember?"

"No, I didn't. He won't play hairdresser." Stephanie buried her face in a pillow.

As Holly waited while Roger's dad called him to the phone, Jordan arrived at the screen door. Her heart fluttered when she saw him standing there, dressed for their casual date in a navy linen sport coat over an open-necked polo shirt and khakis. Despite her qualms after yesterday's lunch, she'd been looking forward to seeing him again all day long.

Holly's last hope for a sitter died when Roger informed her that *he* had a date that night. Feeling as dejected as Stephanie, Holly waved Jordan in as she hung up the phone.

He greeted her with a bright hello, but his smile faded when he noticed Stephanie's muffled sobs. "What's the matter?"

Explaining about the Sanderson twins, Holly sank onto the sofa near Stephanie and began rubbing her back gently. "Finding a baby-sitter at the last minute isn't easy, Jordan. So far, I've come up empty-handed."

"What about Gracie?"

"There's a bingo tournament at the church hall tonight. I couldn't ask her to give that up."

"I see."

The grim tinge in his voice made Holly wonder if he did see. He couldn't have run into this sort of snag very often.

"And there's no one else?" he asked.

She shook her head. "I'm really sorry, Jordan, but I'm afraid I'll have to take a rain-check on tonight."

Jordan said nothing. Yet the disappointment on his face compelled her to apologize again. "I'd cook something to eat here," she added, kicking herself for not yet getting to the supermarket this week. "But all I have is the frozen pizza the baby-sitter was going to heat up for Steph's supper. You wouldn't want that."

"Can't say that I would." Shoving his hands in his pants pockets, Jordan glanced at Stephanie's back. She hadn't yet shown her face to him. "Hey, Steph, want to go out to eat?"

The sulking child didn't respond.

"Honey, Jordan's talking to you."

"No! I want Kelly and pizza," she mumbled into the pillow, refusing to look up.

"Stephanie, Kelly is sick," Holly reminded her. "And that's no way to talk to an adult. I want you to take that pillow off your face right now."

"How about we go out for a pizza, Steph? You can order any kind you want."

"That's not necessary, Jordan," Holly said, shaking her head.

"It's okay, really." He inched closer to the hiding child. "What do you say, Steph? Want to go?"

Holly flinched. It wasn't okay. She didn't like him offering her pouting child a treat—a *bribe*—to get her to do what he wanted. She was about to point this out, when teary brown eyes peeked above the sofa pillow.

"Mommy said you were going to the movies. Can we go to the movies, too?"

"Jordan didn't invite you to the movies, and it's rude to ask." Holly didn't like her child behaving this way.

Steph dove back behind the pillow.

"Hey, kid, come back out." Jordan gave the pillow a playful tug. "There might be a children's movie playing at the Randlestown Mall."

Stephanie poked her head out again. "Really?"

"I wouldn't be surprised. And you know what? If we leave right now, we'll probably have time to have pizza *and* see a movie."

Stephanie jumped out from behind the pillow, raring to go. Jordan got up, too, smiling like a man who'd negotiated his way through a tough deal.

Swallowing her irritation, Holly held her tongue. As a parent, bribery and rewarding contrariness went against the grain. Still, Jordan was inexperienced in dealing with children; he probably had no idea he'd done anything wrong. Besides, she didn't want to chastise him in front of Stephanie.

Holly's annoyance dissipated as the three of them dined at the mall pizzeria before heading to the cinema complex to catch the newest Disney film. Perhaps sensing her mother's displeasure, Stephanie was on her best behavior. Jordan seemed lighthearted and relaxed. Holly decided she should relax, too, and enjoy herself—especially the happy banter between Jordan and her daughter. She couldn't get over how in tune they were with each other.

"Would you ladies like popcorn?" Jordan asked after handing their tickets to the theater usher.

Holly had no room left after their pizza dinner, but Steph was all for it. "I love pupcorn. It's my favorite thing to eat."

"Mine, too," Jordan claimed with a wink. "I have to warn you, though, I like my popcorn with lots of extra butter."

"Me, too!"

"You don't say."

"'Cept Mommy says a lot of butter's not good for me." Stephanie turned to Holly with pleading eyes.

"Can I have pupcorn with butter? Please? Jordan's having some."

"I'll buy a small tub for us to share," Jordan offered. "Would that be all right, Holly?"

At least he'd checked with her this time, Holly silently mused before giving the okay. As Stephanie danced a happy jig around them, Holly shot a teasing glance at Jordan. "Pepperoni pizza with double cheese and hot buttered popcorn in one night, eh? You must have a cast-iron stomach."

Not to mention a wickedly fast metabolism. As he toted Stephanie off to the concession stand, Holly's gaze fell to his flat stomach. She closed her eyes for an instant, remembering the feel of his smooth, hard muscles pressed against her as the river flowed over them.

"Hello there, Holly."

The firm tap on the back accompanying this cheery greeting startled Holly. She turned to find Karin Mahoney, the director of Steph's preschool, beaming up at her. "Caught you daydreaming," Karin said with a laugh. "From the look in your eyes, it must have been a good one."

Holly felt her face grow red. "What are you doing here?"

"Seeing a movie, of course. The Mel Gibson flick— my sister and I adore him." Karin peered over Holly's shoulder. "Are you alone?"

As if on cue, Stephanie came rushing over from the concession stand. "Miss Karin!"

"Pumpkin!" Karin held out her arms for a hug. The two chatted until Jordan returned with the popcorn. The preschool director eyed him up and down, making no attempt to hide her admiration.

"How nice for you to have a friend like Mr. Jordan

to take you to the movies, Pumpkin,'' Karin told Stephanie. But she winked at Holly.

Holly averted her gaze. "Ah, I think our movie's starting soon. We should go inside now."

"And I'd better get back before my sister gives away my seat." Karin gave Stephanie a pat on the head. Then she turned to Holly. "I forgot to mention that I have about fifteen tickets left for the dinner dance. Do you think you could sell a few at the shop?"

"Sure. I'll put up a poster in the window."

"Great. This promises to be the best one yet, Holly. Maybe this year you'll come," Karin added with a pointed glance at Jordan.

"Just bring the tickets by the shop tomorrow," Holly said as she edged Stephanie and Jordan toward their theater.

Talking Stephanie out of the front row, they settled her between them in seats a comfortable distance from the wide screen. Steph dove into the popcorn right away.

"Hey, save some for the movie," Jordan said with a laugh.

"He really means save some for him," Holly teased.

"Your mom's got my number, kid."

Stephanie, entranced by the preshow advertisements flashing across the screen, wasn't paying attention. Jordan looked over Steph's head at Holly and shrugged.

"So, Holly," he continued, leaning back in his seat, "what's this about a dance?"

"It's an annual thing the area preschools put on as a fund-raiser," she explained, surprised he had brought it up. "They rent out the River House and the parents get the chance to dress to the nines."

"You don't ever go?"

"I don't have time for that stuff." She glanced down

at her hands. "Besides, I had my fill of formal affairs back in Boston. Every month there was something. Remember?"

"I remember."

The theater lights dimmed, and the loud music accompanying the coming attractions put an end to the discussion. Holly was glad. There were other reasons she skipped the dance every year—reasons Jordan wouldn't understand.

The movie got under way and soon Stephanie was giggling with the other children in the audience. Holly gazed over her shoulder at Jordan and her child, their faces haloed by the movie's flickering light. Leaning against Jordan's arm as she shared his tub of popcorn, Stephanie kept her eyes glued to the screen. Watching them sitting that close, munching away on their beloved snack, made Holly smile. No doubt about it, her daughter had taken a shine to Jordan. From all appearances tonight, the feeling appeared to be reciprocated.

Finding a mesmerizing peace in their easy togetherness, Holly couldn't tear her eyes away. She had longed to give Stephanie a semblance of actual family, but the obstacles in her heart and mind had been great. Now there was a flesh-and-blood uncle sitting right there for Stephanie to claim as her own. If she knew. If he knew....

Holly would make the truth known—at the right time, in the right way. Yet the memory of her long-ago attempt at the truth still filled her with pain. And seeing Jordan and Stephanie together like this made her feel so very sad that Scott hadn't allowed her a chance to tell him about their baby.

"Come on and play, Jordan," Stephanie squealed over the music blaring from the portable CD player.

"It's fun."

"All you gotta do is dance," added little Tommy Barron as he gyrated wildly with his brother, Sean, in the middle of Holly's living room.

"Mommy plays with us all the time."

As Steph's gleeful brown eyes peered up at him, Jordan fought the urge to scoop her up and swing her around the room. He had to admit, the kid had grown on him in the past ten days. Although quick attachments had never been his style, he felt so connected to her at times. It was amazing, really.

Still, that didn't mean he was ready to surrender his last shred of dignity to a game she called Rock and Roll Freeze. "I don't see your mother playing now."

"That's because she's making lunch for us," Steph said between breathless giggles. "You know that."

He folded his arms across his chest. "I'll play only if your mother does."

In the blink of an eye, Steph had turned tail for the kitchen. *"Mom-mee!"*

Chuckling, Jordan plopped down on the sofa to watch the Barron boys dance to a vintage Beach Boys tune. He couldn't believe he got such a charge out of a bunch of preschoolers. No one back in Boston would believe it, either. But his life there seemed worlds away from Golden and kids and Holly. He wasn't complaining, though. Not in the least. Jordan couldn't remember a time when each day felt so good or when *he* felt so good. The past ten days had just flown by.

"Here she is," Stephanie cried, dragging Holly in by the arm.

Jordan got a kick from the impish twinkle in Steph's

eyes. That same light in her mother's eyes, however, never failed to trip his pulse into overdrive. Like now.

"What's this I hear, Jordan? You're too faint of heart to play a little Rock and Roll Freeze?" Holly taunted with an alluring smile.

"Faint of heart?" He got to his feet. "Them's fighting words, lady."

"Oh, yeah?" Holly came up to him, hands on waist. "Then are you going to play or not?"

She stood so close Jordan could almost feel the tips of her breasts grazing his chest. How he wanted to hold her close against him! After what had happened between them in the river, he'd kept tight rein on his physical impulses. But the more time he spent with Holly, the tougher that got. At this point, it was damn near impossible to keep from touching and kissing her the way he really wanted to.

Stephanie saved Jordan from temptation by shoving herself between him and Holly. "He'll play if you'll play, Mommy. He said so."

"Well, let the game begin," Holly declared with a wave of her hand, and the kids began jumping up and down in delight. Holly peered up at him with a mischievous gleam in her eye. "Do you need us to explain how to play?"

"Very funny, Holly," he replied. After all, the name of the game said it all. "I think I caught the drift of it watching the kids play."

She tossed him a wink before turning to the kids. "Okay, guys, who's going to man the music?"

Tommy Barron shot his hand up. "Let me, let me. I know how to work the player."

"And he *is* the oldest," Steph added for good measure, clearly unwilling to give up her chance to play this round with Holly and him.

Holly slipped on a new CD and let Tommy have at it. The fast beats of an old Beatles song soon pounded from the speakers, and Holly, Steph and three-year-old Sean began to dance. Jordan shifted from one foot to the other, feeling awkward until Holly grabbed his hand.

"You've got to shake it up a little, Jordan."

She yanked him into a rocking jitterbug type step where they pushed, pulled and swung each other around. Moving to the music with Holly was all it took for Jordan to forget himself.

"Freeze!" yelled Tommy as he hit the Pause button on the CD player. They all stood stock-still—even little Sean—until the music resumed.

From then on all four of them took turns dancing with each other or dancing alone while Tommy picked and chose his moments to freeze the music. They had danced through three songs, and although he and Holly were breathing hard, the little ones showed no signs of tiring.

"Jordan, dance with me again," Stephanie called, running to him from across the room.

She jumped into his arms and he twirled her around and around while Holly twisted and jumped with Sean. As the Beatles sang about rock-and-roll music, Jordan swung Steph up in the air.

"Freeze!"

Holly and Sean fell over laughing, dizzy from their whirling dance. Stephanie shrieked with glee as Jordan held her in midair.

"Don't drop her, for heaven's sake."

All heads turned to the front door. Gracie stood inside it with a bolt of sheer pink fabric tucked under her arm, her worried eyes glued on Stephanie.

Jordan set her down carefully.

"We're playing Rock and Roll Freeze, Gracie," Stephanie chirped. "Jordan and Mommy danced together."

"That must've been a sight to see."

The absence of disapproval in Gracie's voice surprised Jordan. And although he wouldn't call her expression cheerful, the look of disdain Holly's housekeeper usually saved for him was missing, too. He didn't know what to make of it.

Noticing the extra two kids in the house, Gracie looked to Holly. "I thought we were going to cut the material for Stephanie's new curtains."

"Is it that late?" Holly glanced at the crystal clock on the mantel. "Nancy asked me to watch the boys for a couple of hours and give them lunch—which I haven't even done yet."

The mention of lunch caught Sean's attention. "Me hungry."

"Oh, darlin', I just bet you are." Holly took his hand. "Everyone to the kitchen."

The kids skipped out after Holly, leaving him alone with Gracie. The inscrutable expression on her face continued to baffle Jordan. "I dropped by to pick up the architect's preliminary drawings for Holly's shop," he said, feeling compelled to explain.

"Oh, I'm not surprised to see you," she said, hooking her handbag on the closet doorknob. "You do an awful lot of *dropping* by."

For some reason, the pointed suggestion in her voice made him grin. "Yes, Gracie, I suppose I do."

Holly emerged from the kitchen, wiping her hands on a dish towel. She apologized to Gracie for running late. "When the boys are finished eating, I've got to take them over to their father's office. Do you mind starting without me?''

Since Jordan had free time before his appointment with the architect, he offered to drive the boys back to town. When Stephanie caught wind of the revised plan, she begged to come along for the ride. She loved the sunroof in his car.

By the time they reached Phil Barron's law office, Jordan's ears were ringing from the kids' nonstop clamor. He couldn't believe three small kids could make such a racket. Jordan handed Sean's car seat over to Phil. ''They're all yours.''

Phil chuckled. ''My boys got a little rowdy in the car, did they?''

''Yeah, but our Stephanie's no shrinking violet herself.''

''Maybe she'd like to come swimming with the boys and me,'' Phil suggested. ''We're heading over to the lake as soon as I close up here.''

Jordan called Stephanie over and repeated Phil's invitation. Her eyes lit up at first. ''Are you coming, too?''

''I can't honey. I've got an appointment in less than an hour. That's why I had to get those papers from your mom.''

''Come with us, Stephanie,'' Phil urged.

Tommy called out his two cents' worth from across the room. ''It'll be a blast, Steph. My dad gives the best flips in the whole world.''

But Stephanie shook her head and hid her face against Jordan's leg. ''I don't want to,'' she mumbled.

Phil followed them out to the car, asking Jordan to send his thanks to Holly for watching the boys. ''I never would've completed this brief on time without her help,'' he admitted. ''Our schedules are in chaos now that Nancy's on the preschool dinner-dance committee. We probably won't see much of her in the next two weeks.''

Jordan hadn't thought about the event since the night he took Holly and Stephanie to the movies. ''This dance is a big to-do, isn't it?''

''It is around here. You know how the ladies are. They love a chance to get dressed up—gowns, jewelry, manicures. And of course they want the men to be in black tie,'' Phil added, chuckling. ''Will we see you there, Jordan? Maybe with Holly?''

The question didn't startle Jordan as it might have a week or so ago. The word was out in Golden. He and Holly had been seen together several times around town, and people were making whatever they wanted out of it. The old guys at the general store even razzed him about it—when they weren't dogging him with questions about his plans for the apple plant, that is.

''I don't think Holly and I will be going, Phil. She doesn't seem interested.''

''I wonder why not.''

Jordan thought that was an excellent question. The reasons Holly gave that night had been on the vague side.

On the drive back to her house, Steph was surprisingly subdued. Puzzled, Jordan stole a glance at her out of the corner of his eye. The air breezing through the opened sunroof lifted and tossed her fine pale hair. Unlike before, however, she took no pleasure in it. She seemed lost in another world, and somewhat wistful, too.

Jordan didn't know what to do.

Although he'd heard it was best not to badger kids into talking about their troubles, Jordan couldn't stand not knowing. He felt helpless. For him, that was almost as hard to take as Stephanie's glum face.

"Hey, Steph, why didn't you go swimming?" he asked. "I hope it wasn't because I couldn't go."

"No." She turned to look out the side window. "I just didn't feel like it."

That was hard to believe. She loved the water. "Did you want to get back home to help make your curtains?"

"No."

"Got something else you want to do this afternoon?"

"No."

Now he understood why the experts said not to pepper kids with questions. It didn't do any good. Casting another worried look at Stephanie, Jordan wished he knew what to say to make her feel better.

After they turned onto Old Paget Road, Stephanie finally stirred. "Jordan?"

"Yes?"

"Do you have a daddy?"

"Yeah, I do. But it's been a few years since I called him 'Daddy.' He lives in Florida now."

Leaning closer to him, she whispered, "Where's that?"

Jordan tried to explain. He quickly discovered that a four-year-old's grasp of geography was practically nil.

"Does your mommy live in Florida, too?"

"No, sweetheart, she doesn't."

"Then where does she live?"

Jordan hesitated. What did one say to a child? Glancing over at her trusting face, he decided only the truth would work. "My mom died, Steph."

"Oh," she crooned, tilting her head to the side in sympathy.

"It's okay, honey. It happened a long time ago."

With a solemn nod, she looked out her window again. Just when Jordan thought that was the end of it, Stephanie turned back to him. "My daddy died."

His hands tightened around the steering wheel. So that's what Holly had told her. He'd been wondering.

"I'm sorry to hear that, Steph." It seemed inadequate, but what else could he say?

"I wish he wasn't dead."

Her wounded voice grabbed his heart. It hurt to hear her say the words.

At least now he had an idea why she had refused Phil Barron's invitation. It would be Tommy and Sean's dad playing with them in the lake, giving the best flips in the whole world. Steph would feel like the odd man out—not for the first time, Jordan was sure. That was probably why she'd wanted him to go with her.

God, he felt terrible.

"What do you think, kid?" He reached out to give her hand a squeeze. "Should I ask Mr. Barron and the boys to go swimming with us next weekend? Would you like that?"

"Yeah!" She brightened immediately. "Will you throw me in the water?"

After mastering shoulder rides and Rock and Roll Freeze, Jordan figured flipping a kid into the water should be a breeze. "I'll give it my best shot."

Seeing Stephanie cheerful and smiling again didn't do much to ease his mind. Learning she'd been told her father was dead revived a worrisome question for Jordan. Was his brother, Scott, actually Stephanie's father?

He still believed what Holly had told him the day he'd come to Golden. He had to. After the past ten days, he'd be crazy to think she'd lied. Yet once or twice, a whisper of doubt had entered his mind.

"Look, there's Mommy," Stephanie announced when Jordan pulled into the driveway.

Holly sat in a rocking chair on the front porch, sewing on the length of pink fabric spread across her lap. As she concentrated on her handwork, her silky hair fell around her face like a golden frame. She looked content and soft and warm. Jordan couldn't take his eyes off her.

"Hi, Mommy," Stephanie called as she climbed out of Jordan's car.

Holly glanced up, her mouth breaking into a dazzling smile—a smile that reached out not only to Stephanie, but to him, as well. She put her sewing aside and came to the top of the steps to wait, arms outstretched, for her child. Sunlight filled her eyes as she watched Stephanie run to her.

Hugging Steph close, Holly sought his gaze and held it, drawing him into her warmth with a welcoming smile. Something clicked deep inside him—a faith, a hope or maybe just a dream. Whatever it was, he felt its power.

Holly made him feel as though he belonged.

In an instant, any doubt he had about her daughter's paternity vanished. He knew Holly had told him the truth.

Chapter Nine

"You should be worried, Jordan."

"Holly, *you* worry too much."

"My livelihood's at stake here," she declared, glancing over at him in the driver's seat. "Not to mention that I have to live in this town after it's all over."

Jordan's eyes remained focused on the road. "We'll handle whatever's thrown our way," he told her. "At CompWare, we had to deal with local governments and ordinances all the time."

"In cities and in suburbs. You're talking apples and oranges when you compare them with Golden."

"Holly, have a little faith in me. Please." Arriving at her house, he parked behind Gracie's old sedan.

Holly sighed. Jordan still didn't get it—even after Gabe Sawyer had advised them that a group of residents had formed a committee to fight the redevelopment of the apple packing plant. In a small town like Golden,

For my big brother, Steve, and my little brother, John.
You two are the best...

With love from the sister in the middle.

that kind of protest often had strong and immediate impact. By the time town meeting came around, their proposed zoning changes could already be dead in the water.

Jordan walked around to open her door. "You and I were having a great time tonight until we ran into *Dr. Gabe.*"

"You have to stop saying his name like that," she insisted. Yet she couldn't prevent a smile from twitching her lips.

Jordan caught her in midgrin as he shut the door behind her. Leaning against the car with his elbow on the roof and chin in hand, he bowed his head in mock contriteness. Unable to hold the pose for long, Jordan shook his head and met her gaze with a pulse-tripping smile.

"I've told you—I'm jealous of him."

The provocative gleam in his eyes made her feel weak in the knees. Tiny shocks of excitement danced along her spine, as they did whenever Jordan looked at her that way.

"Why should you be jealous?"

"Because he's been here in Golden with you all these years."

"As a much-needed friend."

"And I'm jealous because he's A-number-one in Stephanie's book." In a languid move, he reached out to her.

"I think you're closing in on him there," she replied, her voice a breathless rasp as she anticipated his touch. Her eyelids fluttered closed as his fingertips grazed lazy figures on her bare arm.

"And because he has your complete confidence."

Her eyes flew open. The discernible edge in Jordan's voice was a jolting splash of cold water on all the mindlessly warm sensations swirling through her. Was Jordan hinting that she didn't trust *him* enough? Or was guilt making her hear that?

Uncertain, Holly realized she'd have to take his comment at face value. "Gabe has my confidence when it comes to what's happening in this town. That's why we should listen to his advice about this new protest group. We can't afford to ignore them."

"Of course we shouldn't ignore them. On the other hand, I won't pander to unreasonable demands."

"Jordan, they haven't made any demands—not yet, anyway."

"Good," he said with a laugh, cupping her shoulders with his hands. "Let's not waste any more time talking about them or Gabe Sawyer. Or else I really will end up resenting him."

He pulled her to him, curving his arms around her waist. Holly tilted her head back, locking her gaze with his. She found the hungering gleam still there. Shining. Intense. Irresistible...

He lowered his head slowly, drinking her in with eyes the color of the night sky overhead. Holly could scarcely breathe, but she didn't care. His warm breath on her face as he drew closer was all the air she needed. Her hands roamed over his chest and along the steely grooves and hollows of his shoulders. She loved the solid feel of him. Curling her fingers in thick dark hair, she pulled Jordan's mouth down on hers.

At first, his kiss was a mere brush against her lips, as if he were deliberately taunting her. A small cry of frustration hummed in her throat as she pressed her body into his. Finally, Jordan found her lips again and gave her what she desired—a deep, searing kiss.

She wanted it to go on forever. But the last shred of

memory in her feverish head simply would not let go. It needled her pleasure with the nagging fears of past experience. With a moan she pulled her mouth away. "Please, I can't—"

Keeping his arms around her, Jordan spoke her name in a breathless whisper. "Don't run away. I'll just hold you."

Holly sank into his embrace, grateful he understood. But her body and mind were knotted with conflicting emotions and desires. Finally, after all these years, she wanted to be with a man. *This man.* Yet fear lingered in her soul. Her self-protective instincts were still strong and ever on the alert.

Resting her head on Jordan's chest, she heard the wild pounding of his heart; she could feel his muscles tense up as he held her. "Jordan, I must be driving you crazy."

She felt a silent laugh rumble deep in his chest. "You are."

"If it's any comfort to you, I'm driving myself crazy."

"Good." Burying his face in her hair, he whispered, "I hate being frustrated alone."

His light touch of humor did the trick in easing the tension between them, and Holly adored him for it. "Would you like to come in for some iced tea?" she asked, not wanting to say good-night quite yet.

"If it wasn't for the watchdog housekeeper and sleeping four-year-old you have stashed in there, that would be a dangerous invitation."

"I know." She tossed him a sly wink and stepped out of his embrace. "Will you come anyway?" She held out her hand.

Only a couple of lights were on in the house and

Gracie was nowhere in sight. Holly heard the whirring hum of the sewing machine coming from the den. "She must be stitching up the last of Stephanie's curtains," she noted to Jordan before alerting Gracie to their return.

"I'll be out as soon as I finish these up," Gracie called back. "Just a few more minutes."

After pouring two tall glasses of tea, Holly suggested they take them onto the porch. It was too lovely a night to stay indoors. She and Jordan sat in relaxed silence, sipping icy tea and gazing at the stars sparkling like crystals in the sky. The only sounds intruding on their companionable peace were the slow seesawing creaks of their rocking chairs on the plank floor and the unrelenting chorus of chirping crickets.

"I saw Nancy Barron at the post office this morning," Jordan said, breaking the silence after untold minutes. "She tried to sell me tickets to the preschool dinner dance."

"Did she?" Holly was not surprised. "She knows I've been selling them at the shop."

"I told her. So she asks—and I quote—'Then why in the heck aren't you taking Holly?'"

She stopped rocking. "What did you say?"

"That I'd take you if you wanted to go. That I'd love to, in fact."

"Nancy shouldn't be pestering you."

"Holly," he said firmly, putting his glass down on the wicker table between them. "Will you go with me to this dance? Everybody keeps telling me what a great party it is."

"I don't want you asking me because Nancy or anyone else says you should."

His lips curved into a wry smile. "Do I have to kiss you again to prove how untrue that is?"

Holly felt the color rise in her cheeks. "Point taken," she said, glancing at her hands. "But I can't imagine why you'd want to go. You hear everybody talking about it because it's the big date night for homebound parents of very young children. It's not like anything you're used to."

Jordan shrugged. "Maybe it isn't. Still, I can think of worse ways to spend an evening than dancing with you."

Holly wished he'd stop saying all the right things. "Look, Jordan, I've never attended one of these dances, and I'm not sure I want to start."

"Then don't give me an answer now. Think it over for a couple of days." After getting to his feet, he stood by her chair. "This dinner dance doesn't mean much to me one way or the other. I thought you'd like to go."

Moments later she watched Jordan drive away, glad he hadn't asked for an explanation, sorry that she hadn't tried to offer one. Yet how could she put her reasoning into words without sounding foolish and overly sensitive?

Gracie came onto the porch, sweater over her shoulders, tote bag in hand. "The curtains are done. We can hang them tomorrow."

Holly had forgotten Gracie was still there. "You didn't have to stay so late, you know. I could have finished the sewing tonight."

"Well, I knew you had a visitor." Gracie nodded at Jordan's empty glass on the wicker table. After a moment's hesitation, she sat in his chair and looked into Holly's eyes. "Why didn't you accept Mr. Mason's invitation?"

"Were you listening to us?"

"Well, I was getting my sweater and my bag and the

living-room windows were open,'' Gracie explained
with a sheepish shrug. ''I couldn't help overhearing.''

''No wonder you were in there so long.''

''So. Tell me,'' Gracie continued, ignoring Holly's
remark. ''Why are you pussyfooting around about going
to the dinner dance? The man asked you. Why won't
you go?''

The irony was laughable. Jordan hadn't asked for an
explanation, yet Gracie was demanding one. ''You want
me to go with *Jordan?*''

''I want you to go, period.'' She slapped her hand on
the table. ''You hardly take any time for yourself. When
you're not working, you're with Stephanie. When you're
not with Stephanie, you're working.''

''I love running the shop. And I want to be with my
daughter as much as I can.''

''You also deserve to enjoy your youth. Get all dolled
up. Dance with a handsome man. Have a little fun for a
change.''

''You're making me feel like a drudge, Gracie.''

Gracie rolled her eyes. ''Let me help you fix that. I'll
be available to baby-sit for Stephanie on the night of
that dance. Just say the word.''

Holly sold the last of the preschool dinner-dance tickets on Monday morning. Removing the sales poster from
the shop window, she felt dejected and as wary as ever.
It had been three days since Jordan had asked her to the
dance, and she still hadn't given him an answer.

Holly recognized something more was holding her
back than the outright avoidance of the dinner dance
she'd practiced in years past. Maybe it had something to
do with the way Jordan's ''courting'' had snuck up on

her. Now any day that he was not around felt empty. How could that have happened so fast?

Even more, Jordan had awakened longings and desires that had been lost deep inside her for years. Yet as his kisses deepened and his embraces intensified, Holly struggled to keep certain fears at bay. It was a fight she didn't feel she was winning.

Opening herself up to the vulnerabilities of a new, romantic relationship was tougher than she could have imagined. Holly had gotten by on her own just fine after Stephanie was born. She didn't have to worry about pleasing anyone; she didn't have to anticipate disappointment. Now, however, the questions, the doubts, just kept coming at her, fast and furious.

At times, she could think of nothing else but Jordan. More than once, Holly found herself wondering if she, like the rehab of the apple packing plant, was a diversion for the current lull in Jordan's life. Or was he paying attention to her out of a misplaced sense of guilt because of the way his brother had jilted her?

But the ultimate, painful question was how to tell Jordan that Scott was Stephanie's father. Now that they were drawing closer, the truth was critically important to explain, yet more difficult to reveal.

Later that same day, Holly's father called her at the store—something he'd never done in all her years in Golden. "Dad, is something wrong? Are you all right?"

"I was as fine as could be expected, until I received a letter from Lawrence Mason's wife."

"Rachel?" Holly's breath caught in her throat. "Why did she write to you?"

"Because she thinks it would do Lawrence good to hear from me."

"But he's getting better, isn't he?"

"Physically, yes. His spirits are low, though."

"I'm sorry to hear that." Guilt knotted in her stomach. She knew what was coming next.

"Have you told Jordan about Stephanie yet?"

"No."

She heard him mutter something unintelligible.

"How long has it been since he moved to Golden?" he then asked. "Three weeks? Four?"

"Almost three, Dad."

"How can I get in touch with Lawrence now? I can't talk to him in good conscience when he doesn't even know his grandchild exists."

"I'm trying to find the right time. Believe me. But it's more complicated than you think." Holly wondered if her father could even guess at what was going on between her and Jordan.

"The longer you wait, the harder it gets, Holly."

As if she didn't know. "Yes, Dad, it is. You're right."

This response must have mollified him for his tone mellowed. "Did Jordan tell you how he lost CompWare?" he asked.

"Lost? What are you talking about?"

"That's what Rachel said in her letter—Lawrence's heart attack came shortly after Jordan lost the company to a hostile takeover attempt."

She was stunned. "That can't be right. Jordan said he sold it. The newspapers reported that he sold it."

"Oh, you know how those corporate PR departments like to pretty these things up," Ted offered matter-of-factly. "Besides, Rachel wouldn't have written such a thing if it wasn't true."

Holly barely heard her father say goodbye. After hanging up with him, she stood at the front counter, staring into space, trying to make sense out of this news.

Jordan had been evasive the few times she had mentioned the sale of CompWare. But she thought he didn't want to discuss it because he had *sold* out the family business—not because he'd *lost* it.

How devastating that must have been for him! Jordan loved that company as much or even more than his father did. Holly was filled with shame for the cutting thoughts she had had about Jordan's selling out the business. She had been certain he had done it for the money. She had believed the worst of him. And Jordan knew it.

Holly paced around the shop, her mind racing with emotions. She needed to talk to him. Now. She wanted to tell him she knew. She reached for the phone and quickly dialed his home number. Getting no answer there, she tried his cellular phone number. After letting it ring countless times, Holly slammed the receiver down.

Acting on pure emotional impulse, Holly hung the Closed sign on the shop door and headed out to find Jordan. She tried his usual haunts in town. The packing plant, the general store, the post office, the town hall. He was nowhere to be found. She dialed both his house and cellular phones again, but Jordan didn't answer.

Holly's heart was pounding. *Where was he?*

Although Jordan hadn't answered his home phone, she decided to try his house anyway. He had to return there sometime. At the old Paget place, she found the driveway empty, the house locked. Frustrated, she knocked on the back door, even though she suspected he wasn't there.

Since chasing all over town for him had proven fruitless, Holly figured she'd stay and wait. As she walked around the house to the front veranda overlooking the vast pond, she peered into the garage window. Jordan's

Mercedes was inside, parked next to a shiny new pickup truck she'd never seen before. Holly stepped back, while scanning the extensive, unmanicured landscape surrounding the big house. She saw nothing.

"He's got to be somewhere around here."

Holly scurried to the front of the house. After climbing the veranda steps, she turned to survey the huge, rolling green lawn that eventually tapered into Summer Pond. She had to squint to see beyond the sun's glare. Within seconds she was able to focus on the figure standing on the shore, a figure indistinguishable from this distance—save for his shiny dark hair.

She ran across the yard and down the hill as fast as she could. The hill steepened as Holly drew closer to the lake, and it slowed her down. Both her shoes slipped off along the way, but she scarcely noticed. Finally, she could see him clearly, and she felt a rush of inexplicable relief. Dressed in faded jeans and a plain white T-shirt, he was dragging a heavy garden rake through what appeared to be mounds of fresh sand.

"Jordan!" she called from several yards away.

He looked up. A broad grin spread across his face when he realized it was her. He leaned against the rake and waved.

Breathing hard, Holly strode across the sand. "I've been looking everywhere for you."

As Jordan got a closer glimpse of her face, his smile vanished. He dropped the rake and rushed to meet her. "What's wrong, Holly? What's happened?"

Gasping as she tried to catch her breath, Holly revealed what she had just learned about Mason Comp-Ware.

"Is that all this is about? I was afraid something had happened to Stephanie."

"Steph is fine, just fine." Holly brushed the hair back off her face. "What I want to know is why you misled me. You never said you lost CompWare."

Resting his hands on his hips, Jordan glanced over at the lake. "*Technically,* I did sell the company, Holly."

"You're going to play word games with me now?"

Jordan sighed as he turned back to her. "Okay. The truth is I finally gave in to the takeover bid," he said, sounding as uncomfortable as he looked. "I chose to sell before I was forced to."

"Had it really come to that?"

He nodded. "Huge multinational corporations play hardball when they want something badly enough, Holly. The writing was on the wall—no matter what my father would like to think."

"Lawrence had trouble accepting it?"

"He wanted me to keep fighting." He reached for her shoulder, caressing it gently. "But I had to call it as I saw it. Agreeing to sell when I did gave me leverage to negotiate."

"For more money? A better deal?"

"No." His hand dropped from her shoulder. "For job security for my employees. A forced buyout would have meant certain job loss for hundreds of our people. I wanted to save as many of those jobs as I could."

Holly began to understand. "So you agreed to sell if they agreed to retain your employees."

Jordan nodded. "I held out until I got them a guaranteed number of years or a fair monetary settlement."

"And then you gave up CompWare."

"As you and my father and many others have pointed out, I was well compensated," he said with a shrug.

Jordan talked a good game, but she could see in his eyes that the loss bothered him. Holly felt ashamed.

When she had first heard about the sale, she had suspected Jordan of greed and selfishness. But he had actually sacrificed a company he loved and the respect of his father in order to protect the people who had worked for him.

"I'm so sorry I misjudged you." She took his hand. "I should have had more faith."

He lifted his gaze to her. His eyes, a translucent midnight ink, shone with unexpressed emotion. "That's what I've been wanting."

Holly clutched his hand. "Let's sit down over there." She led him to the large, smooth rocks at the edge of the water. Their weathered, flat tops made them excellent benches. They huddled on the rocks, sitting knee-to-knee, their arms entwined.

"People haven't considered how tough the sale has been on you, have they?" Holly held both his hands.

"Hell, it's been a lot tougher on Dad than me."

She gave him a skeptical look. "Really?"

"Selling off the business my mother and father built from scratch was painful, I admit. But I've come to terms with why I had to do it. I just wish..." Jordan paused, turning his eyes up to the powder-blue sky. "I just wish I could have spared my father another loss. First it was Scott, then CompWare."

"Your family's been through a rough time."

Jordan nodded. "Dad still misses Scott terribly."

"Does he?" Holly whispered, sadness rising in her throat.

"You know how close the two of them were—they had a special bond. I'm afraid I haven't been much comfort to him."

"Don't say that. You're his son, too."

"Dad was happy about my engagement to Allison.

He had visions of grandchildren. He would sound out Allison about having kids all the time,'' Jordan explained in an increasingly weary voice. ''You can imagine his disappointment when Allison and I split up.''

Holly winced at the mention of grandchildren. ''You're making it sound like you've failed Lawrence.''

''Haven't I?'' he asked, throwing open his arms. ''I'm not the son he adored and lost. I'm the son who lost the company he spent his life building.''

''You made the tough choice, Jordan—a choice Lawrence might well have made himself if he'd been in your shoes. It took courage,'' she added firmly. ''And that's one thing Scott never had. He would've been incapable of making any decision at all.''

Jordan's gaze widened in surprise.

''I mean it, Jordan. You should never feel second best to Scott.''

How could he? He was twice the man his brother had been.

Scott had been weak and selfish. He had shown his weakness in the humiliating way he had left her standing at the altar. And he had proven his selfishness by refusing even to listen to her when she'd tried to tell him she was pregnant with his baby. Holly felt Jordan had to know this truth about his brother, and that meant telling him about Stephanie.

''Jordan, I loved Scott once, but I was so young and blind—''

''I don't care about you and Scott. It doesn't matter anymore,'' he insisted, a fervent excitement flashing in his eyes. He cupped her face between his hands. ''It means so much to know you're in my corner. It means even more to know I'm not just a substitute for Scott in your eyes.''

"A substitute?" Holly reached up to cover his hands with her own. "Never, ever, Jordan. You've got to know that."

His thumb traced languid circles on her left cheek. "I do now," he murmured, moving closer to her lips.

Enclosing her in his arms, he used his tongue to tempt her mouth open with slow, sensuous licks. Pulling her tight against his chest, Jordan met her gaze for the briefest of moments. Then he reclaimed her lips to kiss her fully, deeply. It was a kiss unlike all the others before, a kiss that went beyond passion and desire. The steamy urgency of his previous kisses had fired her blood and fogged her senses. But the intense, unrestrained emotion of this one did nothing less than rock her soul.

As her hands ran up and down Jordan's long, lean back, Holly could almost feel the happiness thrumming inside his body. It thrilled her to know she had given him that joy. Murmuring her name, Jordan moved his mouth from her lips to her cheeks, to her eyes, to her forehead and back. These featherlight kisses warmed her down to her toes, until she felt like slowly melting butter in his arms.

Then they held each other in an embrace both silent and intimate. As the water gently lapped against the rocks, Holly imagined they were tucked away on a deserted island, far away from the realities that could tear them apart. She wanted this serenity, this closeness, to last forever.

Yet when Holly rested her head on Jordan's chest, the peaceful, easy beating of his heart reminded her what these exquisite moments had cost. To give him this joy, she had had to keep her secret a little longer. There was no other way. How could she reveal Scott was Stephanie's father after everything Jordan had just told her?

That was the last thing he needed to hear. It would have destroyed him when he needed her most. It would have destroyed everything.

"Hey. Where did you go?"

Her head jerked up at the sound of Jordan's voice. She looked at him, puzzled. "What do you mean?"

"All of a sudden you were a million miles away. At least, it felt that way."

Holly was amazed he had sensed her distraction. "I admit it. My mind wandered—but not a million miles."

"Care to elaborate?"

"Another time," she said softly, brushing her knuckles against his cheek, hoping he'd let things go at that. "But I was wondering about all this new sand."

"I had it dumped here this morning," he explained, the smile returning to his eyes. "Don't you think this cove would make a nice private little beach? With some work, I mean."

"It'll make a wonderful beach. But would you happen to be doing this for my daughter?"

He had told her about Stephanie's reaction to Phil Barron's swim invitation. Although she had ached for her child, she'd been extremely touched by Jordan's concern for Steph.

"I did promise to take her and her pals swimming," he reminded her.

"You could take them to the public beach. They'd be just as happy."

Jordan shrugged. "This'll make it extra special. The kid deserves it."

"You shouldn't spoil her, Jordan."

From the way he pulled back to look at her, Holly thought she had offended him. Then she caught the familiar gleam in his eye and knew right away he was no longer thinking of Stephanie.

"Actually, I'm hoping to spoil you," he told her, his voice a low, sexy drawl. "Someday I'm going to get you out here for a moonlight swim."

"That could be a cold day in July," she said, trying not to smile. "I've learned my lesson about going in the water with you."

"You are a cruel woman, Ms. West." Jordan feigned distress. "First you never give me an answer about the preschool dance, and now you mock my dishonorable designs on you. Have you no mercy?"

Dishonorable designs? Holly loved it. "You speak too soon, Mr. Mason. For I have decided to accept your kind invitation to the dinner dance."

"I don't believe it. When did you decide that?"

"Just now," she admitted. "You haven't changed your mind, have you?"

Jordan treated her to one of his more beguiling grins. "Not a chance. But what made you change *yours?*"

"Besides your irresistible charms, you mean?"

"That goes without saying." He kissed the top of her head.

"Stephanie had the most to do with it, really."

"The kid's been rooting for me, eh? And I didn't even have to bribe her."

"She doesn't know you invited me." Shifting around on the rock, Holly nestled her back against his chest. "But after mulling over what happened when you took the Barron boys back to their father, I realized that *I've* always felt like the odd man out where the dinner dance was concerned."

"Seems to me all your friends want you there," Jordan said, sounding surprised. "And Gabe Sawyer must have asked you at one time or another."

"He did—the first year Steph was in preschool. Like you, he'd thought I wanted to go," she explained. "Yet I think Gabe was just as happy that I said no. He's not real fond of black-tie events."

"I still don't understand why you would feel like the odd man out."

"Because in that preschool circle, they're all married couples with young, growing families. I'm the only one who's a single mother."

Holly felt her words inadequate. It wasn't easy to explain how her unmarried status seemed to threaten some of the other young mothers. Or how, now and then, a bored or weary husband got it into his head that her husbandless state made her open to any and all sexual advances. And the minor daily differences between her life and theirs always seemed to get magnified at couple-oriented occasions such as the dinner dance.

"There are just times when I don't feel I belong, Jordan," she finally added with a sigh of resignation.

He wrapped his arms around her shoulders. "Like Steph with the dads."

She nodded, resting her head on his arm. Despite her fragmented explanation, he understood, and that meant so much to Holly. It made her feel less alone.

"Now it's time to forget all that and have myself some fun," she continued, glancing up at Jordan with a smile she felt from the heart. "After all, I'll be going with the handsomest man in town—who, as I recall, used to be one smooth dancer."

Squeezing her gently in his arms, Jordan lowered his mouth closer to her ear and whispered, "I still am."

Chapter Ten

Jordan spotted Stephanie waiting on the top porch step when he drove into Holly's driveway. She was dressed in a strange-looking outfit.

"Jordan!"

Steph got to her feet, her arm swinging in her usual buoyant wave. Instead of skipping down the steps two at a time, as was her custom, she took each step with a careful, regal air.

Jordan bit down on his lip, praying the kid wouldn't trip on the long skirt she was wearing and come tumbling down on her head. But both her little feet touched the ground safely and she headed straight for him.

"Wow." Her eyes popped as they roamed over his tux.

"Not bad, huh?" He made a show of straightening his black tie. "Just don't tell me I look like a penguin, okay?"

"No," Steph replied, shaking her head. "You look like a prince."

The awe in her voice caught him up short. The adoration on her face made him nervous. He didn't exactly consider himself prince material in any sense of the word. But how he'd hate to end up a disappointment in this girl's eyes!

Needing to turn the table, Jordan stepped back and pretended to study Stephanie's dress with great interest. "That's quite the outfit you have on, Steph. Looks like you're dressed for a ball yourself."

"Isn't it pretty?" She twirled in front of him. "It's Mommy's slip. 'Cept she made me wear this T-shirt under it, even though I didn't want to."

"It looks fine to me."

She fluttered the ends of the long, flowery scarf draped around her shoulders. "Do you like my stole?"

"Oh, yes, and your earrings, too. And is that lipstick I see there?"

Her face turned pink. "Please don't tell Mommy. I borrowed it and didn't ask," she whispered, as if it were the biggest secret in the world. "I better wipe it off."

"Here." He took a folded handkerchief out of his pocket and dabbed at her mouth. When he was finished, he planted a kiss on the tip of her nose. "Next time remember to ask your mom."

Then Stephanie took his hand and led him into the house, talking nonstop about Holly's new dress. "Jordan's here," she yelled as the screen door slammed behind them.

"Don't scream, Stephanie," Gracie chastised as she came down the stairs. "Your mother's not quite ready yet."

Stopping at the bottom of the steps, the older woman

gave him a good looking-over. She circled around him twice, pausing each time to examine the front of his coat.

"Is something wrong, Gracie?"

She didn't answer. Instead, she pulled a pair of eyeglasses from an apron pocket and continued her scrutiny. "That's it," she muttered finally. "Don't you move. I'll be right back."

As Gracie dashed out the screen door, Jordan turned to Stephanie. "What was that about?"

The little girl looked at him, wide-eyed. "I don't know, but you better not move."

Gracie returned quickly with a fresh, crimson rose from one of the front-yard rosebushes. "Stephanie, run into the den and get the pincushion for me. Please, dear?"

The older woman trimmed the rose's stem until Stephanie brought her the tomato-shaped pincushion. "This will fix everything," Gracie claimed, taking an awkward step toward him.

Jordan didn't know what to say as she pinned the rose on his lapel. The woman barely tolerated him—yet she had gone out of her way to present him with a boutonniere. It was surprising, to say the least.

"Ooh. That looks nice," Stephanie piped in as Gracie smoothed out her handiwork.

Jordan glanced down at the weathered hands on his lapel. He touched them lightly. "Thank you, Gracie. It's just the thing I needed."

"It was nothing." She backed away from him, taking the pincushion out of Stephanie's curious hands. "But you just make sure Holly has a good time tonight. Okay?"

"I'll do my best."

With a silent nod, Gracie started back up the stairs. "I'll go see what's keeping her."

"Mommy's new dress is so pretty." Stephanie looked up at him with sweet brown eyes.

Jordan scooped her up in his arms. "As pretty as yours?"

"Prettier, you silly." Giggling, she threw her chubby arms around his neck. Then her gaze flew to the stairs behind him. "See?"

He turned to find Holly standing at the top of the staircase in a gown the color of emeralds. "I see," he whispered in Steph's ear.

Smiling, Holly came down the steps. "You two look like you're having fun."

Steph wiggled out of his arms. "Oh, Mommy, you look so beautiful."

Beautiful and dazzling. Jordan drank in every inch of her. Her golden hair was swept high off her neck, leaving an enticing expanse of honeyed skin. Shoulders, throat and soft, soft breasts flowed like smooth cream into her silky, strapless dress. He felt a stirring in his loins and his fingers itched to touch her.

"You look lovely, Holly," he murmured, struggling with his body's strong reaction.

"Glorious is more like it." Beaming like a proud mother, Gracie followed Holly down the steps.

Sounding shy, Holly thanked them all for their praise. "We'd better go, Jordan," she added, "before my head gets too big to fit through the door."

As they walked across the driveway to his car, Holly stopped for one more reassuring glance at Stephanie and Gracie. They stood on the porch, smiling and waving.

"Having second thoughts about the dance?" He reached for her hand.

Holly shook her head. "I'm just not used to leaving them behind like this."

Before Jordan could answer, Gracie called from across the yard. "Remember, I'm sleeping over. So stay out as late as you like."

Jordan winked at Holly. "Sounds like they'll be just fine. Now, how about you?"

Fingering his new boutonniere, she met his gaze. "As long as I'm with such a dashing man, how can I be anything but fine?"

Ablaze with lights, the outside of the River House resembled an ornate, gilded jewel. Inside, the old mansion was alive with music, dance and laughter—as it had been in its heyday, Jordan suspected. And Holly, gorgeous in her stunning green gown, was the standout in a ballroom full of elegantly dressed women. Jordan couldn't help the rush of pride he felt knowing she was with him.

Within minutes of their arrival, however, they met up with the Barrons and the Laceys. After admiring one another's gowns, Nancy and Susan steered Holly toward the table reserved for their party. Holly peered over her shoulder, anxiously mouthing an apology to him. Astounded by the swiftness of her removal, Jordan realized Holly had been right. This event wasn't like anything he'd been to before.

Phil Barron patted him on the back. "Might as well get used to it, Mason. This party is for the girls."

"But look on the bright side. After a dance or two, we can head to the bar to watch the ball game," Jaimie Lacey added with a laugh. "They won't even miss us."

Jordan gritted his teeth. *Not on your life, pals.*

Following Holly through the crowd with his eyes, Jordan was treated to the vision of her bare, beautiful back. All he could think of was how it would feel—how Holly would feel—to hold and to touch. His muscles tightened with a sharp quickness. Male camaraderie was a fine thing, but that wasn't why he'd come to this shindig. And he wasn't about to allow Holly's pals to monopolize her time. Not here, not tonight.

Throughout dinner and dessert, Jordan joined in the table talk, biding his time all the while. When the orchestra struck up again and the waiters with trays full of champagne began circulating through the ballroom, he grasped Holly's hand beneath the table. He leaned in close. "We haven't danced yet."

"I know." She squeezed his hand. The single diamond drops at her ears made her brown eyes sparkle.

Excusing themselves from the table, they began to wend their way toward the dance floor. Yet Holly seemed to have friends or acquaintances at every other table, and they all insisted she stop to say hello.

"Didn't feel like you belonged, eh?" he cracked, tugging Holly along before another round of well-wishers could accost her.

Before they reached the dance floor, however, the town librarian tracked him down. "Mr. Mason, I've been searching all over for you," Annabella Whitney proclaimed between sips from her champagne glass. "I just had to thank you in person for your donation to the children's reading room. I'm writing you an official thank-you, of course. But your gift deserves more than a letter."

Holly gaped at him. "You gave money to the library?"

"He did," Annabella answered for him. "An extremely generous donation, I might add."

"*Extremely* generous?" Holly repeated, her gaze fixed on him.

"Oh, yes." Annabella drained her glass. "And now this town will see what I can accomplish with some decent funding."

"What was that all about?" Holly asked after Annabella left in search of more champagne.

"I'd rather dance first and explain later." He led her toward the far end of dance floor, where it appeared less crowded.

It was not to be.

They ran smack-dab into Miss Karin and her escort, Jonathan Warren, the owner of the general store. "Oh, Holly and Jordan, you did come after all," trilled the preschool director.

As Holly and Karin admired each other's dresses, Jonathan clamped his large hand on Jordan's shoulder. "Hope you're ready for next Saturday. It's expected to be one of the better-attended town meetings."

"That's what I've been hearing."

"Just wanted you to know, I'm on your side. A lot of people aren't, mind you," he remarked gruffly. "But we businesspeople have to stick together. I had one hell of a time getting a permit to enlarge the parking lot behind the store."

"Good gracious, don't let him get started on that parking lot." Karin wedged herself between them. "Come on, Jonathan, you promised me another dance."

Curling his arm around Holly's waist, Jordan was about to follow them onto the dance floor. Out of the corner of his eye, however, he caught a glimpse of Nancy and Susan making their way heading toward the dance floor with husbands in tow. Although he really did like both couples, he wanted time alone with his lady.

"Come on." Grabbing Holly's hand, he turned away from the dance floor.

"Aren't we going to dance?"

"You bet we are."

Remembering the sweeping stone terraces from their last visit to the River House, Jordan headed for one of the large French doors lining the rear of the ballroom. On the way, he spotted a waiter popping the cork on a fresh bottle of champagne. Making a quick detour, Jordan pushed a crisp fifty-dollar bill into the waiter's hand. "I'll take that," he said, lifting the bottle and two empty crystal flutes from the serving tray.

Holly was agog. "What on earth are you doing?"

He gave her the two glasses. "Follow me."

Outside, the terraces were occupied by couples either talking or dancing or smooching. Seeking something more secluded, Jordan peered over the upper railing of the carved stone balustrade. There he discovered what he was looking for.

Taking Holly's free hand, he led her down a curving staircase of wide stone steps, using moonlight and stars to guide them. "Here we are. And we can still hear the orchestra—sort of." He put the champagne bottle down on a marble-topped patio table. "You know, this is just about perfect."

"Perfect," Holly echoed, as if she had to consider exactly what the word implied.

Jordan followed her gaze as she surveyed the lower, ground-level terrace—exactly the same as the ones above except for the faint-sounding music and lack of lights. Still, the natural lighting provided by the glimmering night sky and the precious privacy of the secluded location more than made up for those deficiencies. At least, he thought so.

Holly turned back to him. "Perhaps you're right. It is perfect."

"You sound like you can't believe it."

"What I really can't believe is your romantic streak. I never suspected it of you, Jordan."

At first, he didn't know what to say. Her observation had rendered his trusted stock of wry comments useless. Yet he had to say something to the warm, coffee-colored eyes waiting for him.

"No one's ever brought it out in me before."

Her mouth softened into an alluring smile as she held out the two champagne flutes. "We should celebrate."

The hushed sound of Holly's words triggered an excitement inside him. His pulse raced as he stepped up to pour the wine. He whispered a toast to the rest of their evening. But after the chimelike clinking of glasses, instead of raising his glass to his lips, he lowered his mouth to hers. The wine could wait. All he wanted was to taste *her*.

Closing her eyes, Holly leaned into him. Her soft, tender kiss was like the warm breath of early summer as her eyelashes fluttered against his own closed lids. Jordan was sure he'd never felt a sensation like it before. There was so much he'd never felt until he found Holly here in Golden.

"Jordan," she breathed, opening her eyes. "Aren't you ever going to dance with me?"

Answering her with a smile, he put his untouched champagne down next to the bottle. Then he took the glass from her hand. "I've been waiting all night for this," he murmured, sliding his hands along her waist and up around her luscious back. As he pulled her close, his fingers couldn't resist tracing light, lazy circles on her velvety skin.

Fitting into his arms like a glove, Holly pressed her soft, lush curves against his chest. They began to move together in slow, rhythmic steps, sometimes to the music floating down on a breeze from the ballroom, sometimes to no music at all. They danced like this, drank champagne, talked, kissed, laughed and danced some more until the lights from the mansion flickered out.

Jordan sensed Holly's reluctance to leave. He felt the same way. It had been a wonderful few hours—enchanting, really. She had been sweet, funny, sexy. Unfortunately, these charmed hours had left him hungry for more of her, far more than he knew she was able to give.

He didn't want another evening to end with frustrated kisses at Holly's porch steps. Not this time. As he drove back to Golden, it took all the fortitude Jordan could muster to keep from carrying her off to his house and to his bed. He wanted Holly badly—to make love to her; to feel her hot, lush body let go of the passion buried deep in her soul. He wanted to hear her cries and her moans. He wanted to show her how wonderful it could be between them and how good he could make her feel. But even more, he wanted to prove to Holly that he was different from the others, that he wouldn't leave her hurting and alone.

He wanted so damn much and it was tearing him apart inside.

"You've become awfully quiet," Holly observed as Jordan pulled up in front of her house.

"It must be the hour." He nodded at the dashboard clock before getting out of the car.

As he walked her to the porch, she hummed one of the tunes they had danced to at the River House. With her arm hooked through his, she sounded giddy and light—clearly still under the influence of their magical party for two.

"Want to come in for some coffee?" She stood a few steps above him, her gaze even with his as she curled an arm behind his neck.

"Not tonight, Hol." Although it would be tough to leave her now, this was not the invitation he wanted. Not with Stephanie and Gracie asleep inside.

Holly slipped her other arm around his shoulder, but the dreamy look on her face had vanished. "What's wrong, Jordan?"

Every muscle in his body stiffened. He wanted her so much, yet was resenting her like hell right now. "I think you know," he said, straining to sound calm while his mind and heart churned with the whiplike intensity of a whirlpool.

She didn't answer. Still, the hesitant flicker of her eyes told him she knew exactly what he meant.

"I know you've been hurt before," he continued, "and I've tried hard not to rush you, not to make demands. But patience has never been one of my strengths."

"You've been wonderful, Jordan."

Something inside him snapped. "I don't want to be wonderful. I want to be your lover."

Holly showed no surprise. Why would she? He'd been holding himself out to her, when all the while she'd been holding back. And not just physically. There was a part of herself that she kept from him, something in her heart or on her mind that she wouldn't share. Or couldn't. Either way, it was hurting them both.

"I can't pretend I'm not afraid," she said at last. "I've made mistakes before."

"You've got to put those behind you, Holly, because they're killing any chance we might have." He cupped his hands around her arms, then slipped them off his shoulders. "Not only do I have to contend with Scott's memory every time I'm with my father, but with you I have to pay for his mistakes."

"Oh, God, Jordan, please don't say that."

Her stunned voice came out sounding like both a warning and a plea. She looked as if he'd slapped her.

"Then tell me it isn't true. Tell me you're over what Scott did to you. Tell me that what happened with Stephanie's father doesn't matter a damn where you and I are concerned."

Closing his eyes for just a moment, Jordan willed her to say something—anything to show she wanted him enough to trust him. But when he opened them, Holly was shaking her head.

"I can't tell you that." A single tear escaped her glistening eyes. "Try to understand. *Please.*"

Her words cut like a knife. He couldn't understand—not after the way things had been between them on that terrace.

All of a sudden, Jordan knew he had to get out of there—before he did or said something he'd regret. "Looks like it's time to take a step back."

"That's not what I want."

"It's what I need." His knuckles brushed the tear from her cheek. "And I think you need some space, too."

"There you go again, decreeing what's best for everybody." The tremble in her voice made this more of a lament than a charge. Another errant tear made him want to fold her in his arms.

Struggling against that urge, Jordan turned to leave. ''What happens after tonight is all up to you, Holly.''

''And you're just going to walk away?'' she asked fiercely.

If she only knew how hard it was for him to leave her like this.

''I'm not going far,'' he said with a calm he was far from feeling. ''When you're ready to get beyond the past, you'll know where to find me.''

Chapter Eleven

Holly dragged herself into the shop Monday, still miserable over what had happened with Jordan and exhausted after two nights without sleep. The last thing she needed was to be out of coffee.

"Just great." She slammed down the empty coffee can.

"Somebody got up on the wrong side of bed this morning."

Holly spun around to find Nancy Barron standing at the back room door. "What are you doing here so early? And where are the boys?"

"I sent them to the office with Daddy." Nancy tossed her handbag on a worktable. "I've been dying to talk to you. I must have called you a dozen times yesterday. All I got was the answering machine. Didn't you play back your messages?"

"Not yesterday," Holly said as she searched every

cabinet and shelf in the workroom for anything containing caffeine—a stray tea bag, a packet of hot chocolate, even a forgotten jar of instant coffee.

"I figured you and Stephanie were off spending your Sunday with Jordan."

Holly refused to rise to the bait. Yesterday was one thing she didn't want to talk about. And Jordan was another.

"Ah, come on, Holly," Nancy moaned. "Where did you and Jordan disappear to Saturday night? One minute you were heading for the dance floor, and then— poof—you were gone."

"We just went out to one of the terraces to dance— it was a little less crowded."

"And ten times more romantic." Nancy had stars in her eyes.

But Holly's head hurt and she wanted coffee. She didn't want to continue this conversation. "I've got to run to the general store for a pound of coffee. Watch the shop for me, please?"

Scooting out into the cool, calm morning, Holly hoped her friend wouldn't be too annoyed. She was sick about what had happened after the dance. Recalling how Jordan had left her standing on the porch steps pained her heart. It wasn't the same as being left standing at the altar, yet she *felt* the same shock and disbelief, and the same aching sense of betrayal she had experienced on her ill-fated wedding day.

At the store, Holly skirted around the four old men gathered at the coffee machine and went straight to the beverage aisle. She was in no mood to pass the time of day with them. But Howie McGovern and Earle Stacy spotted her when she headed toward the checkout counter.

"Hey, Holly," Earle called. "Come on over a minute."

"Can't right now. Got to get back to the shop."

"We hear your fella's been spreading some cash around town," Howie added as she brushed by them.

Holly just waved and kept on moving. The General Store Four had been calling Jordan her "fella" for weeks. As far as the spreading of cash was concerned, Holly figured it was just another one of their tales blown out of proportion.

Jonathan Warren rang up the can of coffee. "Those guys are in fine form this morning. They're all up in arms over Jordan's donations."

"You mean *donation*," she corrected, "the one he made to the town library."

The manager shook his head. "The word is he's presenting a check to the PTA's computer fund during their monthly meeting."

She tried to hide her surprise. "What's the matter with that? Everyone knows the PTA's trying to raise money to buy computers for the school. I've contributed to their fund-raiser myself, as I'm sure you have."

"We're not talking twenty-five or fifty bucks, Holly." Jonathan handed back her change. "He's giving them enough money to buy a computer for every classroom in the elementary school."

She felt her mouth drop. "That much?"

"Regina Harwood told me so not more than twenty minutes ago. And she should know—she's PTA treasurer." With a glance over his shoulder, Jonathan lowered his voice. "Like I told Jordan at the dinner dance, I'm behind him on the zoning issue. But Holly, you've got to tell him to be careful. He's not doing himself any favors flashing money around that way. People are getting the wrong idea."

She thanked Jonathan and left. She doubted Jordan would take anyone's advice to heart. He had everything figured out for everybody. And since he'd decreed that the two of them needed to *step back*, Holly didn't know when she'd be speaking to him again.

"Jonathan Warren's missing the boat," Nancy insisted when Holly told her about the conversation. "Every parent in town is going to be thrilled when they hear Jordan's buying new computers for the school. Look, my kids aren't even old enough to attend yet, and I think it's great. And I bet you're glad for Steph's sake, too."

"I suppose I am," she replied, opening the new can of coffee.

She'd be even more glad if she knew how to tell Stephanie Jordan wasn't going to be around much anymore. Yesterday, her daughter had asked about the dinner dance over and over again. Tomorrow, she would be asking for Jordan, wondering where he was.

Holly doubted Jordan had considered what taking a *step back* meant for Stephanie. Of course not. His entire argument that night had been about what he needed and what he wanted. And she'd been left to pick up the pieces. Again.

The week passed at an excruciatingly slow pace. Although she had told Stephanie that Jordan's work would prevent him from visiting, the child kept running to the door every time she heard a noise outside. Stephanie's resulting disappointment was hard to take. As was her own. Without Jordan, each day seemed endless.

True, he had left the ball in her court. When she was ready to forget who had hurt her and how, he'd come back with arms opened. Yet forgetting was impossible. And Jordan's harsh, emotional words had made revealing why just as impossible. If he resented his brother's mistakes, as he had claimed, how would he feel about Stephanie once he knew? Would Scott's daughter become another mistake in Jordan's eyes?

Could she ever tell Jordan now? Perhaps going directly to Lawrence was the only way to reveal the truth. Perhaps it always had been.

When Holly arrived home from work Wednesday evening, Gracie was putting the finishing touches on a tuna noodle casserole. "Haven't made this in a couple of months. I thought it would cheer Stephanie up some. She's been kind of mopey lately."

Holly remembered well the last time Gracie had prepared Stephanie's favorite dish. It was the day Jordan had first shown up in Golden.

"Where is Steph?" she asked, pushing the memory aside. "Out in the tree house?"

"Upstairs reading to Taffy. Or pretending to, anyway."

Holly poured herself a glass of iced tea, feeling Gracie's eyes on her. "Is there something on your mind?"

"Well, ah…" Hesitating, Gracie bit down on her bottom lip.

"Come on, Gracie."

Wiping her hands with a dish towel, Gracie joined Holly at the kitchen table. "It's just that we haven't seen Mr. Mason around here since last Saturday night and, ah, I'd been wondering…"

Why wouldn't Gracie be wondering about Jordan? After all, he'd been at the house practically every day. Still, even after four days, Holly found the entire situation difficult to talk about. So she gave Gracie the same excuse she'd given Stephanie. "The town meeting's this Saturday morning, and he has to have his presentation ready by then."

"Sure, he must be real busy," Gracie said kindly.

But Holly could see she didn't believe her, and the older woman's motherly pat on the hand confirmed it.

"That's what I told Steph. She's been asking, you know."

Holly looked down at her glass of tea and squeezed back an unwanted tear. "I do know."

"Don't worry, she'll be all right." Gracie patted her hand again. "And I hope things will be all right at the town meeting, too. For your sake."

"I suppose you've heard some of the grumbling around town. About Jordan's *donations*."

"That's the last thing you need to be worrying about now," Gracie said, getting up from the table. "People are gonna say what they want, no matter what."

"What have you heard?"

"Not so much. A few eyebrows were raised when he gave the parks association money for installing a new water fountain on the common. But that quieted down real fast until—" Gracie stopped herself in midsentence.

Holly stiffened. "Until what, Gracie?"

"I take it you haven't heard where the retirement home's new van came from?"

"No. Don't tell me he paid for it."

"That's what I heard at bingo last night," Gracie revealed. "Apparently, he gave them the money for it right after he moved to town."

"He never said a word about it to me." She couldn't believe it. Had Jordan been giving away money all along?

"Well, it was the talk of the church hall, I'll tell you."

She could just imagine. "What kind of things were they saying?"

Gracie grimaced. "Not much good. Some, like Howie McGovern and Earle Stacey, say he's trying to buy off the town to make the town meeting go his way."

That was what she'd been afraid of. "I'm sure a lot of other people feel the same way."

"He's gonna hear about it on Saturday for sure. Maybe you should warn him."

She *had* warned him against throwing his money around town. Apparently, he hadn't listened. Or—in good old Jordan Mason fashion—he had simply decided that he knew better. As her ire rose, so did her pulse. Did the man's arrogance have no bounds? What kind of game was he playing with the town? And how dared he jeopardize the future of her business?

"You're right, Gracie." She grabbed her purse. "Jordan should know what kind of mess he has on his hands."

Holly was still fuming when she drove up to the old Paget manse. She pulled in behind Jordan's shiny new pickup truck—the one he'd bought because his Mercedes stuck out like a sore thumb when he parked it in town. She shook her head at the sight of it. It took more than a fat wallet and a truck like everyone else's to be accepted into a community.

A glimmer of surprise flashed in Jordan's eyes when he opened the door. Then his entire face lit up with a smile full of hope. "Are you a sight for sore eyes."

She steeled herself against the resolve-melting effect of his intense blue gaze. "I have to talk to you."

"Of course. We need to talk," he said, drawing her

inside. He seemed happy just to have her there. "I'm fixing myself something to eat. Have you had dinner?"

"Jordan, I'm not staying long," she said firmly as he led into the big country kitchen. An unopened bottle of beer stood on the counter by the refrigerator. A bag of sandwich rolls and several packages of cold cuts were spread out on the round oak table. "Is that your dinner?"

"You know me—I'm not much of a cook," he said with a shrug. "One thing this town could use, though, is a good deli."

She glanced again at the plastic-looking selection of supermarket meats. Sometimes he did need taking care of... Catching herself, Holly pulled back from the undertow of her own tenderness.

Leaning back against a counter, she folded her arms across her chest. "You've upset a lot of people with your extravagant donations, you know."

"What?" Jordan flinched as if he thought he'd heard wrong. "You've come about that?"

His disappointment was palpable, but she refused to acknowledge it. She couldn't.

"Do you know how many people you've upset? I mean really—a computer in *every* classroom?" She flung out her arms in disbelief. "Jordan, what were thinking?"

"I still have a lot of friends in the industry, Holly. I'm getting those machines at below cost."

"That's not the point. People are questioning your motives."

"No one has complained to me." He uncapped the beer bottle with a furious twist of his fingers. "The PTA is thrilled about the computers. I've received notes from little old ladies thanking me for a van with air-conditioning.''

"Jordan, listen to me," she snapped in frustration. "It looks like you're trying to buy votes to get the zoning approved.''

"That's ridiculous. And you're being naive," he insisted, plunking his untasted beer onto the table. "All I'm doing is contributing to the well-being of the town. Good-faith investment in a community is part of doing business.''

"Not in Golden it isn't." She moved away from the counter. "It smacks of greasing palms. The town doesn't like it, and neither do I!''

"Aren't you overreacting?" His voice was calm. Too calm. "I've been in business a long time, and I've dealt with thornier problems than getting a piece of property rezoned.''

His dismissive attitude set her teeth on edge. "I've told you—small towns are different. Golden is different.''

"People are people. Business is business." Jordan's eyes cooled into two steel pools. "I've had a lot more experience handling these situations than you. I know what to do.''

That was the last thing she needed to hear. The last thing she *wanted* to hear. A bubbling anger roiled over the last piece of concern in her heart. "Yes, you always know what's best. How could I have forgotten?''

He took a step toward her, his face hardening. "Holly, please." It sounded more like a warning than a plea.

"You go ahead and handle the town meeting the way you want. I don't really care anymore.''

"I don't believe that.''

"Believe it." Fresh anger merged with days of resentment, and there was no stopping it. "But I've got more news for you, Jordan. When it comes to what I feel and what I need, you know nothing. And when it comes to my daughter, you know even less."

"Wait a damn minute." His eyes were dark and wild as he clamped his hands around her wrists. "I'm crazy about that kid, and you know it."

Although his vehemence frightened her, the hurt she felt for Stephanie was overwhelming. "While you *step back* to pout in your corner, Stephanie's wondering why you dropped off the face of the earth." She yanked her wrists from his grip. "Did you even think how this might affect her?"

The color drained from his face. "I think about her every day. I wouldn't hurt her for the world—not knowingly. I miss her. Almost as much as I miss you."

Holly shrank from his outstretched hand. "The damage has been done, Jordan."

"Look, I'll go talk to her—try to explain."

"She's just getting used to not having you around."

"You don't want me to see her?"

The anguish in his voice shook her. See her? Of course he had to see Steph—he would always have to see her. Blood was the tie that bound Jordan and Stephanie. Not her. With all the confusing emotions swimming inside her head, Holly had lost track of that undeniable fact.

"You have to wait. Please. Wait until—"

His eyes narrowed. "Wait until when, Holly?"

She had almost said wait until she talked to Lawrence. Yet such a slip would be nothing short of disaster. The truth about her child's father couldn't come out in the midst of the anger and hurt unfurling between them.

"Just wait until things settle down after the town

meeting,'' she told him, loathing the lie even as it spilled out of her mouth. After almost five years of protecting her daughter and herself, she'd become proficient at stretching the truth. ''The rezoning may not happen, Jordan. The apple packing plant will be worthless then.''

''You helped me script a great presentation, Holly. The rezoning will pass.''

Despite everything she'd tried to tell him, he was still so cocksure he would prevail. ''*If* the zoning doesn't pass,'' she restated firmly, ''you may decide not to stick around Golden.''

''That's not going to happen,'' he insisted, his voice turning as cold as his ice-blue stare. ''But thanks for showing your enormous faith in me.''

With that dry, cutting dismissal, Holly walked out of his house. She shouldn't have wasted her time. Jordan had his own method of dealing with life—often arrogant, sometimes manipulative. The way he had tried to talk Scott out of marrying her all those years ago was a prime example.

Holly drove off, wondering if she'd been out of her mind to get involved with him. Had loneliness blinded her from seeing Jordan for what he was? Had she let herself be seduced into forgetting what he'd been?

In one particular instance, however, Holly knew she was no better than Jordan. And she knew she had to rectify that. Immediately.

After pulling off to the side of Old Paget Road, she dug through her purse for the telephone number she needed. With her heart pounding in her ears, she tapped out the digits on her cellular phone. Each ring on the opposite end of the line sounded like an alarm warning her that her daughter's life—and her own—was about to change forever.

She drew a deep breath when someone finally picked up on the other end. "Mason residence," announced an unfamiliar, slightly accented voice.

"May I speak to Lawrence Mason, please?"

"He's not here. He and Mrs. Mason visit Palm Beach until after July 4," the voice explained. "I am the maid."

Not there? The ache of anticipation in her chest dissolved in disappointment. The Fourth of July holiday was still a week away. Yet it had to be a good sign if Lawrence was out and about. "Mr. Mason must be feeling better."

"A little. But still he has to be careful," the maid replied. "The doctor told Mrs. M. a change of scene would be good. Would you like to leave a message?"

"Ah, no, thank you. I'll call back. Ah, maybe next week." Then, without even leaving her name, Holly hung up.

"Mommy, Mommy."

Stephanie rushed into Holly's room. "Gracie says I can spend the night at her house with her new kitten. Can I, please?"

"Did you invite yourself again?" Sitting at the vanity, Holly fastened her hair back with a large silver barrette. When Steph didn't answer, she turned away from the mirror. "Did you, Stephanie?"

Nodding guiltily, her daughter stared down at her pink canvas slip-ons. "She really wants me to come—as long as I don't just play with the little kitty, because Jasmine will get jealous."

Gracie appeared at Holly's bedroom door to confirm Stephanie's story. "I've been saying she could sleep over when the kitten got old enough. And since you're going to be busy at the town meeting this afternoon, I'd just as soon take her to my place, where I can putter around.''

"Don't you want to vote?" Holly asked.

"I can't take those long gabby meetings. Too much hot air for my taste." Gracie leaned against the door-jamb. "But I told Sadie Campbell to run over to the apartment if your vote looks close."

With a weary sigh, Holly got up from the vanity. "Then you probably won't be hearing from Sadie. It doesn't look good."

"That's what I've been hearing, too," Gracie said with a sympathetic nod.

The telephone rang as Gracie hustled Stephanie off to pack an overnight bag. Holly reached across her bed to answer it.

"Holly, it's Gabe. Jordan will be starting his presentation anytime now."

"But he's not scheduled until after the lunch break." She checked her watch. "It's not even eleven now."

"I know, but the agenda's a mess." Gabe sounded totally harried. "The architect who's presenting the plans for the new firehouse had car trouble on the way in from Boston. So we had to switch everything around."

"If they break for lunch at noon, there won't be time for adequate discussion before the vote." To make his case, Jordan needed to respond directly to citizen concerns.

"Well, there's another hitch," Gabe grumbled. "The League of Women Voters booked the downstairs hall for their annual ham-and-bean supper. We've got to clear the building by 4 p.m. so they can set up."

"But there must be at least four different items slated for voting."

"The moderator proposed all voting be postponed to a special meeting two weeks from today. For lack of a better solution, my colleagues and I agreed. So it's presentations and limited discussion today, further discussion and voting at the next meeting."

"I don't like the sound of that. Anything can happen in two weeks, Gabe."

"I'm not wild about it, either," he agreed. "Jordan has got to give it his best shot now. And you've got to get over here."

"Did Jordan want you to call me?" An impulsive twinge of hope had compelled her to inquire.

Gabe groaned. "When I asked him if you knew about the schedule change, he shrugged and walked off. I don't know what's going on between the two of you, but your shop is still part of this rezoning package, right?"

"Does it really matter? You've heard all the talk. People don't trust Jordan."

"Have you forgotten how long it took for this town to accept and trust you?"

His question felt like a stiff shake of common sense. "It's really more of the same."

"I think so. Now, how about putting that goodwill you've earned around here to some use?"

"I'm on my way."

"Hurry. Jordan's just been called to the podium."

Discovering Gracie's car parked behind hers, Holly lost several minutes just getting her vehicle out of the driveway. Then, turning onto the narrow road into town, she landed smack behind a tractor hauling a trailer piled high with bales of hay. Not only was the tractor puttering along very slowly, but its load was too wide to pass safely.

Holly tightened her grip on the steering wheel, refusing to believe fate was against her. Gabe's call had made her realize how much Jordan needed her—even if he didn't know it. None of the other stuff mattered now. She bit back her impatience as the tractor continued to crawl at a snail's pace. Although she'd be a little late, she would get to the town hall in time to assist Jordan. Whether he wanted her help or not.

"Thank you for that informative presentation, Mr. Mason," Dennis Metcalf, the town moderator said, reclaiming his position behind the podium. "You might want to stay up here to address questions from the floor."

Nodding, Jordan glanced over at the long folding table where Gabe Sawyer sat with other town officials. Gabe gave him a thumbs-up, confirming that the presentation had gone well. But when he scanned the faces of those seated in the audience of the large cavernous hall, his confidence wavered. With the exception of a few new friends, no one was smiling.

This crowd was tougher than anything he'd faced before—tougher than the platoon of corporate hatchet men who'd wanted to separate him from CompWare. Now he understood that the result of this meeting and the opinion of this group of people mattered more than he'd realized. What he wouldn't give to have Holly standing by his side now. Despite the angry words between them, he had hoped against hope that she'd come to support the rezoning, if not him.

She'd been told about the scheduling changes. Gabe

had taken care of that. Apparently, it hadn't made a difference. Holly was still nowhere to be seen.

"Okay, Earle Stacy, you have the floor," Dennis boomed into the podium microphone. "Keep it brief."

Seated in the front row with his general store cronies, Earle stood up and pointed to the easels where Jordan had displayed visuals of the apple packing plant. "Those are fancy pictures you have there, son. But what about the extra traffic this building will bring? Golden's got enough cars on the roads as it is."

Jordan passed up the moderator's offer of the microphone, preferring to answer directly. "The relocation of two established businesses to the renovated building will actually alleviate traffic congestion in the center of town, which—"

A glimpse of pale-gold hair and a colorful, flowery dress, followed by the sudden hard thud of his heart, derailed his train of thought. *Holly*. His gaze was drawn to her like steel to a magnet. She was all that he could see.

Yet he couldn't make eye contact with her as she slipped into a last row seat. She refused to acknowledge him in any way.

Old Earle tapped his cane on the floor. "Come on, young fella, spit it out. Which what?" he demanded to know.

"Which, ah,..." Jordan's attention snapped back to the question at hand. "My point is that the center of town has the traffic problems. Our location will draw traffic away from the area."

He kept checking the back of the hall, making sure Holly was still there, as the questions continued one after another. Gathering strength from her presence, Jordan handled the comments as best he could.

After the moderator gave a ten minute warning, however, the session took a nasty turn. Jordan struggled to hold on to his temper as he fended off the biting remarks and leading questions. Comments from all sides began flying across the room.

Dennis hammered his gavel repeatedly as he called for order. "No one speaks unless I say so. Understand?"

After the audience had quieted down to his satisfaction, Dennis gave the floor to Dr. Franklin Beck. Jordan girded himself for another onslaught. Dr. Beck was the ringleader of the small but strident group that had banded together to put him out of business.

"Mr. Mason, you must see that the citizens of this town do not look favorably on your effort," the good doctor declared as if his word were gospel. "Many of us feel so strongly about this matter that we're prepared to file suit against you—starting with a restraining order to stop any work on the apple packing plant."

Ah, yes, a lawsuit. Jordan was just waiting for one to be threatened. "Dr. Beck, before you and your *many* friends spend another dime on lawyers, I'd advise waiting until after the vote is taken."

A discordant mix of muffled laughter and vocal indignation filled the hall as Jordan indicated he was ready for the next question. Sounding the gavel again, the moderator recognized another speaker.

"How are we to know you won't add another level with more stores in a couple of years?" one of Dr. Beck's cohorts asked. "Or maybe you'll try to squeeze a new building onto the lot."

Gabe Sawyer answered before Jordan could. "He'd have to come back to us and go through this process all over again."

"Hey, Gabe," Howie McGovern yelled through his

cupped hands, "is he going to buy votes all over again, too?"

"You're out of order, Howie," the moderator charged. "Sit down."

But a chorus of agreement surged through the crowd. And it wasn't just Franklin Beck's cronies rallying behind Howie. Faces Jordan recognized from the everyday goings-on around town and people he had come to know all flowed into the groundswell of doubt.

And all their doubt was about him.

Holly's pleas and warnings—the ones he'd refused to believe—came back to haunt him. Finally, *finally*, he realized just how right she had been.

"Dennis—over here!"

Jordan heard Holly's voice ring over the restless crowd.

"Please, let me speak."

"You want the floor now, Holly?" the moderator asked in disbelief as the meeting slipped out of his control.

"Recognize her, Dennis," Gabe hissed. "Now."

Pounding his gavel and barking orders like a drill sergeant, Dennis battled back. After bullying them all back into their seats, he gave the floor to Holly.

When Holly stood up, Jordan willed her to look at him. To his surprise, however, she fixed her gaze on Franklin Beck.

"Dr. Beck, you've lived in Golden only a year or two. And I haven't been here that much longer. It takes some getting used to, doesn't it?"

Shooting her a wary look, Beck answered the question with a silent nod.

"Golden is one of those rare places where everybody knows everybody else, and that makes for values we newcomers might not grasp at first. I have and still do make mistakes. And so do you, Dr. Beck,'' Holly asserted, her hands gripping the empty folding chair in front of her. ''I suspect threatening lawsuits is not how this town wants to settle its conflicts.''

Dazzled by her courage, Jordan watched Holly as murmurs of encouragement and a smattering of applause rippled through the hall. She seemed oblivious to the support. Turning away from Dr. Beck, Holly faced the audience with challenge in her eyes.

''Jordan Mason's made mistakes, too,'' she declared, finally glancing toward the front of the room where he sat. Her amber eyes touched his gaze briefly. Too briefly.

''Because he's been successful in business for many years,'' she continued, ''he's had a hard time grasping that the rules are different here. While you thought he was trying to buy you off, Jordan thought he was proving that he cared about this community.''

''He shoulda known better,'' one of the General Store Four called out.

The slightest of grins curved her lips. ''I think he knows better now.''

Many people laughed. Although Holly's jest was at his expense, Jordan couldn't help smiling. She was right. And he deserved everything she cared to throw at him.

''In the end, what harm's been done?'' Holly asked when the laughter died down. ''The retirement home now has a safe, air-conditioned van for its residents. The school and the library have been enriched—at no expense to the taxpayers, I might add. And you all still have the power to vote whichever way you think best.''

''Holly, I can give you only thirty more seconds,'' Dennis informed her politely. ''Anything else you want to add?''

"Just everybody, please, keep an open mind for the next two weeks."

When she took her seat, it was all Jordan could do to keep from rushing to her side. His head was swimming with emotions he couldn't begin to describe. He felt grateful and astonished, yes. But there was so much more. The lovely, delicate and warm Holly West of his nightly dreams had stood up to his detractors and faced them down. She had defended *him*. For some crazy reason, that made him feel really proud.

With a whack of his gavel, the moderator adjourned the meeting until one o'clock. Everyone applauded and began to file out of the hall. Jordan headed straight for Holly, struggling to make his way through the maze of people who stood between them. More than once someone stopped him to shake his hand or wish him well. He thanked each person quickly and kept on moving.

Jordan tried to keep her in his sight, but that was next to impossible in the constantly shifting throng. Eventually, he lost track of her halfway through the room.

"Do you see Holly?" he asked when Gabe Sawyer came up behind him.

"She's around here somewhere." Gabe then gave him a hearty slap on the back. "She sure saved your hide. Just keep your nose clean for the next two weeks and you might have a chance. Okay?"

Jordan nodded and pushed on.

He just wanted to get to Holly. He had to tell her how wrong he'd been; he had to set things right again. As the crowd thinned out and he inched closer to her, he could feel his heart pounding against his chest. Jordan realized then that what he wanted, more than anything, was to sweep her into his arms and tell her all the things he should have said a long time ago.

Finally, after brushing past the last straggling well-wishers, Jordan made it to the back of the hall. He looked to his right and then to his left. He turned back to the podium, just in case. And then he peered out into the lobby.

Holly was gone.

Chapter Twelve

Holly sat on the soft summer grass in her backyard, unwilling to get up and leave.

She really needed to fetch Stephanie back from Gracie's or go back to work for a few hours. But she didn't budge. The tension from this morning's session at the town hall had left her drained. And her impulsive, emotional public defense of Jordan now felt like a shock to her system. She felt vulnerable and exposed. Perhaps a little afraid.

So, she'd come home—to her quiet house, to the peace of the sloping back lawn beneath the old willow oaks, to the gentle red dog napping at her feet.

A tall shadow fell across the grass. "Holly, I've been looking everywhere for you."

Taffy lifted her groggy head to see who had come. Already knowing, Holly looked up, too. The suit jacket from the meeting was gone. Light-blue shirtsleeves were rolled up to his elbows and his necktie hung loosely knotted below his collar. Dark hair fell into his eyes. Yet even disheveled and uncombed, he was a man who made heads spin.

"Hello, Jordan."

"It's awfully quiet around here." He scanned the yard.

"Steph's not home."

"I'm sorry to miss her. You're the one I'm here to see, though."

"You didn't have to come, Jordan."

"Did you honestly think I'd stay away?" His deep-blue eyes bored into hers. "How could I after—"

She cut him off by looking away. "I said what had to be said. That's all."

He sat down beside her, taking her fingers in his hands. "That's not all. It can't be."

His touch made her achingly aware of how much she'd missed him. She had neither the strength nor the will to move her arm away. Jordan brushed his lips against her fingertips and then kissed her palms, making her skin tingle and her heart beat faster.

"Never has anyone stood up for me like that." His voice was low as he traced slow, caressing circles along her arms. "I don't know words strong enough to describe how it made me feel."

"You don't have to say anything. I know you're grateful." She looked down at her hands, the feeling of vulnerability that had driven her home stirring within her again.

"This time, something *has* to be said." His fingers tightened around her forearms. "But thank you isn't enough, and I'm sorry isn't, either. I haven't been fair to you. I made selfish demands, said terrible things. I ignored your advice and dug myself into a hole so deep no one would have blamed you if you'd left me there."

"I wouldn't do that to you." Holly couldn't keep from saying it—despite the risk and the fear. Her heart was beyond that now. Pulling back wasn't an option.

"But why?" he implored, searching her face. "After everything that happened, you still stood up to this town for me. You put yourself on the line. Why?"

"Don't you know?" Her throat felt tight, her eyes hot. She didn't know whether to laugh or cry. "I did it because I love you."

Jordan looked as stunned as she felt. Before now, she hadn't admitted that she loved him, not even to herself.

"Maybe that's not what you want to hear," she added, uncertainty compelling her to fill in his silence, "but I do."

"Oh, Holly." His hands cupped her face. "I was afraid I'd never hear it. I thought you wouldn't love me—or couldn't."

"Well, it isn't easy," she teased, feeling her eyes tear up. The emotion surging through her was so intense she had to resort to humor.

"I know." Jordan kissed the one tear dangling from the corner of her eye.

"You're one strong, wonderful woman to put up with me."

The warmth of his breath on her face made her lids flutter. His arms coiled around her back as he pulled her against his chest. Her pulse and her euphoria soared in tandem as his mouth lowered to hers. With half-closed eyes, she breathed his name and opened herself to him.

He kissed her hard, his tongue probing her mouth so deeply it made her sigh. She felt the hunger in his kiss, and his heat and his urgency unleashed her own. Sliding her hand behind his head, she held his lips captive against hers and paid him back in kind.

When she came up for air, Jordan murmured her name over and over as his mouth roamed from her lips to her throat, from her shoulders to the back of her neck, from her forehead to behind her ears.

"I need you, Holly—so much that it made me angry. That's why I stayed away."

She put her arms around him. "I know."

Clutching her to him, he gently lowered her back onto the grass. "I do need you." He kissed her deeply, covering her with his body.

They kissed and stroked with their tongues and fingers until her head was dizzy from the sensations and moist fingers of warmth rippled up from between her legs. And as Jordan caressed and kneaded the soft curves of her body, she could feel his hard desire beneath his clothes.

Holly moaned, unable to stand it anymore. She wanted to feel him inside her; she wanted to express this newfound passion. And more than anything, she wanted the touching, the tasting, the stroking, the kissing and the desire they so obviously shared to reach their natural fulfillment.

"Jordan," she whispered breathlessly after tearing her mouth away from another heady kiss. "I want you."

His eyes locked with hers and he lay very still. "You really mean it, don't you?"

"With all my heart."

Jordan glanced over at the house. "When will Stephanie be home?"

She couldn't suppress a knowing smile. "Tomorrow morning. She's sleeping over at Gracie's."

A silent laugh of surprise vibrated in his chest.

"Feeling like this is your lucky day, Jordan?"

"More like the best day of my life."

As he grazed his knuckles against her cheek, Jordan's gaze fell to her mouth. She ran her tongue across her lower lip, willing him to kiss her again. And with an unresisting groan of desire, he did.

As they continued kissing, Taffy began a restless romp around them. Wanting to play, the dog grew too insistent to ignore. "Let's go inside," Jordan said, his voice a ragged whisper.

He led her into the house and up the stairs to her bedroom. When they reached the second floor he stood back, not knowing which room was hers. Holly hesitated in opening the door to her room. Her heart was pounding in her ears.

"Having second thoughts?"

She leaned back against her closed door. "It's just that I haven't been with anyone since..." She felt her skin redden with embarrassment. "I hadn't planned, and I—I—"

"Holly." He touched her face.

"I don't have any protection."

His fingers lifted her chin, bringing her eyes level with his. "It's all right, Holly. I do."

"You do?"

Her surprise evoked a gentle smile. "After what happened the afternoon we fell into the river, I realized you were afraid of more than just being indiscreet."

Touched that he had understood, she walked into his arms. "I had no idea you thought about it."

"I thought about *you*. All the time." He held her warm against his chest. "It's no secret I've been wanting you."

For Holly, Jordan's concern for her fears, and for her protection, was no small act of caring. After having been left to fend for herself on her wedding day, she'd always had to face any and all consequences alone. This meant more than she could say—yet she could and would show him. She opened the door to her bedroom and drew him inside.

They stood in the middle of the room. The barriers had been banished. Yet she trembled slightly when she saw the fire of her own desire reflected in Jordan's eyes.

He broke the silence by murmuring her name. But Holly couldn't find her voice. She felt overwhelmed by the longing that had been intensifying since the day Jordan reappeared in her life.

"Holly." He held out his hand.

A low, urgent cry rose from deep within her throat. Then she was in his arms again, no longer controlled by anything but the desire flooding her veins. She held on to him tightly, refusing to let even the thinnest of air come between them.

Jordan covered her skin with hungry kisses, his hands roaming down her back to her buttocks and over her hips. Waves of delight rolled through her as his tongue penetrated her mouth, tasting and taunting. She moaned into his lips, her hands never still as they moved over his shoulders and chest. She couldn't stop touching him. Part of her still couldn't believe that he was really here, wanting her, caring for her. She was afraid if she opened her eyes, Jordan would vanish like a dream.

She loosened his tie and let it slip to the floor, then slowly unfastened each button on his shirt. Then she slid her hand inside the fabric to glide her palm over taut muscles and feathery tufts of hair. The feel of his hot, silky skin beneath her fingertips reassured her that what was happening was real. Very real.

"I need you, Holly," he breathed.

His tongue warmed her ear with a moist, tingling caress. Her knees weakened beneath her, but Jordan's arms held fast. Holly opened her eyes to find his face shadowed with passion, his gaze smoldering like blue-black coal. She had seen desire in Scott's eyes long ago. It hadn't been like this; it hadn't made her *ache* to satisfy him. Scott, too, had said he needed her. Yet when Jordan spoke these same words, the fervor in his voice told her he needed all of her—her heart, her soul—not just the release her body could give.

She pushed the shirt off his shoulders, then stepped back and lifted his hand to her lips. He closed his eyes when she kissed it. "Come to bed, Jordan."

Holly felt his eyes on her as she tugged the heavy duvet off the bed, then she felt his arms capturing her again. Lowering her onto the white sheets, he sank down beside her. Between kisses, he undressed her with painstaking care. After he slid her bra off her shoulders, his hands curved over her tender breasts.

"Do you like this?" His voice was a husky whisper.

The sharp breath caught in her throat turned into a languid moan as he cupped his hand over the moist, yearning core between her legs. The sensations were driving her mad and she wanted to swallow him up right then and there. Showing no mercy, Jordan swept his tongue over both her aching nipples and then moved away. She moaned again—this time in disappointment.

Jordan smiled down at her as he tore off the rest of his clothes. Waiting for him to come back to her, she drank in his lean, hard body with her eyes. Just watching him fueled her excitement, and her receptiveness to all this sensual stimulation astonished her. She'd been in love with Scott when she slept with him, yet their encounters had never been quite what she had hoped. But since he had seemed satisfied, she'd always believed something in her was lacking.

Jordan returned, enfolding her in a ravenous embrace. He nuzzled her neck and kissed her sensitive ears, his body rigid with desire as it rubbed against her. She reveled in the feel of him, losing herself in the sensations as if she were floating on a cloud of pleasure.

As his mouth roamed over every inch of her, she murmured his name. Snaking her arms around his neck, she curled her fingers in his thick, dark hair. Jordan strained and pressed against her trembling thighs. The intensity was unbearable; both their bodies needed release.

She gasped when Jordan entered her. He held still within her, whispering his desire in her ear. He began moving his hips against her, slowly at first, and then building and thrusting faster until she arched up to him with a moan. Bolts of white heat shimmered through her loins. Jordan's groans somehow fed the fire spiraling deep in her body and she clutched his shoulders, holding on for dear life as tremor after tremor rolled through her.

Jordan's eyes flew open as his body shuddered inside her; he whispered her name over and over like a prayerful chant. And when they both were still, he kissed her deeply and completely. In this quiet moment—when everything was alive with feeling, yet nothing said—Holly felt the full emotional force of the love she had acknowledged only hours ago.

He stayed nestled in her warm core, smiling down at her with gleaming eyes. "I love you," he said softly, as if he'd been reading her mind. "I've been loving you for a long time."

Wonderful as it was to hear the words, Holly knew Jordan loved her. She knew it from the way he had held her when her body trembled in ecstasy, and she knew it by the way he had called her name when he reached his own fulfillment.

The afternoon shadows grew long across the room as they made love again and again. Lingering in Jordan's arms, Holly sensed he was as reluctant to leave the bed as she was. They were like moonstruck teenaged lovers who couldn't tear themselves away from each other.

Still, even lovers needed nourishment.

The bright digits on her bedside clock said it was fast approaching six o'clock, and her growling stomach reminded her that she hadn't eaten since breakfast.

"I'm hungry," she announced, pulling the sheet over her breasts as she sat up in the bed.

"*Still?*" Jordan's eyebrows lifted in mock disbelief. "I'm doing the best I can."

"Hungry for *food*, wiseguy." Holly tossed her pillow at his laughing face, although she had to admit his best had been pretty darn magnificent. "I bet you didn't have any lunch, either."

"How could I?" he asked, pulling her back down beside him. "I was too busy running around town looking for you."

"I'm glad you did." Her fingers brushed the hair from his eyes. "You know what I want to do for you?"

"More of the same, I hope," Jordan growled, kissing her neck.

She curled away from his playful tempting. "I'd like to cook you a decent meal. I haven't been able to get those mystery meat sandwiches you've been eating out of my mind."

"Hmm. You mean to tell me that when the only thing I could think about was making love to you, you were fixating on my diet? That's *real* romantic, Holly."

"You just stay here and rest your overworked bones.

I'll call you when dinner's ready.'' Dragging herself out of bed, she kissed him once on the lips. ''I'll show you just how romantic it can be.''

''You'll get no argument from me.'' Jordan settled back into the pillows. ''Go ahead, take care of me. I love it.''

Holly loved it, too. Cooking a meal for the man she'd just spent hours making love with added an extremely exciting dimension to a routine activity. With candlelight and flowers from the front garden, she made the dinner table glow. Selecting music for the CD player and uncorking a bottle of wine, Holly felt almost blissful. Back upstairs, she changed into a long gauzy white dress before leaning over the bed to kiss Jordan awake. For her, this was the most exquisite of moments, capping off a glorious afternoon and beginning what promised to be a wonderful evening. It would be, without a doubt, perfect.

Hours later, Holly leaned against Jordan as they sat on the porch steps. Music from the living-room stereo drifted through the opened windows, and the early-summer night was cool and clear.

''I still can't get used to how close the stars seem around here,'' Jordan observed, gazing overhead. ''At the pond, it's sometimes hard to tell where the water ends and the night sky begins. I think that's what I like best about living way out there. It's a fantastic show to have right outside the door every night.''

Holly squeezed his hand. ''Sounds like our city boy has finally found something good to say about country life.''

Chuckling, he tucked her head beneath his chin. ''If I think hard enough, I might be able to think of one or two other things I like about Golden. I know I'll be thinking about them when I'm back in Boston next week.''

"Back in Boston?" she repeated, not really comprehending. Propelled by a wave of unreasoned panic, she whirled around to face him. "You're leaving?"

"Just for a day, Holly. That's all." He drew her back to his side. "I need to sign off on the last of the CompWare agreements."

"Oh, Jordan, I don't know why I'm reacting like this. It's just that I—" She didn't know what more to say, she felt so foolish.

"It's okay. I think I understand." He kissed the top of her head. "But I love you. Remember? *I'm* not going to leave you."

It was exactly what she'd been longing to hear. Still, there was one wary, unrelenting piece of her heart that even Jordan's declarations couldn't melt. It would take a little more time for that last stubborn wound to heal, and time was what Jordan had just promised her. Holly intended to give him every chance to keep that promise.

"Will you stay with me tonight?"

"I was hoping you'd ask." A wry smile twitched his lips. "But I was planning on it anyway."

Waves of affection washed over her. Strangely enough, these two at-odds remarks summed up the essence of Jordan for her—loving, yet wry; surprisingly gracious at times, yet often confident beyond bounds. His tenderness made her melt. His humorous sense of irony kept her amused and on her toes. When his confidence swelled into arrogance, he made her absolutely crazy. But she loved him madly and wouldn't have him any other way.

Turning to him again, she slipped her arms around his

shoulders and kissed him long and hard and with all the love and passion in her soul.

"Whoa," he rasped when she finally released him. "Where did that come from?"

"You."

Puzzled, but undaunted, Jordan reached for her. "Let's go upstairs."

This time when they came together, Holly felt freer to express all the emotions Jordan aroused in her. This time she made love to him. Her passion flared like wildfire, intense and without restraint. In love and loved, she had never felt so alive as when she drew him inside her and loved *him* until he groaned with the ultimate pleasure.

Holly awoke in Jordan's arms hours later, when a gentle rain began to fall outside. Jordan slept soundly beside her. After all the years alone, being cradled all night in a man's arms felt heavenly. She turned her head to watch him sleep. His tanned face with its blossoming overnight shadow was a stark contrast against the white cotton pillow slip. His expensive haircut had grown shaggier since he'd moved to Golden, and she rather liked it. Looking at him like this reminded her of all the things they had said and done together on this extraordinary day.

Holly heard the faint chiming of the small mantel clock in Stephanie's room. It was a delicate chime that had never caused her daughter to stir, and it didn't disturb Jordan now. Recalling how fondly he'd spoken of Stephanie, she smiled and skimmed her fingers along his muscled forearm. During dinner, he had suggested having a Fourth of July picnic on his freshly sanded beach. Since the swim party he'd promised Stephanie had never happened, he wanted to make it up to her with a holiday gathering of all their friends.

Now, in the quiet and the dark, the secret that could shatter what she and Jordan had weighed heavy on her heart. It had been wrong to put off revealing the truth about Stephanie's father, no matter how valid the reasons to do so had seemed. Holly had always known that; she'd felt guilty over it from the first day Jordan walked back into her life. Yet if she had told him that she conceived her child with Scott, he wouldn't have come back to Golden to live. There would be no relationship on the line. They probably wouldn't have fallen in love at all. The irony of it was too bitter to be believed.

She was not, however, about to surrender all hope. Love—real, deep-in-the-soul love—had to be forgiving. If she sat Jordan down and told him everything, absolutely everything, she believed their new love would prevail. It had to.

Holly counted the days until the holiday. Four short days for Jordan to take a business trip to Boston and to organize the big beach party he was determined to have for Stephanie on the Fourth. She'd wait until after the party to tell him, but that was all. After what had happened today, she couldn't bear to hide the truth from Jordan any longer.

"Jordan? Gracie, look! It's Jordan!"

A towheaded whirlwind with pigtails flying jumped off the porch of the modest three-family house and into his arms. He swung her around, loving the sound of her infectious giggles. "Am I ever glad to see you, sweetheart."

"Look, Mommy, Jordan's back," she cried over his shoulder as Holly came up behind them.

"I know." Hooking her arm around his waist, Holly leaned into him. The apricot-and-honey scent of her hair filled his head with instant memories of hot kisses and slow, intense lovemaking. Just thinking about it made him want to carry her home and do it all over again.

Which was the very thing that had made them a half hour late in picking up Steph. As eager as both he and Holly were to see her, one more chance at making love, followed by a rushed but sizzling shower together, was way too much to resist. Besides, finding time alone together was going to be a tricky proposition in the coming days, and they both knew it.

But now that he'd finally linked up with his other lady, Jordan couldn't be happier. With Holly on one arm and Stephanie curled up in his other, the picture was complete. It felt so natural, so right, he could hardly believe it.

"Well, well, look who's back," Gracie said in her usual deadpan tone when she emerged from the ground-floor apartment. Other than her dry greeting, she gave no hint of how she felt about his return to Holly's good graces.

As Holly apologized for being late, Jordan noticed Gracie giving them both a good once-over. Although Holly looked great in long-legged jeans and a lacy white T-shirt, her hair was still wet from their recent shower. And he was wearing yesterday's clothes. He felt sure his slightly rumpled state didn't escape Gracie's eagle eye.

"I missed you, Jordan." Stephanie wrapped her pudgy arms around his neck. "Are you not going to be busy with that meeting anymore?"

The trusting innocence behind her question tugged at his heart. Now he understood the anger behind Holly's accusations when she had come to his house last week.

Before then, he hadn't really realized how much of a factor he'd become in Stephanie's life.

"That meeting's history, kid," he told her, hugging her close. "From now on, I'm going to spend as much time with you and your mom as I can."

"You are?" Her brown eyes widened, reminding him, as always, of the little Holly West he'd known a lifetime ago.

"Do you remember that beach I told you I was thinking of fixing up? Well, it's ready and waiting for some swimmers." He gave her middle a tickle.

Giggling helplessly, Steph turned to Holly. "Can we go to Jordan's beach, Mommy?"

"I've got your bathing suit in the car."

Stephanie wiggled out of his arms. "Gracie, did you hear? Jordan's got a new beach and we're going swimming there."

Gracie patted her on the head. "Sounds lovely, darlin'."

Caught up in Steph's enthusiasm, Jordan found himself blurting out his plans for a Fourth of July picnic. Little did he know his announcement would raise the kid's excitement level more than a few notches.

"And I can really invite all my friends?" she squealed. "Tommy and Sean? Miss Karin? Jenny and Matt and Dr. Gabe?"

"Sweetheart, you can ask them all. Except Dr. Gabe, that is. He's getting my personal invitation." He winked at Holly.

She shot him one of those dazzling knowing smiles of hers, the kind that never failed to take his breath away. Then she scooted Steph into the apartment to get her belongings.

Left alone with Gracie, Jordan took pains to extend a

heartfelt invitation to the picnic. "I would really like you to come join us," he added. "It wouldn't feel like a family gathering to Holly and Steph without you."

"I know it wouldn't."

Something in her flat, emotionless response made him want to try again. After all, Gracie had seemed to be softening toward him on the night of the preschool dance.

"I'll hope you'll come and relax. Have a good time," he continued, trying to gauge where he stood with her. "And Holly and I will do everything. You don't have to lift a finger."

"I don't mind doing my share," she snapped.

Jordan stepped back, unsure what to do next. He always seemed to say the wrong thing to this woman. Fortunately, Stephanie chose that moment to come running back outside.

"Jordan, can Taffy come to the party? She likes to swim, too."

He picked her up. "Sure, kid, the more the merrier."

While Holly helped Stephanie with her seat belt, Jordan threw Stephanie's overnight bag into the trunk. Slamming down the lid, he caught a glimpse of Gracie watching them through her screen door. She looked so alone Jordan couldn't help feeling bad for her. He hoped he wasn't making her feel like a fifth wheel. He certainly didn't want to shut her out, but she had to accept that the three of them needed time alone together now.

He wished he could prove to Gracie how much he cared about them. He wanted her to understand how connected he felt, not just to Holly, but to Stephanie, too. It was as if the heavens had meant for the three of them to be together. And if he got his way, they'd become a family soon.

After spending the better part of two wonderful days with his two special ladies, leaving them became harder than Jordan would have thought possible. He kept reminding himself he'd be away only a day and night. Besides, he had a lot to do in Boston. In addition to officially closing the books on CompWare, he had to put his condo up for sale, see a couple of friends, visit the jeweler's and stop by his travel agent's office. With an agenda like that, the time would fly and then he'd be coming home.

"I thought you weren't leaving until after lunch," Holly said when he stopped by her shop early Tuesday morning.

"The sooner I leave, the sooner I'll get back."

Jordan didn't think he had to add *why* he'd shown up a good half hour before she opened the shop for business. He knew she'd be there, setting up for the day. But he didn't know that Stephanie would be there, too.

"I was hoping we could steal a few moments alone," he murmured in Holly's ear, his hand caressing her firm bottom, making it clear exactly what he'd been hoping for. Her amber eyes flickered with a longing he'd come to recognize.

But almost immediately, this sexy gleam dissolved into disappointment. "Gracie has a dentist appointment this morning," she explained.

He glanced over to where Stephanie was playing intently with her dolls and a tiny set of china cups and saucers. "I don't suppose we can send her across the street for coffee with the guys at the general store."

"Uh-uh," she replied with a smile and a shake of her head. Then she took his hand and pulled him into the back room.

The next thing he knew she was in his arms, firing

him up with a kiss they both knew could go nowhere. But that didn't make him want to stop his hands from roaming over her lush curves or from pressing his burning body against her soft hips. And he really didn't want to stop kissing her. Her lips tasted like the scented flowers blossoming outside her front porch, and her skin was as creamy and smooth as all the sweet-smelling potions lining the shelves of her shop.

Closing his eyes, he filled his head with memories of their actual lovemaking. The touches, the tastes, the sounds flowed through him, reminding him of the profound pleasure he'd never experienced with any other lover. Making love with Holly was an act on an entirely different plane—the intimacies were more intense, the passions deep and the emotions almost sacred.

Holly moaned softly against his lips, pulling Jordan back to his senses. As hard as it was, he dragged his mouth away from hers and kissed her eyes. "I'd better go, before we—"

"Jordan." Her eyes glistened with a startling anxiety. "I asked Nancy to take Stephanie home with her after the picnic—to spend the night."

"You did?" He scooped her up in his arms as his pulse soared with delight. "Maybe we should think about skipping the fireworks display so we can make up for some lost time."

"I would love that."

She stepped back from him, her lips slightly quivering. Jordan couldn't understand why. But when Holly tried to cover up with a weak smile, he was even more puzzled.

"Come here," he whispered, guessing that she might be in need of some reassuring. He held her close. "I'll call you when I get to Boston, and I'll call you the minute I roll back into town. And while I'm gone, I'll be counting the hours until we send all our guests home after the party.''

''We'll have a lot to talk about then.''

Though talking wasn't the thing uppermost in his mind, he nodded and kissed her cheek. She had sounded a little sad. But he felt sad about leaving her, too. Even if it was for less than twenty-four hours.

Jordan rolled back into town and right up to Holly's door while she was making lunch for Stephanie. Butterflies flapped wildly in her stomach when she caught sight of his rangy frame in T-shirt and jeans standing on the front porch. With a cry of delight, she ran out to welcome him and Steph followed right behind her.

''I stopped at the shop first, but it was closed,'' Jordan said after a round of hugs and kisses.

''Business was dead yesterday, so I tossed in the towel and decided to make it a real long holiday weekend,'' she explained as they entered the house. ''And I thought you could use my help getting ready for the party.''

It was all true. More than anything, however, she wanted to savor every minute of their last full carefree day together. As tomorrow night's moment of truth edged closer, her faith was wavering. Her resolve was not. Come what may, Jordan would know Stephanie was his brother's child before the town's annual fireworks show was over.

Hooking her arm through his, Holly led Jordan into the kitchen. ''I'm making Stephanie spaghetti circles for lunch. What can I get for you?''

''Certainly not spaghetti whatever you call them.''

The grimace on his face reminded her of his initial reaction to tuna noodle casserole. She laughed and hugged his waist. "Don't you worry. I'll come up with something just for you."

The kitchen was a busy place, with Gracie at the sink peeling mounds of potatoes for her special holiday salad and Stephanie sitting at the table behind a big bowl of spaghetti circles, begging Jordan to play checkers with her while she ate. Taffy sat at Steph's feet, alert to any and all droppings from the house's designated messy eater. Yet there was laughter and warmth in the midst of the chaos. As she pulled out the makings for bacon-lettuce-and-tomato sandwiches, Holly realized what a difference Jordan's presence made. In five short minutes the house had come alive.

Jordan finally gave in to Steph's plea for a checker game. Holly agreed, but warned her to watch her dish. "She's gonna spill," Gracie muttered from the sink.

"I won't, Gracie. You'll see."

Standing at the stove, frying bacon, Holly watched Jordan and Steph out the corner of her eye. He was so patient with her, calmly explaining which direction she could move her checkers and why she couldn't suddenly switch from red to black in the middle of a game. The look in her daughter's eyes as she drank up Jordan's attention didn't escape Holly's notice, either.

Turning away to finish the sandwiches, she prayed Stephanie and Jordan would never lose that special bond.

"Uh-oh!"

Taffy yelped with delight. And Stephanie, with a tell-tale sauce-covered elbow and a bowl of spaghetti circles on her lap, looked up at Holly in helpless horror. "It was an accident, Mommy."

"I know, honey." She lifted the bowl off Steph's thighs, which were a saucy mess. "We've got to clean you up."

Jordan shooed Taffy out the front door, and Gracie came over with a roll of paper towels in hand. "You go get her out of those clothes. I'll clean this mess."

Gracie wouldn't take no for an answer, so Holly took Stephanie upstairs to wash. Once she was scrubbed clean, they went to her room to pick out some clean clothes. "Can I wear my red-white-and-blue dress now?" Steph asked as she twirled about the room in her underwear.

Before she could answer, Taffy began barking outside, loudly and insistently. Holly went to Steph's window to check on the commotion and was surprised to see Howie McGovern's big lemon yellow taxi sitting in the driveway. Jordan was out there, too, extending a hand to the gray-haired passenger emerging from the rear door. A gasp of recognition rumbled in her throat.

Stephanie stood on tiptoe to peer over the high windowsill. "What's the matter?"

Watching the two men shake hands, Holly froze.

"Who's that with Jordan, Mommy?"

"That's your—" She had to stop—she could scarcely breathe. Her chest felt heavy. "He's—he's my father."

Chapter Thirteen

Holly edged away from the window, her mind in shock. Why her father had come here, how he had come—it didn't connect. All Holly knew was she had to get out there before Ted said more than he should.

She tore past Stephanie and dashed down the stairs.

"What in creation is going on out there?" Gracie called after Holly as she flew out the front door.

By the time she had made it to the bottom of the porch steps, the taxi was backing out and Jordan and her father stood face-to-face, talking. "Jordan!"

Running down the driveway, she called to him again. Her throat burned from her cries. Before she could reach them, Ted turned to her with horrified eyes. They stopped her cold.

"Jordan?"

He looked up, his face ashen, but his eyes were pure ice. "Too late, Holly."

The harsh, controlled anger beneath those three words struck her with the force of a physical blow. But what pained her more was the stricken look on his face. "Jordan, what did he tell you?"

She could see he was literally struggling with the shock racking his body. His hands curled into fists at his sides and he walked away. As she turned to go after him, her father caught her arm.

"Holly, I didn't know. I'm sorry, but I didn't know." His voice cracking with emotion, Ted held up an airline ticket jacket. "He wired me this ticket—to surprise you for the holiday. When it came yesterday, I thought you had finally told him."

He sounded devastated, but there was no time to deal with that now. "Dad, please. Go inside and look after Stephanie for me. Just keep her away from us, *please.*"

She caught up with Jordan just before he reached his truck. "Jordan, you can't leave now."

"The hell I can't."

"No." She clutched his arm with both her hands. "We have to talk. Don't you want to know the whole story?"

"That would be a good question if it wasn't so ludicrous."

His eyes were almost black with rage, and she could feel his anger and hurt vibrate beneath her fingers.

"I know the whole story. Scott is Stephanie's father. You told me he wasn't. Like a fool, I believed in some phantom lover of yours. But lo and behold, your father shows up to finally clue me in."

"I was going to tell you tomorrow night. That's why I arranged for Stephanie to go to Nancy's. So we could talk."

Jordan yanked his arm away from her. "Tomorrow

night? Even if that were true—which I doubt—that's five years too late.''

She wiped her hand across the tears on her cheek. ''You don't understand how it was.''

''Damn you, Holly. I don't know which is worse— hiding Steph from Scott and my family all these years or lying to me all these weeks. After what we've been to each other? Even after we made love?''

The pain in his voice sliced through her. He might not know which was worse, but she could see which hurt him more. ''I've been wrong, I know. God, how I know. I did try to tell you, though, several times. But something always happened to interrupt us. And after the way you talked about Scott and the way you resented him, I was afraid of hurting you.''

''Well, congratulations, Holly. You've done it anyway.'' He leaned back against the cab of his truck, shaking his head. ''If I hadn't come to Golden, would you have kept this secret forever? If your father hadn't blurted out the truth by accident, would you have kept lying to me forever?''

''No!''

Jordan didn't hear her; he didn't even look at her. ''No matter what Scott did to you, he deserved to know about that little girl. And my father...I told you how much he had grieved for Scott. How dared you keep part of my brother away from him? How could you?''

Holly closed her eyes, absorbing every verbal blow, yet trying to steel herself against his unbearable rage. Although she felt as though she was dying inside, she was determined that Jordan know her side. She could see Jordan was deeply wounded, but she was in pain, too.

''I deserve everything you've said, Jordan—and more.'' She struggled to keep her voice calm, hoping to soothe the inflamed tension scorching them both. "I take total responsibility for this unbearable mess. Still, I beg you—let me tell you what happened all those years ago. *Because* of what we've been through together, and *because* of how it was between us when we made love."

Jordan's eyes were cold, his mouth still tight with his seething pain. But he didn't object. He didn't try to leave.

So, with her heart in her mouth, Holly traveled back to that distant, almost unreal time when she was with Scott. "We did use birth control, but there were slipups now and then—like the last time we slept together, about a week before the wedding."

"When he was already having second thoughts."

Holly nodded. "Unfortunately, I found that out after the fact."

She hadn't realized she was pregnant until months later. Young and upset, she had convinced herself that stress had thrown her cycle out of whack. "When my pregnancy was confirmed, I did try to tell Scott. I spent weeks attempting to get hold of him on the phone when he was gallivanting across Europe. But when I finally did, he scarcely listened to anything I had to say. All he could talk about was *his* life, *his* choices." Holly swallowed hard as the bitterness from those days merged with the hurt in her heart now. "You remember what he was like then."

Jordan gave a somber nod. "I remember."

"Then he hung up before I had a chance to tell him about the baby. He had to be somewhere—or something like that."

Holly found it still hurt to talk about that phone call. She peered up at Jordan, hoping for a comforting glance or a sympathetic word. But no.

"You can imagine how angry and hurt I was then,

and how scared," she continued, wishing Jordan would at least look at her while she spoke. "I resented Scott terribly—even after I had the baby. I didn't want him to think I was trying to trap him or burden him with a responsibility he had no interest in. I was bound and determined to prove I didn't want him or need him when I did finally tell him about Stephanie. That was why I came to Golden—to give myself the chance to build that life."

"But Scott died."

Fresh tears sprang from her eyes. "The day my mother told me about his motorcycle accident was the saddest day of my life. I had a hard time accepting he was really gone." She bit down on her lip to stop the trembling. "All I kept thinking was that Stephanie would never ever know her father."

Holly wiped her tears with the back of her hand as a deafening silence followed.

"You could've told Dad."

"I should have told him. I know that now." How could she make Jordan understand the emotional climate she had lived in all those years? What more could she say about her youthful fears, her parents' difficulty in dealing with her pregnancy and the incredible guilt that buried the truth deeper and deeper with each passing year?

When he finally looked at her, she realized it didn't matter what she said. The Jordan she knew and loved was lost in a hard, cold shell of anger.

"You lied to me about Stephanie that very first day. Why?"

"You scared me half to death," she declared, as an angry resentment began to mount inside her. "I didn't know what you wanted. I felt I had to protect Stephanie."

"Protect her from her own uncle?" Jordan's voice grew fierce. "That doesn't wash, Holly."

"You haven't been appointed my judge," she snapped. "Just because I didn't react in the way you think I should doesn't mean my feelings aren't real."

"Why should I believe anything you say now?" he demanded, his eyes flashing. "When I was falling for you hook, line and sinker, lady, you kept on lying to me."

"Stop it. Stop it, Jordan!" The high thin voice strained to be heard over the shouting. "Why are you mad at Mommy?"

Stunned, Holly looked down at Stephanie, who was tugging at the hem of Jordan's T-shirt. Jordan looked equally stunned as he stared openmouthed at her little girl.

"Stephanie! Stephanie!" Both Gracie and her father came running out of the house, visibly distressed that Stephanie had slipped away from them.

Kneeling low to meet Stephanie's eyes, Jordan cupped his hands over her little shoulders and gazed at her for one long moment. The tough, steely facade he had shown to Holly melted almost immediately. "We're just a little upset right now."

Stephie's mouth drooped. "Why?"

Jordan clearly didn't want to say. "Look, kid, I've got some disappointing news—about tomorrow. I'm afraid we won't be able to spend the day as we planned. Something unexpected came up."

"There's not going to be a party?"

Struggling to control his emotions, Jordan shook his head. "I'm really, really sorry, Steph."

"But why not?"

"Remember I told you my father lives in Florida?

Well, he's been sick and I need to go see him. We've got some important things to talk about.''

Stephanie's eyes began to water. "When are you coming back?"

Unable to bear it anymore, Holly looked away. Hot tears streamed down her face. Gracie came over to put a hand on her shoulder.

"Soon, sweetheart. Real soon," Holly heard Jordan answer. "Besides, now your grandpa's here to see you. Why don't you go inside and show him what a mean game of checkers you play?"

Her father walked up and took Stephanie by the hand. "Come on, honey. I've been hankering for a good game of checkers."

As her father led Stephanie back to the house, Holly turned back to Jordan. Straightening from his kneeling position, he let an unguarded glance fall her way. Hope rekindled briefly when she realized some warmth had returned to his deep sea-blue eyes. But then, without so much as a goodbye, Jordan climbed into his pickup and drove away.

Holly watched, absolutely shattered that he'd leave her standing alone like this. She had truly believed that the love she and Jordan had was untouchable. Sacred.

What a fool she was.

"Come inside, dear," Gracie said, putting an arm around her shoulder.

"He said he loved me, Gracie. I thought he'd understand," she murmured, feeling dazed. "I thought I could trust him, no matter what."

Settling her on the den sofa, Gracie spread a crocheted afghan over her. "I'm going to make you some soup."

"Will you check on Steph? She doesn't know my father very well."

"I'll take care of her, dear. Don't worry."

"Did you see her face out there?" she asked, her eyes filling up again. "How could I have let this happen to her?"

"No, it's not your fault. It's not anybody's."

"You know all about it?"

Gracie nodded. "Your father told me. Now you have to calm down. This will get all straightened out, you'll see."

After Gracie left, Holly sat in the darkened room, worrying about Stephanie, aching for Jordan. Although she was upset with him, she knew he was suffering, too.

Her father knocked once on the door and then entered, carrying a bowl of steaming soup on a tray. "Gracie says you're to eat this."

Food was the last thing she wanted. "How's Stephanie?"

"A lot better after she beat me at checkers three times. Gracie just put her down for a nap." He put the tray on the coffee table. "She's a pretty resilient kid. I'm a lot more worried about you than I am about her."

She sank back into the couch. "I've made such a mess of everything."

"That's all spilled milk now. The question is, what are you going to do about it?"

"You saw what happened out there. It's over."

"It will be if you let it go without a fight."

"Oh, Dad," she groaned. "You have no idea what's been going on."

He sat on the edge of the sofa. "That's because I haven't been the father I should be. I didn't think you needed me around. After what I saw today, I may have been wrong."

"Dad, I do need you, and so does Stephanie. Now more than ever."

"Okay. Then answer my question, what are you going to do about this?"

"Do you have any suggestions?"

"Not a one, honey." He patted her blanket-covered foot. "But I think your mother and I did too much of that after your wedding. We told you what to do, how to feel, what to say. And we worried too much about what people would think. Maybe we did more harm than good."

She reached for his hand. "You only did what you thought best."

"Now you have to figure that out for yourself. But I'll stick around if that's all right with you. Your old dad's still a good hand holder." He gave her fingers a squeeze.

"Dad? Stick around for a long time, okay?"

Jordan took a look at the rented folding tables and chairs piled neatly on the front veranda and cursed them under his breath. The last thing he wanted to be reminded of was that damn party. Feeling the full force of the fury that had been twisting in his gut all afternoon, Jordan knocked down the metal tables with one hard, violent kick. They went clattering across the plank floor, the sound bouncing off the pond in a reproachful echo.

Too bad it didn't make him feel any better.

He felt wild inside. There was no other way to describe it. It was as if all his emotions had been swooped up by the tornado spinning around his heart. If he could only block Holly from his thoughts, he'd calm down then. And if he could get Stephanie's disappointed face out of his mind, he'd stop feeling miserable.

When the back doorbell rang, he was tempted not to answer. There was no one in this forsaken town he cared to see right now. But the visitor was insistent. He walked from the front of the house to the back, telling himself it wasn't Holly, it couldn't be Holly, that it had better not be Holly. But in truth, Holly was the last person he expected show up at his door.

"What is it?" he growled as he swung open the door. But then he stiffened, suddenly at a loss for words as he faced the *next-to-last* person he expected to show up at his door.

"Gracie."

"Mr. Mason, I have to talk to you."

She sounded on the verge of tears, and her red eyes suggested she'd already done some crying.

"Look, I have nothing else to say about what happened this afternoon." He couldn't believe she had actually come here.

As her eyes began to tear, she walked past him and into his kitchen. "You don't know how terrible it is back at the house. Stephanie's upset, and Holly's beside herself. She's worried about Steph and she thinks she's ruined your life."

"I'm going to make it up to Stephanie. She's my niece—or did you know that?"

"Not until today. Holly's never said a word about it to anybody."

"Seems to be her pattern."

"Please don't talk like that. She's the sweetest, kindest girl in the world, and you know that." She dug around in her handbag for a tissue. "Haven't you ever made mistakes? Do you expect to pay for them for your entire life?"

He sat down across from her. "What do you want me to do?"

"Go back. There's nothing so terrible it can't be worked out."

"I don't know, Gracie. This is pretty bad."

"I've seen the three of you together. Stephanie adores you, and she needs a man around, you know?" She choked back a sob. "And Holly used to work so hard, rarely taking any time for herself. But then you came along and that all changed. You made her so happy."

He was amazed she was saying these things to him. Gracie, of all people. Still, they weren't easy to hear. Not the way he was feeling.

"And she made you happy, too. I see the way you stare at her when you think no one's looking." She began to cry in earnest now. "You're a decent man—Holly wouldn't care for you if you weren't. So, please, don't walk out on them. They're the dearest people in the world to me."

He got her a glass of water and waited for her to collect herself. "I'm not walking out on Stephanie. But under the circumstances, I couldn't go ahead with tomorrow's party. It would have been a farce," he said, trying to explain. "I know I disappointed Stephanie, but I told you, I'm going to make it up to her—in every way I can."

Gracie shook her head sadly. "You can't make up for the family she almost had. Not if you turn your back on her mother."

Jordan sat down at the bar and ordered a beer. The jukebox was twanging away in the darkened lounge adjacent to Kelsey's Kountry Haven dance hall. In deference to the upcoming holiday, tiny little flags lined the long wooden bar and the handful of tables in the room. The place seemed to be doing a bang-up business. The room was full of men just like him—sad, sorry stiffs drinking alone.

He would have been all right if Gracie hadn't shown up at his door. Up to that point, righteous indignation had been working in his favor. He'd been too angry to feel the real pain. But the old lady's tears and pleas had sapped the fury right out of him. Now that his anger had simmered down, a sense of loss took hold. Now—just like the crooners of the woeful country ballads on the jukebox—he felt wronged by love.

As he gestured to the bartender to bring him another, he felt a strong hand on his shoulder. "Make that two," Gabe Sawyer called, pulling a stool up beside him.

"Somehow, I don't think this is a coincidence," Jordan observed. "This can't be your usual hangout."

"I remembered you'd stayed at the motel across the road for a while. So I took a stab at it." The bartender put the beers down in front of them. "Where have you been?"

"Just driving around."

"Holly's been looking all over town for you." Gabe took a long first swallow of beer. "She got so frantic she called the posse out after you. Nancy, Phil, Susan, me."

"Great. That's all I need."

"Hey, consider yourself lucky I found you. It could have been Miss Karin."

They nursed their beers in silence through at least three increasingly mournful jukebox songs. Finally, after draining his glass empty, Gabe turned to him. "I understand why you're so upset. When we're crazy about a woman, it's hard to accept she isn't perfect—that she, like the rest of us, can make mistakes that hurt."

Jordan plunked his glass down on the vinyl-covered counter. "She played me for a chump, Gabe."

"I don't believe that, and I don't think you do, either. Look, she's sitting out in front of your house right now. Go home. Talk to her." Gabe stood up to pull out his wallet. "If Holly were waiting home for me, I sure the hell wouldn't be hanging around this dive."

"Maybe you'd just rather have me out of the way, pal."

Gabe chuckled and threw some bills onto the bar. "Fat lot of good that would do me. She's so in love with you she can't see straight."

Jordan followed Gabe out of the bar. As he drove home, he tried to get a handle on his feelings. Maybe he was being too hard on her. Maybe they could find some common ground... Maybe...

She was sitting on the veranda steps, just as Gabe said she'd be. Her silky fair hair shimmered in the moonlight, and her eyes were wide and deep as she watched him approach. Now he realized why he hadn't wanted to see her. While the sight of her made his heart melt and his arms itch to hold her, it also riled up his uncontrollable resentment and an increasingly bitter sense of betrayal. When he saw her like this, anger at the mockery she'd made of the most intimate, sacred hours of his life shook him to his soul.

"Are you all right?" she asked, obviously relieved to see him.

He sat down beside her, but not close enough to touch her. "Gabe said you wanted to talk."

"That's why you came back?" Her voice lilted with hope.

When he didn't answer, she sighed and asked him to put aside his conflicted feelings about Scott. "Don't mix them up with what's happening between you and me."

"Easier said than done, Holly."

"Everything I felt about Scott pales in comparison with how I feel about you," she murmured softly. "When I think about my wedding day now, it's not about Scott leaving me. It's all about you. You were the one to take on the responsibility. You were the one who came to me.''

''That was so long ago.'' Yet he had never forgotten it.

''I love you for being there for me back then. And I love you for teaching me how to trust again.'' She touched his arm with her warm, soft hand. ''You've got to believe in me now. What we shared was real, Jordan. My love is real.''

''I wanted so much to believe that. I can't now.'' He slid his arm from her grasp.

''But why?''

''There were a couple of times when I really wondered if Stephanie was Scott's child. I questioned whether you were being straight with me about it.''

He glanced up at the sky and noticed the stars weren't shining so bright tonight. It had to be a sign of something.

''Then as you and I got closer, it was unthinkable that you'd be dishonest with me about anything.'' He stood up and moved off the steps. Her familiar scent was tugging at his memory.

''So I put the doubts out of my mind. And when you said you loved me, when we made love, I honestly believed nothing could come between us. Not Scott. Not the past.''

She looked up at him with a clouded gaze. ''What can I say to set it right? Tell me, please. I'll do anything.''

''Holly, what I'm feeling inside can't be wiped away with apologies—although I wish to God it could. And the sad, cold reality of what's happened can't be absolved with acts of penance.''

Holly came to his side. ''Are you saying you can't ever forgive me?''

The pain in her eyes tore at his heart, and he had to

fight the desire to take her in his arms. "Time always takes care of that, doesn't it? I'm angry, yes—but I don't hate you."

"But you don't trust me." Resignation flooded her voice.

He couldn't think of what to say that wouldn't hurt her, so he said nothing.

Holly turned away from his silence. "Well, Jordan, you're a man who appreciates irony. Isn't this one perfect? When I finally come to trust you, your trust in me is shattered."

"Trust is the whole ball game, Holly. Without it we've got nothing to hold on to."

The truth of this stirred his resentment anew. He and Holly could have had it all. It ripped him up inside to think how close they'd come to it. If only she had told him the truth…

Jordan pulled himself out of the pointless trap of *if-onlys*. It was finished between him and Holly. It was time to move ahead.

"Holly, you should know that I'm leaving for Florida tomorrow."

"So soon?" Her eyebrows lifted in surprise. "You're going to tell him about Stephanie."

"It's about time someone did," he snapped, his anger flaring.

"Are you coming back to Golden?"

"Count on it. I'm not going to let you keep Stephanie away from her family anymore."

"Our trip to Palm Beach was just the thing your father needed," Rachel declared as she drove him home from the airport. "The color's back in his cheeks, his appetite's good, he's strong enough to take some exercise. His doctor said he's turned the corner."

"You don't know how glad I am to hear that."

Rachel smiled as she pulled onto the expressway. "When I told him you were coming, he started planning things to do. I really think he's getting to be his old self again."

"And his doctor said it was okay to tell him about Stephanie?"

"I told him everything you told me on the phone. He thinks it might even help." Rachel glanced at him from across the front seat. "Actually, I'm kind of excited about Stephanie, too. I can't wait to meet her."

Thinking about Stephanie made him smile. "The kid is something else. You're going to love her."

Lawrence was halfway out the door before Rachel had even parked the car. It had only been a couple of months since Jordan had last seen his father, but it felt like a lifetime ago. A startling sense of relief washed over him as Lawrence approached. Jordan realized he'd been missing him.

"Jordan." Lawrence greeted him with his usual casual embrace. This time, however, when his father's long arms curved around him, something compelled Jordan to hold on. The grueling emotions of the past few days welled up inside him and he pulled his father closer.

Finally, he felt Lawrence's big hand ruffling his hair, just the way he used to. "I'm glad you're here, Son."

On the second day of his visit, Rachel went out shopping so he could talk to his father alone. Sitting together on the handsome leather sofa in the study, Jordan told Lawrence everything about Holly, Stephanie and Golden—everything except his personal relationship with Holly. In this version, he made it sound strictly platonic.

After the initial shock and emotion, his father accepted the news better than Jordan had hoped. Although he reminisced about Scott a little, Lawrence was more taken with the notion that he had a living, breathing granddaughter. "Stephanie." He said the name aloud for at least the fifteenth time. "And you say she looks just like Holly."

"I've got pictures." Handing them to Lawrence one by one, Jordan was surprised by his father's lack of animosity toward Holly. He had expressed disappointment in her, but none of the indignation Jordan felt. In fact, Lawrence sounded almost sympathetic when he spoke of her.

"These could be pictures of Holly at that age. She's really precious," his father noted. "Holly's blossomed into a real beauty."

Jordan stiffened. "You've always had a soft spot for her, haven't you?"

Lawrence gave him a curious look. "It's true. And I'll always regret what Scott did to her. It was terrible how it split our families apart."

"She could have rectified that." He handed his father the last snapshot.

"Well, well, don't you look handsome!" he exclaimed, ignoring Jordan's remark. "And from the way Stephanie and Holly are looking at you, it appears they thought so, too."

Jordan peered at the photo in his father's hands. It was a shot Gracie had taken of them in their finery on the night of the dinner dance. He had forgotten Holly had given him a copy.

"From some of these pictures, it looks like you and Holly were—"

"Looks can be deceiving, Dad."

Lawrence glanced up sharply. "I detect a definite hardness toward her in your voice. Something's going on between the two of you, isn't it?"

"Nothing's going on. Certainly nothing for you to worry about."

"Jordan, when are you going to stop shutting me out? We've been through so much, and here you've just found my granddaughter—and yet you continue to keep me at arm's length when it comes to what's important to you," he declared with an adamance that stunned Jordan. "I'm not blind. This woman means something to you."

Shaken by Lawrence's outburst, Jordan reluctantly admitted having had a relationship with Holly. "But it was a mistake, Dad. I never should have gotten involved with her."

His father shook his head. "There's got to be more to it. From what I can see, you're hurting more than you're willing to admit. Tell me."

Jordan stared down at the aging hand resting on his arm, and something inside him gave way. He told his father the entire painful tale.

Lawrence sighed deeply when he'd finished. "Don't be so hard on Holly, Son. She made a mistake. We all do."

"Everybody keeps saying that. But nobody but me knows how much that mistake hurts."

"Nobody does. Nobody can." Lawrence tried to calm him with a fatherly rub on the back. "Just as no one can know the hell Holly went through back then. How can we sit in judgment of what she did?"

"Why are you defending her like this?"

"Because I see a changed man in front of me. When you hugged me yesterday, I felt it. Something about you was different."

Jordan felt weary. "I don't know what you mean."

"Look at you now. You're full of feelings. You're

opening up to me, letting me in. Surely Holly had something to do with this change in you.''

His father was right; Holly's love had changed him. Yet now it was making him miserable beyond endurance. He leaned forward, head in hand. ''What am I going to do, Dad? There were things that were said, things that were done... They can't be taken back.''

''Says who? You're a strong man, Jordan. You can do anything,'' Lawrence insisted. ''I've always been proud of that. I wouldn't have had the courage to sell CompWare in order to save it.''

It meant the world to hear that from his father. But he was surprised. ''You didn't want me to sell.''

''I was wrong. I see that now.'' Lawrence got up from the sofa. ''I think I was also wrong in believing you didn't need me the way Scott did. When your mother died, I guess I let a lot of things slide.''

Jordan looked up as his father lifted a silver-framed photo from the credenza. He recognized it right away. His throat tightened as Lawrence sat down beside him.

''This was the last picture taken of the four of us together, remember?''

He nodded, not trusting his voice.

''Not a day goes by when I don't think about your mother and your brother.''

''I think about them, too.''

''Good. We can't forget.'' He placed the photograph on a side table. ''Now we have some new members for a family portrait. Rachel. Stephanie.'' He turned to Jordan, encouragement shining in his eyes. ''And maybe Holly?''

Chapter Fourteen

As soon as he saw the emerald green common, rich and lush and welcoming on this beautiful summer day, Jordan realized how much he had missed Golden. Annette from the bakery waved to him when he parked outside her window. And the driver of the retirement home van—whose name he kept forgetting—tooted his horn as he drove past.

When he spotted Holly's car in front of the boutique, his chest tightened. He still didn't know what he was going to say, nor did he know what kind of reception he'd get. Things just might not work out. When he crossed the street, however, he saw the big Closed sign on the store door. But Saturdays were the shop's busiest. Puzzled, he walked over to her car.

He smiled at the stuffed bear tossed in the back seat with Steph's coloring books and markers. The kid liked to keep busy in the car. In the front, he recognized one of Holly's sweaters, her hairbrush and one of the many paperback mysteries she loved to read. Small, incidental items that belonged to the two people he loved best in the world.

He had to make things work out. Holly and Stephanie were everything and he'd fight to the death for them. There was just too much love at stake and too much love to lose.

"Hey, Jordan," Jonathan Warren called from the front of the general store. "On your way to the town meeting? It's already started."

The second special meeting—he'd forgotten. That's where Holly must be. When he reached the town hall, debate on the rezoning was in full force. He searched the vast room with his eyes, but was unable to locate Holly. As he listened to the discussion, several of Franklin Beck's cohorts began taking verbal potshots at newcomers who tried to make money off the town with no regard for its rural landscape. Jordan didn't care that his name was derided several times. But when Beck and his army started taking snipes at Holly, Jordan saw red.

He gestured furiously at Dennis Metcalfe to recognize him. Gabe Sawyer spotted him and gave the moderator a poke in the ribs.

"Mr. Mason, you have the floor," he announced with a smile.

All heads turned to the back of the room where Jordan stood. He scanned the faces but still couldn't find Holly. Then he fixed his gaze on Dr. Beck and friends. "I'm going to make this short and sweet, because—as Sadie Campbell so kindly reminded me at the door—I can't vote because I forgot to register."

A sprinkling of laughter greeted him.

"Perhaps the good people of Golden are right to be suspicious of outsiders like me who can pull some foolish stunts at times. But you people have no reason on God's earth to suspect Holly West of anything—anything—but trying to make a decent life in this town for her daughter and herself.'' He looked at Dr. Beck's cool face once more. ''And Golden's damn lucky to have her,'' he added for good measure.

The crowd broke out in applause and Beck's guys actually booed. Then the moderator called for a vote and chaos reigned.

Holly sat stuck in a corner behind three rows of people eager to cast their votes. She saw Jordan leave the hall, but she couldn't budge an inch. Her knees were still trembling from his beautiful words of support. It didn't matter which way the vote went. Jordan was back. And wonders of wonders, he'd stood by her when she needed him—one more time.

When Holly managed to squeeze out of her corner she ran outside to find him. He was nowhere to be seen, and no one could recollect which way he'd gone.

Since experience had taught him that it was impossible to find anybody in the town hall after a meeting, Jordan decided to go directly to Holly's house. She'd turn up there eventually. Besides, he was eager to see Stephanie, too.

He was almost as surprised to see Ted West still in town as Ted was to see him back in town.

''I'm baby-sitting my granddaughter this afternoon,'' Ted claimed proudly. ''And I'm looking to buy one of those summer cottages on the pond. I realized I need to spend more time with my girls.''

Jordan was happy to hear that. He knew what it would mean to Holly. He hoped his return would mean something to her, too. When Ted called Stephanie downstairs, Jordan felt another sliver of apprehension. How would she react to him? Was she angry at him for leaving the way he had? Would she forgive him?

"Jordan!"

Her high-pitched squeal pierced the air as she jumped into his arms. She kissed and hugged him, and Jordan held on to her for dear life. He had talked about her a lot to Rachel and his father, yet the real thing proved too delightful for words.

"Mommy said you'd come back."

"She did?" He hugged her close.

"Every night when she tucked me in bed."

"Your mom's a smart lady."

"Jordan, I know something you don't know," she claimed with all the seriousness a four-year-old could muster. "You're my uncle."

He was floored. "I am?"

"Your brother is my daddy who died. And Mommy says I have another grandpa who is going to love me like crazy."

"It's absolutely true, honey. He can't wait to meet you."

It gave him hope to know Holly had already told Stephanie about her other family. It meant she recognized how important it was for Steph, and how much it meant to his father and himself.

The screen door squeaked open, and Jordan turned as the soft, warm scent of the woman he loved reached out to him. Holly met his eyes and everything went still. Joy and relief filled his soul. The bundle in his arms began to wiggle away.

"Mommy, Jordan's back," Steph announced gaily. "I don't think he's mad at you anymore."

"Come on, dear." Ted managed to capture his reluctant granddaughter's hand. "Jordan and your mother need to talk."

As Ted coaxed Steph out the back door, Holly walked up to Jordan. "Are you?"

Uncertainty flickered in his dark-blue eyes. "Am I what?"

"Still mad at me?"

He smiled. "Not anymore. It took a few days, but I got over it. I let the anger go."

"I'm so glad." Her heart fluttered with relief, and she longed to touch him.

"It's time we let go of the past, too." He moved an inch closer as his finger skimmed along her arm. "We've got to trust each other in spite of it. So, do you?"

"Do I what?"

"Still trust me?"

"Oh, yes." She touched his face, caressing his cheek gently, and then she melted against his chest. She could hear his heart pounding wildly.

Jordan closed his arms around her. "Will you have me back? I want us to have a life together—you, Stephanie, me. Here in Golden."

She tilted her head back slightly. "Golden? Really?"

"Somewhere along the way, I discovered I belong here."

"Correction," she said, sliding her arms around his shoulders. "You belong here with me, and I belong here with you." And then Holly set about to prove it with the first of a lifetime of kisses that would always be there to welcome him home.

Three weeks later, Stephanie ran dripping out of the water, with Taffy licking at her heels. "I'm gonna jump in again. Watch me, Grandpa. Watch me!"

Two heads swung around at the same time, sending Stephanie into gales of laughter. "I forgot. I meant

Grandpa Lawrence. But you can watch, too, Grandpa Ted.''

Holly smiled as the two men who'd been estranged too long watched and clapped with delight at the grandchild they shared.

"Holly, here it is." Gracie showed off the elaborate cake she had made for Stephanie's "half-year" birthday.

"Steph's going to love the little checkerboard on it."

Gracie's mouth pursed into a proud smile. "That was your father's idea. Rather ingenious, wasn't it?"

Holly had suspected Gracie and her dad were spending time together, and now Gracie's smile confirmed it.

Gracie covered up the cake box and lent Holly a hand setting the table. "At first I wasn't crazy about the idea of having Stephanie's little party on Jordan's beach, but it's really very nice down here.''

"Tell him when he comes back from rowing Rachel around the pond. He loves it when you compliment him."

"I think I'll save the compliments for the wedding tomorrow. Tell him exactly what I think of him all at once—sort of as a special wedding gift just for the groom."

Holly's heart was full of affection for her dear old friend. "Gracie, thanks for helping me through the past five years. I wouldn't have survived to see this day without you."

Gracie's eyes glistened as she squeezed Holly's hand. "I know it's kind of presumptuous of me. But I'm so excited about your wedding I feel like the mother of the bride."

"You are to me."

"Jordan's coming back in." Her father walked up to them. "What are you two yakking about now?"

"Bride stuff," Gracie said, turning away to wipe her

eyes with her hand. "Now, come over here and look at this cake."

Holly looked out at the water where Jordan was guiding the small wooden boat toward the shore. She couldn't believe that tomorrow they'd be married. It was everything she wanted and more wonderful than anything she could have dreamed.

"That daughter of yours is a little dynamo, Holly," Lawrence said as he strolled up to her. "She's just perfect."

Holly had seen the instant love in Lawrence's eyes yesterday, when he had first met Stephanie. Now it was even brighter. "She really likes you, Lawrence. She wasn't shy with you at all."

"Oh, I think we're all going to be just fine." He curved his arm around her shoulder.

He really was the dearest man; not one word of reproach had she heard from him. Yet she still felt guilty about having kept Stephanie a secret from him for so long. She felt she should say something. "I hope you'll be able to forgive me one day, Lawrence. I'll try to find a way to make it up to you."

"Dear, you already have." Squeezing her shoulder he pointed toward Jordan "You've given my son back to me. And to see him this content for the first time in his life is more than a father could ask."

"Everybody, come and see my cake," Steph called out at the top of her lungs. "Grandpa Ted, Grandpa Lawrence, come see it."

Lawrence planted a kiss on her cheek. "I'm going to get my wife and go look at that cake."

Holly followed him down to the shore, where he helped Rachel step out of the rowboat. "Why don't you two go for a little ride yourselves," he suggested to Holly and Jordan. "Let the grandparents run the party."

She looked to Jordan. With a smile that made her start counting the hours to the honeymoon, he held out his hand.

After they pushed out, Holly glanced back at the beach. The center of attention of four loving faces, Stephanie stood over her birthday cake, chattering away a mile a minute.

With a full heart, she turned back to Jordan, whose gaze was drinking in the happy reunion. His eyes were brimming with joy.

Holly couldn't remember feeling this happy before her first wedding day, and she certainly hadn't been as deeply in love. But she was a different woman, and Jordan was her groom now. She knew he'd be there tomorrow, and every day forever after.

* * * * *

SILHOUETTE

SPECIAL EDITION®

COMING NEXT MONTH

TENDERLY Cheryl Reavis

That Special Woman!

Wealthy Eden Trevoy is desperately seeking the truth about her lost heritage. But her searching reveals more than the hidden past as she captures the heart of Navajo policeman, Ben Toomey.

FINALLY A BRIDE Sherryl Woods

Always a Bridesmaid!

Katie Jones is finally getting married, the only hitch is that husband-to-be, Luke Cassidy has business—not love—on his mind. So, it's up to Katie to convince Luke to swap business for lifelong pleasure!

THE RANCH STUD Cathy Gillen Thacker

Hasty Weddings

Patience McKendrick has just come into an unusual inheritance. Knowing she's desperate for a baby, her eccentric uncle Max has left her handsome Josh Colter to sire her a child! But will she take her own advice and throw caution to the wind?

LITTLE BOY BLUE Suzannah Davis

Switched at Birth

Bliss Abernathy is stranded with her old foe, exasperating, but thrilling, Logan Campbell. But, once bitten, twice shy and Bliss is not about to lose her heart to Logan for a second time. After all, once they got back home everything would return to normal, wouldn't it?

DADDY'S HOME Pat Warren

When town bad boy Sam Rivers skipped town under a cloud of suspicion, he also left heiress Liza Courtland pregnant. Now Sam is back, but how can Liza let him be a part of her and her daughter's life after he has abandoned them once before?

HER CHILD'S FATHER Christine Flynn

Trapped by the weather with reclusive Jack Holt, Carrie Carter never dreamed that their isolation would lead to passion. But now Carrie is expecting Jack's baby, and it is up to her to break through Jack's reserve—for the sake of their child!

COMING NEXT MONTH FROM

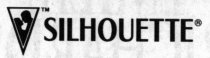 **SILHOUETTE**®

Intrigue
Danger, deception and desire

HER HERO Aimée Thurlo
FORGET ME NOT Cassie Miles
FLASHBACK Terri Herrington
HEART OF THE NIGHT Gayle Wilson

Desire
Provocative, sensual love stories for the woman of today

THE COWBOY STEALS A LADY Anne McAllister
BRIDE OF THE BAD BOY Elizabeth Bevarly
THE EDUCATION OF JAKE FLYNN Leandra Logan
HER TORRID TEMPORARY MARRIAGE Sara Orwig
THE KIDNAPPED BRIDE Metsy Hingle
THREE-ALARM LOVE Carole Buck

Sensation
A thrilling mix of passion, adventure and drama

CAPTIVE STAR Nora Roberts
A MARRIAGE-MINDED MAN Linda Turner
BRANDON'S BRIDE Alicia Scott
KNIGHT ERRANT Marilyn Pappano

EMILIE RICHARDS

THE WAY BACK HOME

As a teenager, Anna Fitzgerald fled an impossible
situation, only to discover that life on the streets was
worse. But she had survived. Now, as a woman,
she lived with the constant threat that the secrets of
her past would eventually destroy her new life.

1-55166-399-6
**AVAILABLE IN PAPERBACK
FROM SEPTEMBER, 1998**

JASMINE CRESSWELL

THE DAUGHTER

Maggie Slade's been on the run for seven years now.
Seven years of living without a life or a future because
she's a woman with a past. And then she meets Sean
McLeod. Maggie has two choices. She can either run,
or learn to trust again and prove her innocence.

"Romantic suspense at its finest."

—Affaire de Coeur

1-55166-425-9
**AVAILABLE IN PAPERBACK
FROM SEPTEMBER, 1998**

CHRISTIANE HEGGAN

SUSPICION

Kate Logan's gut instincts told her that neither of her clients was guilty of murder, and homicide detective Mitch Calhoon wanted to help her prove it. What neither suspected was how dangerous the truth would be.

"Christiane Heggan delivers a tale that will leave you breathless."

—Literary Times

1-55166-305-8
AVAILABLE IN PAPERBACK
FROM SEPTEMBER, 1998

4 FREE
books and a surprise gift!

We would like to take this opportunity to thank you for reading this Silhouette® book by offering you the chance to take FOUR more specially selected titles from the Special Edition™ series absolutely FREE! We're also making this offer to introduce you to the benefits of the Reader Service™—

★ FREE home delivery
★ FREE gifts and competitions
★ FREE monthly newsletter
★ Books available before they're in the shops
★ Exclusive Reader Service discounts

Accepting these FREE books and gift places you under no obligation to buy; you may cancel at any time, even after receiving your free shipment. Simply complete your details below and return the entire page to the address below. *You don't even need a stamp!*

✂

YES! Please send me 4 free Special Edition books and a surprise gift. I understand that unless you hear from me, I will receive 6 superb new titles every month for just £2.50 each, postage and packing free. I am under no obligation to purchase any books and may cancel my subscription at any time. The free books and gift will be mine to keep in any case.

E8YE

Ms/Mrs/Miss/Mr..............................Initials ....
                                                          BLOCK CAPITALS PLEASE

Surname ....

Address ....

....

....Postcode.................................

Send this whole page to:
THE READER SERVICE, FREEPOST, CROYDON, CR9 3WZ
(Eire readers please send coupon to: P.O. BOX 4546, DUBLIN 24.)

Offer not valid to current Reader Service subscribers to this series. We reserve the right to refuse an application and applicants must be aged 18 years or over. Only one application per household. Terms and prices subject to change without notice. Offer expires 28th February 1999. You may be mailed with offers from other reputable companies as a result of this application. If you would prefer not to receive such offers, please tick box. ☐

Silhouette Special Edition is a registered trademark used under license.

JAYNE ANN KRENTZ

A Woman's Touch

He was her boss—and her lover!
Life had turned complicated for Rebecca Wade when she
met Kyle Stockbridge. He *almost* had her believing he
loved her, until she realised she was in possession
of something he wanted.

"...one of the hottest writers in romance today."

—USA Today

MIRA®

1-55166-315-5
AVAILABLE IN PAPERBACK
FROM AUGUST, 1998